MONSTER'S BRIDE

MUCH ♥!

Stasia

Black

USA TODAY BESTSELLING AUTHOR

STASIA BLACK

MONSTER'S BRIDE

*We are all worthy of the most
spectacular love.
From one disabled girl to another <3*

MONSTER

PREFACE

It is a tragedy when the One who created you cannot love you. Enough almost to destroy a man's soul. I suppose it is presumption to call myself a man, though.

You see, I was not perfect enough. Not created in *his* image perfectly enough. Which, let's be honest, was more *his* fault than mine.

But then, I was the fool who sought his love for far too long. Almost to my own destruction. Because he would destroy that which was not beautiful.

And so in the end I killed god, my father.

Now I am a wild thing set free. A terror upon this earth.

I do not think it was my destiny.

But a child unloved will turn to violence.

Or perhaps what he said before he died was true, and I have always been a monster.

CHAPTER ONE

The path is rocky and I struggle with my crutches up the mountain.

I'm seeking a monster who can perform miracles, after all. So what else did I expect if not a struggle? But still, sweat pours down my forehead.

"How much farther?" I ask my guide, a young guy from the nearest town. He's stopped up ahead. He doesn't like moving as slowly as I do, so he keeps hiking further, then waiting till I catch up. But he's the only one I could find who would even take me this far.

These mountain paths are treacherous, or so the locals have warned me. There's no cell service out here, and though I have a sat phone, I'm not sure it will help me.

It certainly didn't help the others who took this trail before me in search of miracles, and they were all able-bodied folks. We had to abandon my walker half an hour ago when the path became too narrow, and my balance is dicey at the best of times. And now that I'm so exhausted? I try to hug the side of the mountain path that's by the forest; the other edge is a sheer cliffside. It's not like there's even a railing or anything to grab if I go stumbling that direction.

My guide—Keith—points up the path. "The cave is about a half mile more. That way. But this is as far as I go."

I frown, confused. "But I paid for you to take me the whole wa—"

"I told you, lady. You're crazy. No one comes back from here, and if anyone knew I even took you out this far..."

He shakes his head, looking worried. Then he slices his hand through the air. "No. You come back with me now. You got to see it. You can say you came up the mountain, and that it just didn't work out. Look, I'll take a picture of you so you can put it on your Insta and prove you did it."

He pulls out his phone, obviously only for its camera function, since there's no cell service.

"I'm not turning back." I frown as he taps the screen, taking pictures of me, I can only assume. "I paid for you to take me as close to the cave as possible."

He gestures around him. "This is as close as possible, and my mama would kill me if she knew I even went this far. I told you what happens on this mountain."

He covers his eyes to block out the sun and look up the path toward the mountain that looms above us. The air is thick with mosquitos, but I've quickly learned that swatting at them is futile. They just swarm right back.

Keith shakes his head as he turns and starts walking back toward me. "Yeah, we should head back before the sun goes down. We have just enough time to make it to town. This went a lot slower than I expected." He glances at my elbow crutches. "But if we leave now, we should be able to get far enough down to be safe."

I dig my crutches into the dirt stubbornly. "I'm not turning back."

The only person who has made it back alive from this trek is a child—a previously disabled child who has somehow been cured of his terrible scoliosis after visiting the mountain. He speaks of a monster so fierce and deadly, it's scared away most since. Or so the rumors say. Most people think it's just a story, one of those local legends. Especially since no one can find the boy, whose family has apparently moved away after the miracle.

But the legend has only grown. Especially since other adventure seekers coming this way recently, most seeking out the mythical beast, have a habit of going missing.

So why am I, a disabled woman alone, who has difficulties navigating a downtown street much less a mountain, attempting such a hike?

Likely because I'm a fool.

And because I've always had more heart than brains, or so my fifth-grade teacher said when I jumped off the swing-set when the swing was at its highest, so for once I could pretend to be like all the other kids.

What that teacher and many others along the way have tried to instill is that I am *not* like the other kids. My twisted spine, club foot, speech problems, and the neurological condition driving it all have placed limitations on me that mean I *have* to live differently—from the time my condition was discovered at age ten and onwards.

So I dig my arm crutches in, careful to wedge the spikes at the bottom between rocks to make sure I'm steady as I head up the steep path.

Considering the steep, treacherous fall to my left, I'm determined to be extra careful before swinging my body forward.

But forward I *will* go.

"I'm not going back," I huff out through my teeth, heading toward my guide as he approaches me.

"Yeah, you are. Cause I'm not going any further, and you can't stay out here."

He's getting that look on his face my fiancé likes to get. The one where he's decided he knows better than me. Even when it comes to my own body and its limitations.

"No." I stubbornly dig in and swing myself forward again. "I'm not. If you need to go back, no one's stopping you."

He rolls his eyes at me. "Look, lady, you can barely stand up, and there's grizzlies out here. Probably what got all those dumb hikers."

When I just stare him down, he says, "Wolves, too. Real hungry wolves, and cougars." He lifts his arms menacingly. Like this skinny boy making claw-hands at me is going to intimidate me.

"I'm not afraid of bears or wolves."

That gets me another eyeroll. "Fucking tourists," he whispers not so quietly under his breath.

What Keith doesn't know is that I'm actually not like other *fucking tourists* he might have brought up this mountain and then scared with all this *lions, tigers and bears, oh my!* talk.

It takes a lot more than that to scare a person who's gone through as many surgeries as I have as just a little kid. One to correct the curvature of my spine. Another on my feet. Another to shave off my too-thick sternum so my heart can beat without constraint.

I've looked death in the eyes too many times already. It doesn't strike fear into my heart to meet it with a different face. Even if that face has a mouth full of teeth.

I have come here seeking monsters, after all.

"We're going back." Keith reaches me and grabs my upper arm. *"Now."*

I yank hard away from his grip. "Get the fuck *off* me."

I hate people thinking they have the right to touch me just because I'm different. When his grip clamps even harder, I flip my left cane and hold the spiky foot end to his throat. He freezes in place. Especially since I'm shaky on my feet and the spikes wobble.

"I said to let me fucking go."

His mouth drops open like he's not sure how he got in this position. But he does let go of me, roughly tossing me away from him so that I tumble into a bush on the side of the mountain. "What the fuck ever. I did my job."

"Hey!" I cry, trying to right myself and get out of the thorny bush without falling off the mountain. "Asshole!"

I stop struggling with the bush long enough to flip him the bird, not that he gives even a single look back to see.

I heft out a breath, bite back tears, and set about getting my legs free without tangling my arms even more. He knocked one of my crutches out of my hands during the fall, and when I finally roll out of the bush back onto the path, I grab for it desperately.

Keith is hoofing it down the path so fast he's around the bend before I fully regain my breath so I can curse him out properly.

Then he's gone. And that's when it sets in.

Well shit. I'm out here, all alone, on a mountain trail that's famous for people not returning from it. With a face full of dirt and mosquitos swarming my teary eyes.

I grit my teeth and, using my crutches, slowly, painfully, make my way back to my feet. It takes longer than I wish, and I'm glad that asshole is gone so he doesn't see the awkward process.

By the time I manage to get upright again, the sun is indeed dropping toward the horizon. It's far closer to sunset than I'm prepared for.

But I don't care if the guide was telling the truth about the time or if he was just scared shitless. There's never a need to be an asshole to those who are weaker than you.

I look up the ever-darkening mountain. At the path that seems to grow even narrower.

I'd rather not die of stupidity in my search for my miracle.

The thought makes me giggle out loud.

Some would—and have—said that this entire trip is a fool's errand.

As thorns catch *again* on my long-sleeved shirt, I'm

inclined to agree with them. I almost got caught in a patch of briars about a half-mile back where I had to abandon my walker. It almost made me give up—like it is nature's barrier trying to scream at me: what do you think you're doing? You can't do this! Even healthy people don't come back alive!

The path narrows even further and is thorny with overgrown brush. I'm glad I'm wearing long sleeves and jeans despite the mid-October warmth. I mean, I know Alaska can't be cold *all* the time, but I haven't quite been ready for this heat—or the number of mosquitos apparently native here after summer when the snow melts into thousands and thousands of lakes.

And I am far from healthy, as my mother, fiancé—well, ex-fiancé—and everyone else around me tried to remind me when I first told them about using my savings to go to the three most promising sites around the world where it's rumored miracles have happened.

As if they have to remind me of my body's limitations. Why can't they understand? That's the entire point!

I wake every day with pain that wracks my unnaturally curved spine, and spasms that cramp my legs. My childhood was nothing but surgeries and yet still, my body refuses to cooperate. I'm always in the losing percentile, even with the best doctors.

My mother didn't know what to do with me. She supported me as best she could, but my father left us not long after my diagnosis and the first surgery. Mom started carrying a thermos of wine with her everywhere she went after that. A beauty pageant queen, she'd considered it her life's highest ambition to become a trophy wife. But then I came along—a poisonous combination of her and my dad's genes—ruining everything.

One night I came out to get a glass of water after she'd got really sauced, and she sat me down beside her on the couch, eyes red.

"Look honey, so you'll never be beautiful, let's just face facts," she said, reaching for her large coffee cup that declared "World's Best Mom"—a Mother's Day gift from my father a few years before he took off. She uses it for wine when she is at home. "But if you work hard enough, you can still be useful." Then she laughed humorlessly. "And really most of them just want a warm hole to stick it in, anyway."

She can only see a woman's worth defined by whether she can catch a man. And by that definition... well what is the point of me?

So, I think she was more surprised than anyone when I came home and told her about Drew. Drew isn't just any man, either. He is successful and handsome, and for some reason no one around me seems to be able to fathom, he'd wanted *me*.

So, my mother was absolutely furious with me when I broke off the engagement to go in search of my miracle.

"What do you think you're doing?" she'd raged at me as I stopped back home to pick up a suitcase. I certainly didn't have any of those at Drew's place. Even though we lived together for two years, I still think of it that way—as Drew's place. "You're ruining everything! Go back and grovel. He'll take you back, I bet. He's such a good man. He'll take pity on you."

Take pity.

Her words lit me up inside with burning rage. "Take pity?" I seethed, so angry I could barely see straight.

But, of course, that's what she thinks. That I should be glad to for whatever scraps of kindness I can get from this world, take the forty years of life my condition might afford me with gratitude before my weak heart gives out, and then die with grace so everyone else can go back to their regularly scheduled programming without any more fuss.

Except that lately I've become a creature of rage. Very unbecoming of a petite disabled woman.

And I've decided that, fuck it. if conventional medicine won't work, why not try the miraculous? I am twenty-five and still able to walk with my rollator walker and occasionally my arm crutches, but in another year or two, I'll be in a wheelchair. If I am going to try this, it has to be now.

Maybe some god or spirit will have pity on my poor, broken body if no one else will. So I finished stuffing that suitcase with clothing and went for the nuclear option even though no one in my life supported me. I started traveling in search of a miracle.

First, I visited a basilica in Ireland where the Mother Mary is said to appear. It is a simple but beautiful church, and when I visited the holy statue that is the place of miracles, I did feel quite at peace.

The monks prayed over me, and I held vigil for three days and nights, waiting for my miracle.

But I was not healed.

So then I went to India, to visit the Jwalamukhi Temple. Travel is much more difficult there, being constantly jostled, but I managed. All the things I've been told my whole life I can't do—I managed. Yes, I lost my balance and fell plenty. But I got back up again.

The temple is beautiful. Beyond anything I could imagine. Nine eternal flames burn continually from stone in sacred spots throughout the structure. There is no recordable source of the fire, but they have still been burning since time immemorial. The flames are said to be part of fifty-one remnants of a girl of fire, who happened upon the spot where fire flamed brightly from the gods to banish a mounting attack of devils.

I thought a fire goddess might hear my prayers.

I have a heart of fire.

Fury and rage and a lust to live burn so brightly in me despite my broken body.

The temple is also beautiful, in a more elaborate way than the church. It is filled with pilgrims in beautiful colors, and the flames dance as brightly as foretold.

I stayed there two weeks, hoping my persistent vigil might sway a goddess's heart. But then I saw others around me, who had waited many months, years even, for the goddess to touch and heal them. And in the end, I decided, if there are miracles to be doled out there, those waiting deserve them more than I do.

But I am not done with my quest.

I still have one more spot left to visit. One last hope.

Because what I hadn't told my family or Drew when I broke off our engagement one week before I left is that I know in my heart this might be a one-way journey for me.

Time is running out, whether they wanted to admit it or not. I have these last few mobile years left, and then I'll be in a wheelchair. That's not the bad part. I'll make a wheelchair my sexy bitch... it's just that the other risk factors go up at that point.

That I've had this long on my feet is lucky, considering my condition.

But I still might not live past forty. And my survival rate past that is discussed in percentage points.

So, I returned to my own continent to visit the last place, a holy site in Mexico thronged with worshippers. I was so overwhelmed with bodies I could barely stand without being knocked against. And while I was standing there, waiting for a third day to enter the sacred place, another seeker who had also been waiting for many days spoke to me.

"Where you headed after this?" She only had a cane. Many around me were in wheelchairs pushed by other family members waiting to get in—a familiar sight by then.

I just blinked at her. I had made friends with strangers while waiting at different places I'd traveled. But usually I was the first to speak.

"What do you mean?" I asked.

"Well, you look like you've been traveling awhile. You're on the hunt, like me."

"The hunt?" I wasn't quite following.

"For a miracle." She smiled up at the church in front of us, the hope obvious in her face. "I'm hoping this will be the one but doubt..." She looked to the ground. "It's a tricky thing. If I let doubt in my heart, will the holy Mother know and not give me my miracle because I lack faith?"

I shook my head. "I don't think it works that way."

She gave my unsteady legs the once-over. "No offence, but I'm not sure you're really one to say."

Ouch. But maybe fair. I hadn't got my miracle yet, after all.

"This is my last stop," I confided. If this didn't work then I'd... do what? Go back home, accept my fate, and try to pick up the broken pieces with my fiancé if he'd even talk to me? I sighed. The thought was exhausting.

The woman merely nodded knowingly. "Many turn back from the path."

I frowned at her. "What about you? Where are you going after this?"

She smiled at me, a peaceful, calm smile I envied. And then she rattled off a list of locations, many I'd read about online. Her eyes gained a faraway, slightly worried look. "At the end, if nothing has worked, then I'll try the nuclear option."

I straightened, alarmed. "What's the nuclear option?"

"Well, there's rumors of this place in Alaska.

Deep, deep up in Alaska. A little boy who'd been deformed since birth came down from a mountain completely healed."

I blinked at her and swiped sweat from my brow underneath the cap I was wearing to shade my face from the blistering sun. We were all baking out here. "And that's it? Just a rumor? Has anyone else gone to check it out?"

She regarded me again, solemn. "They have. None came back alive."

I laughed out loud.

Of course, I assumed she was joking. A magic mountain deep in the Alaskan wilderness? Who wouldn't laugh?

But she just kept staring at me, dead serious.

"Well you can't really be thinking about going there, can you?" I asked.

She tilted her head. "Why not? Maybe all these places"—she waved her hand at the church—"are all out of miracles. Maybe the mountain gods in Alaska will only bless the pure of heart, like the little boy. Maybe others went with bad intentions."

She inhaled, and as exhaled out, the peaceful smile settled back on her face. "But I believe."

Neither of us was healed by the weeping statue inside the church.

But I remembered her words.

And even though I knew I should have booked my flight home back to safe San Jose, California... on a whim at the airport I asked for the earliest flight to Anchorage.

Two weeks later, after sleuthing, tracing down rumors, and researching missing hikers and adventure seekers, I found my mountain.

And so here I am, slowly digging my crutches in then dragging one leg forward and then the other. And repeat.

I try not to let the anxiety battering at my heart overwhelm me as the sun falls lower and dark shadows are cast over the side of the mountain. Taking a moment to look outwards from the mountain, I can't deny it's beautiful here.

But then my attention zooms back to the ground in front of me. For all the beauty of the world I've just seen these past few months, my vision is mostly glued to the ground wherever I go.

I try to move faster as the sun drops lower, but after tripping and stumbling forward, only catching myself with my crutch at the last minute before plunging off the side of the mountain... Yeah, I think I'll go a little slower and more carefully.

I have no tent. No supplies other than the water bottles in my pants pockets, already half gone, and a flashlight... I click on the flashlight when the path gets too dark to see, but it's difficult to hold along with my crutches. Maybe if I put it in my teeth?

By the time it's almost full dark, I'm *so* exhausted.

Ready to drop, really. What the hell do I think I'm doing trudging up this dangerous mountain into darkness all alone? There's no way I'll have the energy to get back down again.

I try to bite back my tears, but they flood down my cheeks anyway.

Mother Mary, I pray, *and Fire Goddess and God and anyone else who might be out there, hear my prayer: don't let me die tonight.*

It's right after I finish praying that I first hear the inhuman *roar*.

MONSTER

CHAPTER TWO

When you flee from the world, there are few places that will allow solitude.

At least, if you're a monster like me.

But my Father Creator made me and then left me this way. Misshapen. Half-baked. Trying to fuse multiple creatures together which nature never intended to meet in one body.

I am an experiment gone terribly, terribly wrong.

And there is no kindness in this world for one like me.

I've sought out many haunts for my life of solitude. Soon I must go back home. I have responsibilities back in that place I detest. And besides, everywhere else, they will not leave me alone. I am an object of interest. Something out of scary stories made real for hunters to hunt. For adventurers to capture. A curiosity like they see in their zoos.

But I will never be fenced in.

And those who are not wise enough to back away from a lion's roar will meet its teeth.

I let out another mighty roar, but the light below bouncing up the path does not turn back.

I watch, alert, from the entrance of my high mountain cave. All other predators have vacated the area. They, at least, have enough sense and survival instinct to stay away from me.

It's only these human predators who have no instincts left. They ignore the tingle at the back of their necks. They think they know everything, that *they* are the gods. Ha!

I laugh in their faces every time before I devour them. I simply help them meet the true gods they have so casually disrespected.

Someday soon, they may come with their guns en masse, at which point I will have to vacate yet another sanctuary. These humans will not allow me among them, but I know enough of them that when too many gather, they can become pests. Like stepping into a bed of swarming fire ants. Far from deadly but annoying enough.

I will leave before that happens.

And certainly this one bobbing, shaky lantern light coming up my mountain at such an hour is no army.

I let out another mighty roar from deep in my unnatural belly. It shakes the ground I stand on. The lantern bearer is close enough, I imagine they are shaken, too.

Turn back, I urge them silently.

But after only a moment's pause, again the light comes steadily forward.

I let out a great, beastly sigh.

Oh well. I have not feasted on a good meal in a while. This doomed wanderer will meet their end in my belly, and then I will sleep well.

Still, I occasionally let out a loud growl to continue to warn them to turn back. It is not their hearing that lacks, for the little lantern pauses and wavers each time I do. But still, invariably, they come straight toward me.

I barely bother to hide my large shape when they get near enough to the small ledge that is my cave's entrance.

It does not smell good here. The cave was a home to bears before I took up my haunting here. I did not bother with cleaning it out, because why bother with all the upkeep? I intend to allow myself to be what I am here without any pretenses—just another animal. If it's what they treat me as, why fuss with all their human pretentions like cleanliness? Especially since it was also Creator-Father's obsession, and I have turned my back on all his ways.

At first, all I can see is the lantern light's glare. Or flashlight, I suppose, since the beam is so small and stinging. My eyes don't like the unnatural light.

After my incubation surrounded by godlight, I find all these human-lit filaments as abrasive as a curse on the lips of a child. Give me darkness any day to their false light.

I pull back just that much more as the creature does the most foolish thing any of them have yet.

They have come here with their popping guns and arched bows and nets and equipment to catch my likeness to prove my existence and bring swarms more of their kind—

But this one—a female I surmise by her form as she flings away contraptions she was using to hold herself up, along with the small light—falls face-forward to the ground.

The light rolls away from her and shines back her way, illuminating not my cave, but her face.

She is beautiful. Long red hair is caught by a tie at her nape, where the rest flows down her back. She lifts her face blindly toward my cave.

"Please," she cries. "God of darkness, I beg your mercy. I come alone. And I know you can turn me away, or worse. But I still beg your help."

Ah, so she comes wanting something. As all of them do.

She throws her arms out and crawls awkwardly forward. Only then do I see her slightly shrunken legs and the strange curve to her back. Unlike the other humans who have come to me, though, she crawls on her knees in supplication. I shift slightly so I can get a better look.

"God of the mountain, what offering might I give that would please you? Heal me, and I will give you anything you ask!" she cries out.

I pause.

Curious.

And I have not felt curiosity in a long time. It feels strange curling in my belly. To feel anything at all other than anger and bitterness is novel.

I tilt my head and take one step out of my cave. Quick as lightning strikes, I kick the little object making light away so that she will not see the face of the one she has come to beg favors from.

Not yet.

Apparently, I'm in the mood to play with my food.

"Anything?" I growl. "You will give anything for this great favor you ask?"

She raises her head, but I know without the sudden light, she cannot see anything more than my large shadow, if that.

No one ever makes offerings, only demands. Humans *used* to know the correct way to approach a god, but they have forgotten. All except this one.

"To heal costs me great suffering," I bark into the night.

She lifts her head, eyes darting to the left and right in such a way that I can tell she's been blinded by the lack of her light. I have perfect night vision. She does not.

"Healing me would hurt you?" The look on her face tells me the thought distresses her, and for a moment I'm taken aback.

No one has ever cared about the cost to me. I am merely a means to an end.

Her face falls, and I am astounded by the bright glint of a tear upon her soft cheek. "Then I am sorry to have come and bothered your sanctuary, God of Darkness."

I pause, astonished. She would turn back and cease her demands of me? Simply because I have informed her that it would hurt me?

"You come to me because you are displeased with the shape of the body you have been given?" I growl the words. She is still beautiful. Her world tolerates her to move among her kind. Whatever suffering she imagines she has is—

"It is killing me," she says simply, face still bowed to the ground. "And I am in daily pain."

"Many experience pain," I spit. "Many die. Why is your case special?"

She bows her head, and my eyesight is acute enough that I can see the tears rolling down her cheeks when she looks back at me.

"It's not. I'm not special, and I know there are plenty out there that suffer more than I do." But then she raises her head higher, though the rest of her body remains prostrate before me. "Perhaps you. We who suffer do not find kindness in this world."

I tilt my head, mind whirling at these unexpected circumstances. I *have* done it before, I suppose. Of course I am *capable* of the healing. And my life is full of pain, so what is a little more?

This—or at least the dark twin of healing—was part of what my Creator-Father intended when he created me. Had he loved me, I might have granted gifts such as this creature now asks for happily. But love is the one thing he could never manage. Not when it came to me. And so I have been essentially left alone, all these many years.

Yet this tiny, weak creature comes to me asking what she knows to be impossible, no doubt warned about this mountain and the creature that lurks here of late...

It must have required a lot of bravery and determination for her to make the journey.

Or perhaps she just hates her deformity and loves beauty that much.

Either way, I am enjoying the feeling of this fresh curiosity when I thought it long dead. I am cursed to live this life, and if this creature seeks the miraculous, then I will merely ask for the same in return as payment.

"I will give you this miracle you seek—"

Hope lights her face like the glow of heaven. "—on one condition."

"Anything," she says, too quickly, because she does not know what I will ask.

"I will heal you on the condition that you remain with me as my consort."

Shock hits her face at my request.

"For how long?" she asks.

I grin into the darkness, my sharp teeth clenching hard for a moment before I tell her my demands. "For forever, of course. In exchange for what you ask, you will become mine."

CHAPTER THREE

He's a monster to ask such a thing.

Maybe the roar and the deep, terrifying voice in the dark is just some boys with a voice modulator who wait up here in a cave to scare stupid girls like me for shits and giggles.

I can almost trick myself into believing that except... I can *feel* his—*its*—presence. And it came out of the cave to kick my flashlight away. I didn't imagine that. In the dark, I can feel him hulking over me. I look frantically up, left, and right but can't see a thing. It's just this... this, darker darkness.

But he is *big*. And while my eyes won't give me much information, all my other senses are taking in a lot.

He doesn't smell good, that is for damn sure. And all the hairs along my arms stand on end.

Every time he speaks, the ground seems to rumble

along with his deep bass. My bones vibrate inside me, too, I swear.

All of it adds up to...

Crazily, I believe what he says.

I believe he *can* heal me.

But the price he's asking. To be his *consort*? What the hell does that even mean? It's an old-timey word. Does it just mean companionship or is he asking for...?

"Let me see you," I say, heart pounding in my ears.

"So you can judge me as you have been judged?" His voice rumbles above me, and he sounds angry. "Do the eyes of mortals judge kindly those they do not deem beautiful?"

My whole body shakes now. I'm both ashamed and terribly, terribly afraid.

I would never judge anyone for not being beautiful.

... I don't think, anyway.

I have a feeling whatever this... creature is... will test me in ways I have never expected.

Deep down inside, some foolish part of me hopes that once I am healed, I can go back and pick up my life as it was. Except I'd be healed. I could fix things with Drew. The engagement fell apart because he didn't like the idea of me tramping all over the world looking for a miracle-cure he said we both knew wouldn't work.

Except... here I am, bowed before a miracle maker.

And if I take what's being offered to me, there won't be any going back to Drew. Or my mother. There may never be any going back, not if this creature meant his demands of *forever*.

But then, forever means I'd be alive to see it, doesn't it? I have to be alive to see any sort of forever.

Forever means longer than just another fifteen years on this earth, the whole time wondering if death is right around the next bend in the road, never being able to make plans for my future without worrying I won't be there to see them—

"Yes," I say before I can think it all the way through and talk myself out of it.

I have come looking for miracles. Beggars can't be choosers when it comes to these things. "I said I'd pay any price."

"I'm glad to hear that, I think," booms the dark voice from high above me.

And then things happen quickly.

So quickly I can barely register what's happening.

There's a swooping of wings, and then I'm surrounded by strong odors. I cough but there's nowhere to turn my face because strong hands grab me underneath my armpits and lift me up, up—

I scream when I'm lifted not just off the ground but up into the air.

The whoosh of air around me gets even louder while I'm dragged against the creature's chest. *Whoosh. Whoosh. Whoosh.* The sound is everywhere around us. Deafening.

My scream is drowned out as the earth drops away, and my stomach swoops wildly.

Oh my God!

We're in the air.

It—he—has *wings*!

I open my eyes for the first time to see wings spread out further than I can imagine—huge dark feathered wings that block out the stars.

I freak out, but there's nothing to grab onto. He's the one holding my crumpled body against his huge chest. The chest feels human—or more human.

At least until it starts to glow.

The glow starts from where I'd imagine a heart would be. Right where my face is smooshed up against his warm chest. I pull back and try to look up at his face—

Which is a mistake. Because his face is truly terrifying.

It's the hybrid face of a human and lion, with long, wicked black goat horns curving out from his temples on either side.

I scream right into his face.

He turns his face down to me and opens his mouth, full of razor-sharp teeth. Inches away from my face.

And he roars a deafening roar. Which only seems to make his chest glow brighter.

We were heading higher into the sky, but he pulls his wings back in, so we suddenly drop, swooping low.

My scream is cut off, not because I don't want to keep screaming—believe me, I really freaking want to keep screaming. But I physically can't, the downfall is so extreme, nothing will come out of my throat.

Meanwhile his chest burns brighter and brighter until I have to close my eyes as the freefall continues.

Even through my closed eyelids, though, I can see the shine.

It's burning my retinas it's so bright.

And then my own chest starts to get hot. Oh shit, he's burning me.

So this is what happened to all the disappeared hikers.

The monster in the mountain took them on a little flight and fileted them to charbroiled brisket. Will he gnaw on my bones after I'm cooked? At a glance I'd barely seem like a meal, but from the heat burning along my bones and coating my lungs—

I open my mouth and finally my scream is back.

I howl out my fury at being cooked alive from the inside out.

He's a liar and a cheat, and I'm a fool for walking straight into the lion's den when everyone from the mountain guide to Drew tried to warn me away. Thanks to my stubborn pride that was so certain *I* could find a solution to heal my body when doctor after doctor has told me it is helpless, there is nothing to do other than manage symptoms—

"Stop screeching," comes the monster's roar in my ear. "It is done. You are healed."

I pause, cutting off my death-scream to consider his words.

I'm sure it's a trick, considering we're still speeding through the air. He hasn't stopped flying. If anything, we're moving faster.

But the light which had been blinding white from his chest is now receding. And when I consider how my own chest feels. The burning heat that felt like it was cauterizing my insides as it jolted through me is... well it's all gone.

Sweat is quickly drying on my head from the cool air blasting my face as we speed through the air.

The monster's surprisingly human arms rearrange me in his grip so that I'm not even hanging precariously over the—

I twist my head to glance down at the ground—

Oh shit! It's so far below that in the break from the clouds where the moonlight shines through, I'm far up enough it's like the view out a plane window. Everything below is broken up into tracks of land like on a map.

And when I gasp for breath, even though the air feels thinner up here, I nevertheless feel it fill my lungs.

Not just halfway, like usual, because previously my bones constricted to keep me from drawing a full breath.

No.

No way.

Have I truly just been healed mid-flight by some sort of ancient chimera-like beast?

And if he fulfilled his part of the bargain, then when we reach wherever we're going, does that mean—

I'm his consort now. Oh shit.

MONSTER

CHAPTER FOUR

We fly long and hard.

It feels good to use my wings like this. I can attract attention, so I've only been hunting underneath the tree line lately. Which means I haven't been able to fully extend like this and it feels—

I let out a bellow as I flex and slice through the air with my body.

I'm not going as fast as I might because of the burden attached to my front. But at least she's stopped shrieking. I healed her with my holy light, and I suppose she can feel that.

Once we arrive it will be time for her to begin fulfilling her end of the bargain. To start her forever with me.

I won't be alone any longer.

It would have been too much to ask for a willing

partner to go through this life's journey by my side. With a face not even a father could love…

Even a slightly willing captive is far more than I ever expected to ask for.

She gave her consent, though, and I have fulfilled my end of the deal.

And, besides, if she disappoints, as every other creature I have ever come across always does, then I can simply go back to plan A—having her for dinner.

I frown as I flap my wings faster, speeding us toward our destination.

Not that she'd be much of a meal. She barely weighs anything in my arms. Her illness has kept her small and scrawny. Now she'd be worth little more than the toothpicks I could use her tiny bones for.

Barely a mouthful of meat on her entire frame.

I can certainly work on fattening her up, now, though.

A smile curves my wicked face at the thought.

She might be tiny, but she is still female. What meat she does have is distributed in the right places. Tiny little hips. Sweet breasts that swing from her chest, strapped to her body by some devilish contraption the female mortals like to wear here.

And now, for the first time in ages, I feel that male organ which so often lies dormant for me come to life at the feel of the woman in my arms.

She consented to be my consort.

Forever.

Tonight will be the first of many nights. And tomorrow,

the first of endless days. For now there is a female to receive my—

I swell and harden.

And at the same time, I swoop low, for we have finally arrived, thank the Sword I struck through the Creator's foul heart.

Her screeching starts up again. We are not going slow. Not now that I have my destination in my sights. And my consort's warm, squirming little ass right over my hard maleness.

I will fuck her first thing, I think.

We speed toward the ground, white with snow. It is still dark out, and I have flown far.

Morning will greet us shortly. I can smell it on the air.

I head toward the snow that glimmers below.

My consort's screams escalate to a fever pitch. My hearing is far more sensitive than any mortals, but I am too focused on the ground and our landing zone to tell her to stop. I squeeze her to me more tightly, hoping that will send a message.

It does not, apparently, or it sends the wrong one, because she screeches louder. I would not have thought it possible.

I heft her higher in my arms as we come in for a smooth landing.

I hop a few times on my large feet.

Her squalling does not stop.

I shake my consort. "We are on the ground," I growl. "Stop with your noise."

"Let go of me!" she screams. "Put me down!"

I roll my eyes but acquiesce, letting the heap in my arms roll onto the soft snow.

She immediately scrambles away from me. "My crutches," she says, looking around. "Where are my crutches?"

"You are healed."

Behind us, the sun crests the rim of the earth.

And with those first rays of light, my consort takes her first look not up at me, but down at her own legs.

I see the hope in her eyes, and as one familiar with hope and its disappointment, I watch it seep from her face.

Only then do her eyes fly to me, and they are full of accusation. "You didn't heal me!"

She impresses me, because even though she is now looking at my full monster's face—though perhaps I am still in shadow because the sun is behind me? still I am massive compared to her—she does not shy away in fear.

She is only fury and accusation.

She sits up, and in her fury, hops to her feet to come point her tiny finger in my huge face. "You said you'd heal me! We made a deal."

I smile down at her, and she only moves back a small bit at my mouthful of sharp teeth.

Hmm, I'm not sure if it is bravado or stupidity that drives her now. Most creatures naturally seem to have more survival instincts than this one. I am obviously a predator, but she is not predictable prey.

"Yet you are standing," I growl through my teeth. "And where is your pain?"

She opens her mouth, obviously with a retort ready on

her lips. But at my words, she freezes and looks down at herself.

"But— But—" She looks up at me, then down at herself again, as confused as a child. "I don't understand. I look the same."

When her eyes come back to me, I smile with all my teeth again. "Did I misunderstand your request? I thought you asked to be healed. Not to be made beautiful in appearance to others' eyes."

Her mouth drops open and she sputters. "But how can you— They're all tied together! The bones and—"

"Says who?" I growl, bending down so I am close to her.

She jerks back, but judging by her expression, and way she grabs for her nose, I am not sure it is self-preservation or simply my overwhelming... stink.

"Stay here," I order harshly. "Don't move."

"What?" she starts. "Where are you—"

I rise into the air before she can finish her inane question. I don't go far. I'm still within her field of vision, and her eyesight should be perfect now, along with the rest of her that I have healed from within.

I deposited us at my castle, which happens to be on the edge of a lake.

The lake is frozen over at present, but that's never stopped me before.

I ascend high into the sky then turn upside down and rocket with my claws extended toward the ice.

There's only a moment of brusque airtime before I smash into the icy surface. The pain is momentary, and then I'm plunged into breathtakingly cold water.

The angel-spark inside my chest strikes up and warms

me as I extend my wings fully outwards in the water. Flapping them quickly back and forth, I wash out the filth that has accumulated from my months in the bears' haunt.

I quickly scrub myself up and down, including my lion's mane, and then I head back toward the hole I created in the ice with its circle of sunlight beyond.

When I break from the surface with a bellow, my eyes immediately seek out my consort on shore.

And there she is.

Fleeing across the endless snow away from the lake.

Oh, sweet consort.

I roar, and my monster's laugh echoes out across the lake and back from the mountains on all sides of us. I explode out of the freezing water to chase down my prey.

HANNAH

CHAPTER FIVE

I flee.

I don't care if it doesn't make sense. I now understand fight or flight, and I am all *flight*.

There's an elation and terror in my legs' new-found strength. They shouldn't work as well as they do, considering they are the same legs I woke with yesterday—at least to see them from the outside.

But somehow there's fresh muscle inside—

Or maybe it's just absolute terror and the instinct for self-preservation at seeing a monster up close like that. Like the adrenaline that allows moms to lift thousand-pound cars off their kids. Yeah. Like that.

Cause when the sunlight broke over the horizon, and I saw its *face*—

His bulk has already told me that he is an unnatural thing, but to see it with my eyes and fully realize that while all this time I've been praying to the heavens...

I've accidently unearthed something straight from hell.

And when you look a demon in the face...

Well, you run.

You run as fast as the legs you've got can carry you, regardless of how those legs function.

When he explodes through the ice like a torpedo, I'm already running.

He's going to kill me. He's already taken me to a secondary location. I don't know why I suddenly forgot all the stranger-danger instruction I've been taught my whole life.

Especially as a disabled woman, I've taken as many self-defense classes as possible. When the first class and first lesson had the instructor say that a person's best chance is to *run*, I thought, well I'm screwed.

But here I am, *running*.

The problem is, I'm not being chased by any ordinary predator.

And I *am* being chased. I see that when I look over my shoulder and scream. Because the bird-man-lion monster is up in the air again, flinging water from the lake off his great wings with a mighty flap.

His head moves around as if he is searching.

Maybe he has bad eyesight with those strange cat's eyes of his. Maybe he's like those dinosaurs in *Jurassic Park* and can only see things when they're moving. Not that it stops me from sprinting like my life depends on it. Especially considering that I'm pretty sure it does.

A fresh burst of energy burns through my blood, and I sprint for a rocky outcrop ahead. If he is like the dinosaurs, maybe I can hide in the rocks and he won't—

I scream as clawed hands grasp me underneath my armpits, and then I'm being lifted off the ground. I bicycle my feet uselessly in the air as the crunchy white snow disappears in front of me, and I'm swung up into the sky.

"Let go of me!" I scream. "Let *go!*"

I look around wildly as I'm whipped through the air. Unlike when we took off from Alaska, there's nothing below us—no separated tracts of land. It's all just... unending white. No lights of human dwellings *anywhere*. It's only October. Where are we that it's *this* snowy, this time of year? Somewhere in the Arctic Circle, or what? How is there a *castle*—

"Are you sure of that?" he growls.

My entire body is wracked with shivers from the freezing air... and his voice. This is all wrong, wrong, wrong. *Unnatural.*

"Let me go!" I scream again.

And then—dear Jesus—he does.

He drops me, and where moments before, there was controlled flight, now I'm freefalling.

I can't even catch my breath to scream as the white, packed snow comes at me faster than—

I flail uselessly as if my tiny, bony arms will do anything to soften my impact, moments from hitting.

And then I'm caught again. Awkwardly by my middle, clawed fingernails slicing into my shirt as I'm captured from above.

Harshly my descent is stopped, and then we're ascending again.

No longer able to fight, I go limp, all my adrenaline spent.

My body is spiraling in the wind, the swoop of his huge wings stirring the air all around us and making a loud *whoosh-whoosh-whoosh*.

I expect a hard landing, if not to be dropped again.

Instead, when the clawed hands do release me—

I scream, but do not hit anything hard. Not even cold, packed snow.

No, I land on a soft...?

I look down and then scurry so that I'm sitting up, tangling myself in sheets and a fur blanket.

A bed?

He's brought me to a bed.

And then I scramble to the wall, remembering what I promised in return for my healing. To be his *consort*. Oh shit.

I hold up my hands as the creature drops down to... hooved feet!

He takes a step toward me, and the light comes in full through the window. I look furiously around, trying to get my bearings.

The walls are stone, like I'm in an old castle, and the window looks out on a vista of white snow and the iced-over lake. He's just flown us in through the window.

I scan the view frantically, but there's more snow. More lake.

And that's all.

I don't see the lights of a town, or any other human habitation. Where the hell am I?

I look back to the demon.

He takes another step toward the bed. His enormous black wings span the entire width of the room, and while his face is fairly human, his nose is still somewhat leonine. His lip is split in the middle, and his eyes have cat-like slit pupils. Instead of skin, he's covered with short fur, and sports a lion's mane for hair. Now that he's clean, I can tell his fur is a golden color, but the curling horns extending from each side of his crown are an intimidating, inky black, like his wings.

The short fur also covers his man-like chest but it stops when it gets to his—

I drop my gaze then feel my eyes grow wide. Naked. He's totally naked.

Oh God. He's man-like down there, too. Exceedingly manlike, and... *excited*, if that log hanging between his legs is any indication.

I back up even further against the wall, even though I don't have anywhere else to go. I burrow my back against the corner and hold up my hands.

"Whoa, whoa, whoa, buddy! Let's just slow down a second here!"

"Slow down?" he growls. "I did not see consort slowing down as she ran away. You run, I will chase."

I laugh nervously, still keeping my hands up as a useless barrier between us. "That was just a misunderstanding. You flew away like that and I—"

I'm not sure how, considering all that fur, but I can tell

he's lifting a sarcastic eyebrow at me. "And you run the opposite direction from me, forgetting your promise after you got what you wanted?"

I shake my head. No, not that, definitely not that. "I wasn't sure if you healed me."

"Now you see. Your legs work well. See how fast you run."

My mouth drops open to make an intelligent retort. To point out the moms-lifting-cars-thing. But then... then I really stop and think about it.

The way I was running... sprinting really. I haven't been able to do that... *ever*. Not even when I was a kid. It was one of the things that had my parents thinking something might be wrong with me. I couldn't run around like the other kids. Instead, I just tripped and fell a lot.

I certainly didn't sprint so fast I felt the wind in my hair. Like ever, in my whole life.

"But I—" I start, and that furry eyebrow of his arches even higher.

What can I say? I asked for a miracle and didn't really think the consequences all the way through, even when I agreed to... gulp... *forever?*

Oh shit, I'm gonna be dizzy.

I swoon a little forward.

"Yes," says the demon. "Lie down for first time as my consort. Good idea."

I reach back and for the wall stones again. "Whoa!" I say, "Not so fast."

"Why not fast?" He reaches toward me with one

dark-clawed finger. "I healed you fast. Did we agree or not? Should I take back the healing?"

I freeze, hand still out toward him, his finger halted an inch from my palm.

Shit, this is all happening so fast. Why did I agree to it? Now he expects me to— To give my *body* to him?

I start shaking my head, my refusal on my lips. Ready to tell him that yes, I want him to take the healing back, that I want out of here, that I've made a terrible mistake—

But the words freeze in my throat.

Because running like that, even if it was while experiencing the most terror I've ever felt in my life, was also... *exhilarating.* I mean, it was beyond. I've been trapped in the cage of my body my entire life. And just because I couldn't escape today doesn't mean I never will.

Even if I spend ten years with him as payment for this new body, that's as much as I had left to live on earth.

I look at the beast, who's a little less terrifying every moment I become more accustomed to his face. "How long will the healing last?"

"Forever. Now you have been touched by angel-spark, you will live longer than most humans."

I blink, thinking of all I could do with... life without limits. I can finally begin a career without worrying that there is no point because I'd never see retirement. Or I could focus on my art and not because I hoped to flash like a shining star before my life is extinguished.

Is a blank canvas full of possibility really worth—

I raise my eyes to the demon. My head still spins with all that my life can now be that the term *future* isn't a curse word.

Am I not willing to sell my soul to the devil for even the *chance* at all that?

The demon in front of me grins big, all those sharp teeth of his glistening. A wolf in wolf's clothing. And I'm lying to myself if I think I didn't walk into this with my eyes wide open.

"Okay," I whisper.

The claw he still has held out moves forward the last inch, flips over, and slices through my clothing as smoothly as if it were silk.

"Then you are mine," he says, and drops one knee on the bed.

MONSTER

CHAPTER SIX

She is ripe for me.

The scent from between her legs speaks of her readiness and sparks the fire in me.

I have shorn her of the cloths covering her small body. She is bare as a furless kit.

Her eyes go wide as orbs when I shift her underneath me.

"Don't hurt me," she gasps.

I frown. Does she misunderstand? "You are my consort," I say as if this explains all.

And lick my lips.

CHAPTER SEVEN

He puts his large hands around his absolutely ginormous shaft. It takes everything I have not to scramble off the bed. Is he seriously about to try to shove that goddamn thing in me?

I mean I've heard of jumping in the deep end but Jesus Chr—

His huge body leans over me, and his wings flare outwards around us, blocking out the light.

He doesn't stink like earlier. I figured he was going into the lake to hunt some food or something but was he actually... taking a bath?

My mind races as I cling to the sheets as his still-dripping lion's mane dips down toward my breasts. Oh shit, with those teeth, he could shred me—

But I barely have the thought before a warm, wet tongue contrasts the freezing water from his hair.

And while I can feel his hot log of a cock against my thigh, he just lets it rest there.

He licks all around my left nipple with his rough, rasping tongue.

I gasp and my back arches up in my surprise. Which he apparently takes as a good sign, because his leonine mouth closes around my suddenly hard nipple.

I blink in confusion and shoot one hand from the sheet underneath me to clutch—his mane. Jesus why am I clutching onto his wet hair?

Like I'm—

As if I'm—

He maneuvers his mouth in such a way that the barest edge of his teeth bite against my now rock-hard nipple. And he pulls back, and then does it again.

As if with those huge, man-eating teeth, he's just intentionally *nibbling* on my breast.

I screech, but it's not in fear this time. It's a breathy little moan of… of pleasure.

What the absolute *hell* is happening?

Is he a literal demon? He mentioned angel-spark? Is that why one touch of his raspy tongue and those menacing teeth against my rock-hard nipple—

My hips lift unintentionally up off the mattress.

Where my inner thigh again encounters his absolute ship's mast of a cock. He pulses and leans up and into my thigh.

My entire body jolts at the indecent action while I snake my other hand to his head. Where I encounter one of his massive horns and grip onto it. But I'm not sure if I'm trying to pull him away or urge him on.

One more swipe of his tongue and my stomach spasms. Really low. And this intensity suddenly tingles between my legs.

Holy crap! My eyes pop back wide open again. Is this what it feels like to…

… to come?

I blink rapidly, trying to understand the sensations the demon is raising in my body even as he releases my left breast with a wet little *pop* and moves on to the right one. Immediately, he goes after the nipple again. It was soft but after a second's attention of his tongue and the nip of his teeth, the nipple hardens right up to a little pebble.

I mean with my ex-fiancé, we had sex sometimes. Not too often because… well. It's not that it was painful… though sometimes it was. I tried to suggest positions I'd read online could make it easier on my body and bone structure, but that wasn't the way he liked it. So we just did it the way Drew preferred, and we used lube because I never got very wet. He said some women were like that, and that it wasn't my fault.

I took comfort in that.

I was just one of those broken women, in more ways than one.

I've made my peace with it.

So, what the *hell* does my body think it's doing now?

I study the ceiling, my fingers clenching in the lion's mane and his horn as he continued doing what he was to my nipples, that warm, solid log against my thigh occasionally twitching.

Holy shit, when he said he healed me, did that mean he healed *this* part of me, too? Whatever it was that made a woman be able to—

I grab his horns with both hands and wrench hard as I cry out, my groin arching up into him. Without exactly meaning too, my legs... open a little.

He growls and releases my nipple. I barely have a chance to gasp for breath, still confused about what's happening. I let go of his horns and dig my elbows into the bed, boosting myself up so that I can tell him to wait, that we should slow down, to tell him *something*—

But at this angle I can see his long, unnatural tongue extend. With one strong, clawed hand, he takes the small opening I've given and shoves my leg against the mattress.

So that I'm completely exposed to him.

Okay.

This is it.

He'll fuck me with that giant log now, and it'll hurt. Like when Drew forgot to use lube that time, and I handled that just fine.

You can do this. Just close your eyes and go over what you'll make your next painting look like.

I clutch my eyes closed and drop down to my back, not wanting to look anymore. It's fine. We can do this any day of the week. And it's a good exchange, my health for just letting a man... well, mannish-type-creature... spend a little time getting his rocks off with my body, that's fine—

He grasps my hips, and he must've retracted his claws

or something, because they don't pierce my skin. They just graze me tantalizingly.

And despite myself, this *won't* be entirely without lube.

Because I'm slick for the monster-man above me.

Not just slick, either, if I'm really being honest.

I finally understand what they mean when they say *wet*.

I'm wet for this.

It feels like I'm betraying Drew. Yes, I broke up with him, but part of me sorta thought that if I managed the impossible, and got my miracle, I could show back up on his doorstep as a whole woman, his equal—

Instead I'm here, squirming under a clawed hand holding my leg open, the other one at my hip. My wet center open and exposed. The cool air of the castle tower room hits my pussy.

I wish he would just stick it in and then I could be distracted by the burning and the stretching instead of this torment of thoughts in my head—

The icy wetness of his mane against my hot inner thighs shocks me, and I quickly tilt up my head. Wait, what the hell is he—

And then that long, rough tongue of his licks up my pussy slit.

CHAPTER EIGHT

Consort tastes good. Salty. Like the best meal I've had in a long time.

I never knew what a woman would taste like.

I always just went hard at the thought.

The reality is—

Better.

My tongue is long and strong. I stick it inside her little hole and explore all around.

She heaves and squirms above me. More juices flow out onto my tongue. I like the way it tastes. I like it very much.

I've heard much of fucking. I've read much about it. Watched occasionally.

None of it can compare to this soft wet flesh in my mouth.

Or the live woman squirming and jerking beneath my heavy body. She is so small, but her little mewls of pleasure make my rod *big*. Big and harder than I have ever been before in my life.

I withdraw my tongue from its exploration of her hole and move up her slit.

She makes noises. I think she misses my tongue.

I lift a knuckle and press it to the rim of her opening. At the same time, I move my tongue to swirl all around the soft little nubbin at the top of her sex I coax to life with my tongue. I have heard of this legendary spot and want to explore.

Indeed, when I latch onto it a little and suckle, she comes to life more than I have ever yet seen her.

Her hands come back to my horns. I like it when my little kitten's paws seek my horns, like handles. Especially when she is pulling me to her flesh like that, her thighs flapping wider than ever.

It is as it is meant to be.

My consort is ready for me. I push my fat knuckle in, and I stretch her while I continue to suckle her.

She cries out and her body spasms against my face.

I taste her fresh pleasure.

Now it is time for mine.

After a lifetime of solitude, for the first time in my life, I will fuck.

HANNAH

CHAPTER NINE

I'm still spasming in the aftershocks of what I'm pretty sure is my first-ever orgasm...? Holy shit, I just came. I finally *came*... from being eaten out by some sort of demon monster.

When he rises, mouth glistening with my juices, I let go of his horns as he takes his giant cock in one hand. He's terrifying. He's so big, his large hand doesn't even close around his shaft. Not even including the claws.

"Now we fuck," he proclaims.

My mouth drops open.

There's time to protest.

But nothing comes. Because... I don't *want* to protest. As hard as he just made me come, my legs fall open wide to him. In this wild moment, oh God, I want to see what might come next.

And then he's there, his absolutely *obscenely* large cock

at the rim of my pussy, stretching as he pushes forward.

Is it too late to ask about demon-human sexually transmitted diseases? Is my pussy going to light up like a glow-stick after this?

Wrong question for my brain to ask right now, considering that demon-lord dude's chest literally begins to glow as he presses forward and the angular tip of his cock begins to breech me.

It takes my breath away.

But not from pain.

The stretch feels... incredible.

My eyes roll back in my head. Especially when he leans his hips forward so that the girth of his cock slides against my clitoris.

He's too big!

It's a desperate thought in my head even as shame washes me at the pleasure quaking down my spine at having this huge beast-man penetrate me.

What if I... just give in to the pleasure?

God, is that *my* voice or his somehow inside my head?

What exactly *are* his powers anyway? Beyond healing and somehow knowing how to drive a woman absolutely insane with his sexual prowess?

I look down our bodies between the valley of my breasts.

And then wish I hadn't.

Because he's impossibly large. His cock gets even wider as it goes down toward his groin. "It won't fit," I gasp through heaving breaths. I feel panicked. My hands scrabble against the sheets again. I'm not sure I can—

"I fuck you now," was all he growled in response.

And his hips move inescapably forward, pushing in another impossible inch. And dear God, I don't know exactly how, but my body receives him. There's nowhere else to go against such a thick battering ram.

My body stretches.

He keeps pushing in.

I start to howl, a panicked, unsure noise.

When I look up at his face, his lion's teeth are bared. He whips out his long tongue to lick his glistening bottom lip when he notices me looking.

"Submit," he growls, and brings one of his clawed hands to my throat. He doesn't hold me hard or even clench his hand.

But he could. It is so obvious who is the predator with the control here and who is the helpless subject getting fucked.

So why the hell does the grip of his hand around my vulnerable neck and the slightest scrape of his clawed thumb at my pulse point make another spurt of wetness help ease his passage as he pushes even deeper inside me?

"You engorge me," he hisses through his teeth.

I look down. He's not even halfway inside me. And he's right. I have apparently engorged him—he's even thicker around than when he first started.

"It won't fit!" I cry, my breasts heaving.

One knee on the bed, spearing me with his huge cock, he gives me his terrifying smile again. "You will. You will love to engorge and fuck me. I will teach you how."

I think I squeak at that because a part not so deep down inside me is quickly coming to think he might be right. Oh

God, what the hell am I supposed to do with that? I've never felt anything like this; I never knew a body *could* feel anything like this—

And then his wings, which have so far have been still, or as still as they could, rush to life.

"I call for the angel-spark over this consort," he roars.

And then his giant wings began to flutter as they curve in and around our bodies in such a way that— I have no idea what he's doing since it's not like he's trying to fly. Until I realize that the very *tippy tips* of his silken black wings are fluttering—

"Oh God!" I scream as his wings flutter against my clit while he thrusts his log cock as far in as it can go, and then pulls it out again with such force that I slam against his chest.

The tips of his wings are still between us. Unnaturally and indecently fluttering against my sex like the most unusual vibrating sex toy anyone could ever imagine.

With his human arms he clutches my body to his. I reach for his horns, holding on for dear life as he rides me, fucking me so deep while his wings *flutter-flutter*, and it all makes me quake—

He presses his thumb at the pulse point of my throat, locking his bright, tiger-colored cat's eyes at me.

"God cannot help you now. Gush over me, Consort," he orders, "and I will gush for you."

God help me, I do.

I come and come and come while the most enormous object I can imagine thrusts in and out of my pussy.

And then he roars, and I'm blinded by the light

exploding from his chest. His wings flap faster, and I feel it inside me.

It's liquid light.

It's only milliseconds before the hottest pleasure I could never have imagined spikes through me from my tailbone up my spine and then reverberates back.

Oh God.

He has magical cum.

And.

I.

Can't.

Stop.

Com-

ing-

around-

his-

giant

shaft

split-

ing

me

open.

CHAPTER TEN

When I awaken, I'm alone.

And filthy with the remnants of...

I blush and shift in bed, only to find each of my limbs sore. I look around the medieval castle room, brief hope filling my chest when I see two heavy doors to the chamber.

I hop out of the huge bed as quickly as my aching limbs can manage and push one of the doors.

Thank God it's a bathroom!

And while it's no modern luxury suite or anything, the toilet is recognizably a toilet, and perfectly clean, as is the clawfoot tub. After I finish relieving myself, I twist the brass knobs, and clean water spurts out of the tub spigot, and after a few minutes, it even starts to run warm, then hot.

God bless modern plumbing. I genuinely had no idea what I'd run into.

I get in the tub while the water's still running and do a first quick wash of myself to get most of the… well, *excess* off. It still glows a little as it swirls down the drain, and my cheeks heat with embarrassment.

Then I plug the tub and let the hot, steamy water fill all around me. And really take a chance to look at my surroundings.

As in the bedroom, it's just cold stone walls in here, too. The only nods to modernity are the plumbing and a rug tossed carelessly on the floor.

But it's *freezing* in here. I'm not sure whoever made this place ever heard of the wood insulation, and my bathwater feels like it's cooling down as fast as I pump hot water into it. I sink my body into the water that's steaming as soon as it hits the cold air.

The warm water is magic on my achy muscles.

My brain seems to skip around the *reason* I'm so achy.

But now, like an object I've been trying to glance away from for too long, my mind's eye locks straight on it—my muscles are so sore because I used them quite extensively *having sex!*

And not simple, safe sex like I had with Drew.

No, the monster and I had intense, all-consuming, mind-altering *sex*.

I came.

Maybe more than once. I'm not sure. Or maybe that was all wrapped up in one super-intense orgasm? How is a girl who's never had one before to really know?

I wrap my arms around my body in the warm water and shiver. And then, as I try to absorb the hot water beyond my sore, cold muscles, I swear I hear a faint, distant scream.

I sit up straighter, water sloshing out the sides of the tub, my eyes wide. Is someone else here? I mean besides me and the—

But as I strain to hear if the sound repeats, there's nothing. It's just the wind and my imagination.

I sink back into the water, and as I warm up, my mind drifts back to the mind-altering sex. Dear *God*. It couldn't have really been as good as my memory is trying to make it out.

But even just thinking of how it felt when he opened my legs and pushed in, and how my body stretched so impossibly wide around his *huge*—

I slip my hand down my hip and between my thighs.

"It is good to find my consort naked and ready for me." The huge voice booms from the doorway.

I sputter and sit up in the water, which again exposes my finally heated, wet flesh to the cold air. Which has me dropping back down into the warm water again.

"Get out!" I shriek. "I'm not decent!"

But the monster just leans one huge forearm against the door jamb, his wings in their folded position behind him, blocking out most of the morning light.

I can't decide if he's more terrifying as a silhouette, like this, or in direct sunlight where I can see his lion's face, black horns, mouth full of teeth, and occasionally glowing chest.

"Naked consort is very decent," is all he says, and there is enough light to see his lion's mouth creep up into a wide smile—something between a Cheshire cat's smile and a predator who looks ready to devour me.

"Bath time's over. Your training begins today."

I feel my brows lower. "Training? What do you mean?"

But he just approaches, reaches down into my bathwater, and plucks out the plug holding the water in.

"Hey!" I protest.

"No time to waste," is all he says. "Let's go, little pink consort."

I look down at myself, flushed with embarrassment and furious at him for making me feel this way. I cover my breasts with one arm and my pussy with the other as I stand up confidently. It's obvious he's not going to be gentlemanly and wait outside. And my clothes are in the other room anyway. Well... what's left of them.

I grab for the towel, but the monster-man is quicker. He yanks it away faster than I can reach for it. Again, with that smile that borders on a smirk.

He approaches, his hand full of a towel. Okay. So it's clear he wants to be the one to dry me. My first instinct is to push him away.

Yes, I let him fuck me last night but that is just part of the gig, right? Sexual favors in return for my healing.

But this doesn't seem to have anything at all to do with the deal we made, and I'm not sure how I feel about it.

When he approaches with the towel and slowly begins to wipe down the water droplets, though, it makes my head a little dizzy.

I want to pull away or tense at his ministrations, but instead my whole body relaxes.

For all this bulk, he can be surprisingly gentle.

So gentle, in fact, as he dries me off, that, like a fool, I let my eyes close.

I hear the *tinkle-tinkle-clank* far too late to do anything else but jerk back to the present right as I feel the cold kiss of metal close around my neck.

"Hey!'"

But he's already gotten the heavy iron collar around my neck, with attached medieval chain, and he locks it into place.

I grasp hold of it, and it's so thick, my thin little fingers barely make it around the thick metal band. What I wouldn't give for a fresh set of bolt-cutters right now.

"Are you kidding!" I cry. I hate being constrained. It's one of the reasons I've always hated my body so much. For someone who's always *go-go-go*, it's infuriating to have a body that's so often kept me inside and still, away from the adventures I've always dreamed of.

"Why are you doing this?" I hate my voice when it trembles.

He just stares uncomprehendingly at me with his cat's eyes. "Because you are my consort, and you will behave as one."

He starts to back away to the bedroom, the long chain trailing behind him, stretching between us...

But he jerks me forward when I don't move.

I stumble forward, disoriented after being torn from

the warm bath back into the cold. And hello? I'm still completely naked!

But the monster doesn't slow for me. He obviously knows where he's going as he drags me back through the bedroom and then drags open the other door through which he strides.

My thoughts are chaotic and random. If he has this place, why in hell was he squatting in that filthy mountain cave back in Alaska? Why has he waited until this morning to collar me?

He jerks me forward by the chain when apparently, I've been dithering too long—pulling me toward the bedroom's second door, other than the one leading to the bathroom.

Oh God, what have I gotten myself into?

Is it any solace that as I stumble after him, it's on sturdy, steady feet?

The sensation is still so new, I still can barely believe it.

"Where are we going?" I gasp as I'm pulled through the door into a hallway.

All I get back in return is a growl.

A freaking *growl*. Ever the reminder I'm not dealing with a human man.

First, we head down a long, claustrophobic stone hallway. Where to, God knows. My mind whirs non-stop as I wonder what's next, when we reach a steep, curling staircase.

The monster's huge wings flop and flutter ahead of me as he stomps.

I'm a Taurus and have been stubborn since the moment

I was born, or so my mother says. I came out of the womb kicking and screaming.

I was a wild child before the bounds of my illness tamed me. And since I got sick when I was so young, I didn't appreciate the wild years when I had them.

I kept trying to do everything the other kids did. Climbing on the playground. When a boy taunted me in junior high for sitting out during recess, I challenged him to a race.

Naturally, I lost dismally, of course—I'd just got my arm-crutches then, and I wasn't very good at using them yet. But I still raced around that track as quickly as I could stumble.

"What were you like as a little kid?" I ask suddenly as we start to head down the staircase. Try to humanize yourself in captor situations, isn't that what they always say?

At least rectangular windows punched out in the walls allow light in. But, naturally, there are no glass panes in them, and freezing air with wafts of snow burst in at intervals.

I grasp at the metal around my neck as I try to make casual conversation. I can't believe something so medieval still exists—much less that I'm chained up by it and being dragged around by this... whatever he is.

"Never child," he growls back over his shoulder. I can just see the corner of his jaw in the space between his shuddered wings. "Always this."

I blink. Okaaaaaaay. "Well, what was it like when you first... uh... started existing?"

The silence extends so long I think he's not going to answer me.

At least we're finally done descending the endless staircase. He pulls me into a large anteroom that has a long, long table running down its center with a plate and drink in front of the large chair at its head. The room is totally empty except for a fireplace in the center of one wall. Otherwise, it's just cold, stone walls.

No fire is burning, and flurries of snow gust in through several more open windows, while ice gathers in the corners and along the heavy beams that stretch across the ceiling. My teeth jitter in my freezing nakedness, and I cross one arm uselessly across my chest.

"Cozy," I whisper.

The beast whips its head around toward me. "First existence-time was bad. Creator-Father was cruel. Creator-Father liked to beat me because I did not turn out as desired. I displeased him."

I blink again, not sure where to focus—on his unnerving cat's eyes or his even more unnerving lion's mouth.

Or most disconcerting of all—how even though he is most obviously monstrous, there is still something unalienably *human* about him.

"Only good time," he continues, much to my surprise considering he hasn't been all that talkative in my limited experience, "was when Creator-Father had a consort. She was obedient and took care of me. She fed me and fucked my Creator-Father well."

"Oh," I say.

"Now *you* are consort."

I nod. "Yeah, I got that part."

"You fuck *me* well now."

It takes everything I have not to roll my eyes. Especially at the way his terrifying mouth turns up at the edges in what I think is his... smile? And staring at him now in all his towering monstrousness as the morning light pours through four large eastern windows...

Dear God, what happened last night has to have been a dream. Some hallucinogen-induced nightmare. In fact, I'm pretty sure all of this— Maybe that cave was full of some kind of mushrooms, and that's why hikers don't come back. We all get exposed to a toxic fungal gas, that makes us hallucinate and have wondrous, ludicrous visions of—

Tree-trunk cocks?

I slap a hand over my mouth to stop a hysterical giggle. What else am I supposed to do? Because this is all suddenly feeling like a terrible nightmare.

But then I'm yanked forward again by the metal collar around my neck, which makes all laughter stop abruptly in my chest.

Oh God. Nope, this is all far too real again. And whatever I might have thought this could be last night, in a crazy moment of lusty, romantic fancy—it's clearly not. He's dragging me around by a collar and chains, freezing and naked.

"Look, about this whole consort business," I try anyway, as he jerks me forward until I'm only a couple of feet away from him. I'm nimble on my feet now and able to hurry. I try to keep ahead so he stops with the *yanking* me around business. Moving quicker helps against the lung-clenching cold, too. My feet are already blocks of ice.

"I think it's about time we establish some boundaries," I say frantically. "And get me some clothes? Maybe we could go back for the comforter if there's nothing else?"

He pauses and stares at me, the chain loose in his hands. "What is boundaries?"

I blink but before I can speak, he's dragging the heavy chain so that it rattles and sparks along the stone floor as he starts forward again. I scurry to keep up before the metal collar can tug at my neck again.

"Well," I hurry to explain, "boundaries are helpful between two people—say two *strangers*—like us, for example. It's about personal space. And sometimes I'll need some alone time."

His wings shake, and a few huge black feathers flutter to the floor. I noticed them all over the bedroom earlier. Normal men shed hair; he sheds feathers.

And then he whips around to face me, and his wings flare to their full extension, enormous in the big room, stretching probably thirty feet in diameter. And he grabs the chain right close to where it links to the metal collar around my throat, jerking me roughly to him.

I squeak as he draws my face forward so that it's just inches from his.

And he gives me that terrifying smile again.

Except it's up very, very close.

"There is no per-son-al space. Or a-lone time." He even says the words like they are foreign concepts. "You are my consort. Your time is my time." He pulls me even closer, so that my nose touches his cool, leathery lion's nose. His liquid amber cat's eyes blink sideways as he peers straight into my soul. "Your space is *my* space. Your body, *my* body."

I nod, terrified. Terrified... and something else I'm not prepared to name. But nothing gets past him and that damnable nose of his.

He pauses and sniffs, then puts his hands underneath my armpits and lifts me up straight off the ground until my—

"Hey!" I screech and bat at his face—which is now avidly sniffing me... *down there.*

He grins up at me. "My consort is not opposed to these ideas. Your body tells me so."

I'm freezing and upset, and I can't even believe— Just because my dumb body happens to remember how good last night felt has absolutely nothing to do with how pissed off I am at him chaining me up and dragging me around—

I kick, hoping to get in a good smack in with these strong new calves, and put some real force behind my efforts.

But he's lowered me, gently placing my feet back on the freezing stone.

"Time for that later," he says, which he amends with a sideways tilt of his head. "Soon. First, we eat."

I'm about to tell him that no, *first,* we finish the conversation about boundaries, and then we find me some clothes because not all of us can regulate our temperature with fur because you know, I don't *have any*—

But then my stomach rumbles with hunger. Dammit, when *was* the last time I ate?

And by that point, he's already dragging me over to the long table.

He points down to the floor where a small cushion rests beside the large chair at the head of the table. The steak on the plate in front of his chair smells delicious as steam wafts off it—it's freshly cooked. I look around for my plate.

"On your knees. Not a morsal unless you are in consort position."

My mouth drops open, and I'm sure my eyes blaze as I stare up at him. We've been in the morning light for about half an hour now. And well, after the first shock of how damn *big* he is has finally started wearing off... He's not all that terrifying, I suppose.

Yes, it is still somewhat frightening to see a man-shaped guy with lion's features, short golden fur like a lion might have all over his face except for his exceptionally furry eyebrows. Yes, those big, black goat's horns are a smidge disconcerting... And those unnerving eyes. Not to mention the dark lion's nose and that split-lipped mouth that I remember all too well from last night...

As if he knows exactly what I'm thinking, he flips out his long, long tongue and licks those self-same lips.

I step back from him, hands on my hips. "Why the hell did you give me working legs if all you're going to do is order me to my knees?"

That wicked, terrifying mouth of his twists up in a grin. "You only get to your knees when *I* tell you. It is I who gave good legs to you, and I who can take them away. So you bow to me on your knees when I command it."

His answer only infuriates me more.

"So this is how it'll be?" I ask, totally pissed now. I'm not new to people thinking they can take advantage of me. There's this general idea out there that people are nice to the disabled, but that's BS. I've been treated like crap my whole life. When I'm not being looked past as if I don't even exist, I've had people try to take advantage of me because they assume I'm helpless.

When I visited Chicago, I was robbed. Naturally, the pickpocket looked around and thought *I* looked like a perfect, weak target.

Even my own mother. She always assumes I can't do things. And rather than let me figure out how to do them on my own, she just quickly grows impatient with my slowness and does them for me.

It's why I like Drew so much. He trusted me to do things for myself. At least until he didn't. I frown, even more angry and not sure why.

I focus on the monster in front of me.

Yes, that's what he is. A monster. I rattle the solid metal ring around my neck as if to prove it to myself.

"You'll just threaten to take back my legs if I don't do exactly what you want? If I don't bow and scrape to your every whim for the rest of my *life*, you'll just keep threatening me? I thought we made a deal."

His face is unreadable. He's not exactly smiling anymore, but all his teeth are still all bared. "Do not question my honor. I am not like Creator-Father." He bends so his face is in mine. Invading personal space seems to be a favorite pastime of his. But I don't move back or let him know he intimidates me. "I do not lie."

Well now I'm currently losing my momentary inoculation against his size. Jesus he's a large... whatever he is. He's almost twice as tall as me.

"You don't lie?" I scoff. "What's that supposed to mean?"

"Deal is deal. You will bow on your knees out of *respect*. For I am worthy of your respect. I am the being that restored your legs. And so you will bend them to bow to me now."

"You aren't a god," I bark at him, not quite sure where I'm getting my bravado.

"I may as well be yours"—he glares right back—"for I will give you freedom only when you bow before me and acknowledge me as your master."

I just stare at him. "What the hell does that mean? You'll take this stupid thing off?" I rattle the heavy chained collar around my neck.

He pulls back, a motion so fast it's absolutely inhuman. Another reminder, as if I need any, that he is anything but a normal man.

"The ways of angels are above the ways of men," he says in a rote manner, like he's quoting some sort of scripture.

I tilt my head and frown.

His grin is back. "Now." Again, his sharp claw finger points toward the cushion on the floor beside his chair. "On your knees."

A shiver starts in my legs, but I force my spine straighter. It still feels strange to stand straight so comfortably.

"No." My voice only shakes a *little* as I say it.

His cat's eyes flare and blink rapidly a few times, and his hand tightens around the chain he's allowed to go slack for several minutes.

I arch my eyebrow at him. "Are you a coward? Only cowards use force."

His eyes flare again, and then, hand by hand, he draws me closer with the chain. But he does it slowly so that I'm not yanked, just urged, inch by inch. And then he grins again. "On that we agree. So you will bow before me because it is your desire."

I laugh in his terrifying face. "Fat chance."

He yanks me the last inch forward until he is gripping the large metal collar around my neck. "Fine," he growls.

I yelp a little as his knuckles graze against the tender flesh of my neck, right at my pulse point.

He reaches down, and I blink. Jesus, is he reaching for his— Are we about to... again—?

My pulse starts to speed up, and oh shit, he can feel it with his hand at my throat. Because I've just drawn a line in the sand about bowing down to him, but what about—

What about sex?

Why didn't I get this feisty and defiant last night? Does some part of me really want... Oh shit, I can't breathe—

And then he produces a key and unlocks the neck-collar with a metallic *click*. It springs open at a tiny latch, and I stumble backward, massaging my neck after being encased in the chaffing metal for I don't know how long.

I look up at him, confused.

"Only cowards use force," he growls. "Follow me."

He turns and heads across the large antechamber.

I immediately check for all the other exits. A doorway is situated opposite where he's going.

"Please—do it. Run," he growls. "I will delight in chasing you. And then it will be *you* who is the liar. You promised forever."

He pauses and looks back at me, where I feel trapped in his sharp gaze like a rabbit in a hunter's sights. "I *despise* deceivers."

By his emphasis and the way he spits the words, I do believe him. Quite a lot.

I scurry forward to follow at his heels.

Well, I'm not on my knees.

But my confidence grows a little dimmer when we descend another set of spiral stairs that goes down.

And down.

And down.

And down.

For a while, windows allow daylight in, but the further we descend the steep staircase, we finally hit a layer where there is no more daylight. We must be underground.

In fact, there's no light here at all.

And we just keep going down.

So many levels down that the daylight from the many stories above now only casts a mere memory of light.

I quickly reach out to hold onto the walls. The stone becomes more rough-hewn the further down we go. And it's so, so cold, though I wouldn't have thought it possible to get colder than it is above.

"Where are we going?" I whisper.

And that's when I hear it.

The much-louder version of the distant echo I thought I heard this morning—a gut-wrenching scream so piercing the hairs on my arms immediately rise.

"Do you keep... pigs down here?" I with my fingers for a grip against the stone.

"No," is all he says as he continues descending, his voice echoing back to me. I don't move. And then I take a step backward.

"What's down there?" I hate the way the stone amplifies and multiplies my quivering voice.

"Follow," he commands. "Follow or we return upstairs, and you kneel."

I shake my head, then realize it's all but blackout dark down here, and he can't see it. "No. Neither."

"You are not a seedling," he growls. "You must choose. Choose to see what is at the bottom of these stairs or go back up, and you kneel."

Jesus Christ, what kind of choice is that?

My heart starts beating even faster. He's gotta be kidding.

He stays silent.

Another absolutely horrific straight-out-of-a-horror movie scream comes from down below.

Yup, that's it. I turn around and *fly* back up the stairs.

The exhilaration of escaping whatever horror is down below is equaled only by the novelty of feeling my hair flying from how fast I'm running. *Me.* With my own two legs and no motorized assistance.

It's a wild, giddy sensation.

Until the pang in my side hits because *damn*, I'm not really sure what the limits of this new body are, and sprinting up ten flights of stairs all at once might not yet be within its endurance radius. Yet, anyway.

At least when I'm huffing for air by the monster's big, sturdy chair at the head of the large dining table, it really doesn't feel *that* much like giving in to drop to my knees.

I am exhausted, after all.

And if him feeding me off his plate does make me feel a little like a pet, and him the human master... well, considering the situation, can I blame him?

By the time I'm back upstairs and on my knees, yup, I'm ready to blame him again.

Especially when he feeds me from his leather-padded fingers, each piece of surprisingly good-tasting meat speared by those sharp, sharp claws.

It feels like taking bites of meat off the tip of a knife.

I glare up at him after chewing an especially juicy bite. I need a napkin. I'm making a mess of myself. But when I try to wipe my mouth with my forearm, which is really the only thing available to me considering there aren't exactly any napkins around—the beast just lets out a low, disapproving growl.

Then he leans down and licks my chin free of juice himself.

I'm so stunned, I stay still and let it happen.

Then he goes right back to feeding me the next bite from his claw-tip.

And I... well, I eat.

I consider briefly going on hunger strike.

But won't that just end up with another march down to the basement and whatever terrors live down there?

Plus, while being on my knees might be a little humiliating, I am free of the heavy collar. I don't know if I could trust—okay, scratch that. I'm not entirely naïve—obviously I can't *trust* him. I've lived long enough to know that no one is good, or kind. Not really. Not deep down, at least as far as I've ever seen. No matter how much I've wanted to believe so and given person after person the benefit of the doubt, waiting and believing the best of them...

I've been disappointed and hurt in so many ways.

So, I'm obviously not going to go around believing anything this "guy" says, even if he promises to set me free someday. But, like the best of them, I can still play along. Having been so naïve for much of my life, I think I can still play a believable enough version of the sweet ingénue.

It's a tricky balance—you can't be agreeable all the time. Or be a doormat. That's too easy, and easy isn't fun for the type of manipulator who really likes to play with their food, which this guy obviously does. Plus, it's not believable.

So I'll keep pushing back, but only to a point.

This beast seems to like it when his prey gives him a run for his money.

But it's obvious that if he's keeping whatever creatures

are down in that basement in a state that has them screaming in that kind of agony, there's no true kindness in him.

Maybe just enough kindness to want his "consort" willing enough to keep that monstrous cock of his wet.

After holding the heavy glass to my mouth so I can drink some cold, pure water, he spears another piece of meat that's especially dripping. "Eat, and suck the juices off my fingers."

He holds it suspended over my mouth so that I have to rise on my knees to reach it, and then he teases by holding it a little further away still.

I glare at him until a noise I suspect to be a chuckle rumbles out of his giant chest, and he plops the morsel into my mouth. He immediately retracts his claw from the meat, but his thumb remains in my mouth.

"Suck," he repeats.

And God help me, I do. Which confuses me as much as it seems to please him. I've just decided he's some sort of horrible masochist serial-torturer. So why the hell do I feel a buzz between my legs right now? He should *not* be turning me on. None of this should be turning me on!

Another noise emits from his chest, but it's not a chuckle this time.

His wings, which have gone slack since he first flared them out to their full wingspan like a morning stretch when we entered the room, have been slack again at his sides since he sat down.

But as my lips close around his thumb, and I apply the

slightest pressure to clean it of the meat's juices, they flare to life again, fluttering around him in a mad flurry.

"Now I will reward my consort. When she does well, rewards follow."

I barely realize what's happening, chewing and swallowing quickly when I'm lifted by my waist up off of my knees and onto—

My ass plunks onto the table in front of him with a *thud*. He apparently shoved the plate off the table with his wing even as he lifted me up to put in front of him in its place.

Wait, by reward, does he mean...

Unceremoniously, he yanks my hips open. And ya know, since all I've got on is my birthday suit, I'm immediately exposed to him.

Is he really just going to— Here?

I look around. Somebody had to cook this giant hunk of meat we were eating this morning, right? Or did he do it?

"Hey!" I grab his horns when he dips toward the apex between my legs, my cheeks flaming. I'm so confused right now. Sometimes, he seems good-natured, almost playful. But when he took me downstairs... Those screams...

He pauses, arching one of those devilish eyebrows at me. "Do you not want your reward? Because I promise it is far nicer than my punishments."

Wait, wait, wait? What?

"Punishments?" I squeak.

He nods, and the unholy light in his eye burns. Right before he leans down and that long, leonine tongue of his—

I immediately drop my elbows back to the long table at

the still-unexpected sensations that the feel of his tongue...
there... brings.

I think I swear a blue streak, but again, I'm not sure.
I'm not sure of anything. It feels like my head floats a little
away from my body. Not because I want to escape what's
happening to me, but simply because I can't believe how
good what he's doing feels.

It's *wrong* that it feels so good. I *shouldn't* like it so
much.

I very much shouldn't like it when this morally
questionable captor-like monster—*oh!* I shudder in
pleasure as his tongue licks inside my depths. With that
long, *long* tongue of his. It's not just long. It's *strong*.

So strong and the way he snuffles around my pussy...
Like the scent of me makes him mad to taste me even
more. To get more of me on his tongue.

I shouldn't like it.

Shouldn't like that he's a messy eater.

He smears his lion's face back and forth, motorboating
my pussy and then pulling my ass up off the table to get
me deeper in his mouth, to plunge further.

My back is flat against the table now, he's knocked me
back in his ferocious pussy-eating.

And as the pleasure rises within me, I can only have
the disloyal thought that this was part of my body that
disgusted Drew.

He liked it when I went down on him, but he always
refused to do the same for me. Women "smelled funny"
down there, to use his words. And he didn't like that I
didn't shave it.

Maybe if I kept it tidier, he said once. So I tried to shave. But I couldn't really do it very well, the way my spine was curved, and it just got almost immediately spikey instead of smooth—which he complained about, too. And then he didn't want to have sex at all. Except for blowjobs. Which frankly, at that point, had felt like a relief.

So, there is just absolutely no precedent for what I'm experiencing in this moment. Being so voraciously eaten out by someone—who, for as sloppy as he is—really seems to know what he's doing. Or maybe he just really enjoys it, and that makes up for all the rest. It's like he can't get enough of me. My spine shudders as pleasure begins to quake through me.

Even harder as, oh God, *yes*, his nose starts snuffling and sucking on my clitoris. And while his teeth are terrifying, he's flattened them so that they don't feel dangerous even as he opens his maw so he can lick and press his gums against my whole pussy.

And his *tongue*.

Dear God, that rough, perfectly textured tongue of his as he drags it in and out of me. Along all my inner walls. And then darting inside me again to *thwang* against those needy spots I never even believed were inside me. Like my G-spot. Which I seriously thought was just fiction before this very moment.

But oh!

Definitely—

Not—

Oh *God*!

Not fictional. Oh God! Oh-oh-*oh*!

I start heaving and shuddering on the table, my thighs shaking and my toes pointing toward the ceiling as all the feelings inside me galvanize, and the volcano deep within me starts to erupt—

I grab his horns and ride his face through my orgasm.

And he sucks and slurps and licks me until I'm a broken, wet, slippery mass left shuddering on the table.

Only then does he stand, swipe his forearm against his sex-slicked jaw, and declare, "Good meal. Now we fuck."

MONSTER

CHAPTER ELEVEN

Things are going well with my consort's training.

She shudders beneath me like a female should, her legs open and her eyes awash with want for me.

Beyond that, her scent sings for me to fuck her.

She is staring at the ceiling, still seemingly lost in the pleasure I have brought her. That is good. I will keep her in a pleasure-hazed state. I like that for my consort.

And... an idea has come into my head that before meeting her I had rejected on sight.

But feeling her warm rump against me in bed all last night, I began to think man-thoughts. Creator-Father thoughts.

As if I might want... offspring.

Which startled me and kept me awake the second half of the night. Even as I put the collar around her neck that I had once worn for many years.

But I did mean what I said to her. Only cowards use force.

I am glad I unlocked it and freed her. See what luscious things resulted.

Well, that, and she is not yet ready to see the basement.

If you implant her with your seedling, and it grows in her belly, surely it will make her heart kinder toward what is in the basement?

I frown down at her.

Will she yet hate me? And what grows in her belly, should I manage to put it there, will she hate it also?

The thought infuriates me. And so perhaps I am less gentle than I ought to be as I lift my masthead toward her drenched sex.

She raises her head off the table, obviously a little surprised to feel me there.

"Put me inside you," I order stiffly. It takes control not to shove myself there.

Her face blanches, and I grow harder. I like to see her war against herself and what she truly desires. Her sex pulses around my cock's tip in anticipation for what will come.

"Consort," I warn, lowering my eyebrows. "Put me inside you. Reach your hands down, take hold of me, and feed me into—"

"I get it," she snaps, still breathless, so the words come out little more than a gasp.

She must sit up in order to manage the task. Her arms are not as long as mine. All of her is so much smaller. Weaker. More helpless.

And yet, when those tiny little hands shake as they close around my maleness—not that they can even begin to close around me or apply much pressure—it still does something to me that no amount of stroking myself in the dark can manage.

I almost gush all over her before I am even fully inside her, right there just primed at her opening.

But she does as I ask. She begins to pull me into her narrow little opening that seems to magically expand to fit around the three-inch girth of my circumference.

Her eyes go immediately wide.

She is afraid. Afraid perhaps I will not fit? I do understand I am larger than the males of her kind, but as we proved last night... I *will* fit, given the right circumstances.

She is a little stiff below me, though wet enough from my ministrations moments earlier.

I must bring her back to gushing.

"Now lay back," I order gruffly, not able to even pretend gentleness when the bulbous head of my shaft is an inch inside the grip of my consort's cunt.

She groans as she leans back, and I follow her, bearing down and entering another inch. She shakes beneath me as I lay my groin on hers and roll my hips, both smoothing further entrance and simulating the motion we will engage in several moments from now, once her body remembers how to accept me.

Now that I am over her on the table, it is easy to bend down with my mouth and latch onto her breast with my mouth while playing at her sex nubbin with my hand.

My wings flutter above us, holding me perfectly steady while I begin to torture her little nipples.

My consort's nipples fascinate. They way they immediately harden and bud under my attention. She strains away from my touch one moment and her back arches, thrusting them into my mouth the next.

And in a brief flash, I imagine these teats full of milk for our young.

I harden more fully than I have ever in my life and suckle her hard nipples, determined more than ever to have her gushing.

And it happens as predictably as night follows day.

Because this consort has obviously been designed for me

The Fates cursed me until the day she hobbled up to my mountain, but finally they gave me the kindness my own Creator-Father would not.

In her they have given me hope and a future.

So as her slick explodes forth from her pussy to make passage for a cock as large as mine, I take advantage and shove in, to the hilt.

Not my hilt, but hers. My understanding of consort anatomy is limited, but my cock is shoved in as far as it will go before meeting a soft wall. Only about as half as long as my cock is, but it is enough to have even the front half fully encased in her cunt.

I drag out and briefly break from her succulent teats to look down at my cock, drenched with her fresh slick, and then I grin and shove right back in.

It is still a fit so tight as to be almost impossible.

She heaves and curses and her legs come up around my back, almost spread-eagle as they attempt to wrap around me.

I grab one with my hand, careful to retract my claws. And I hold her open to me while I pull back again and plunge back in.

She howls, but the way her eyes are rolled back in her head and the fresh wetness that springs on my cock, she is enjoying all of this, even if it surprises her.

A fresh charge enters my veins.

I am a good lover to my consort.

I grab her underneath her back and allow my wings to do what they naturally want. We lift off of the table and then there is nothing to hold us except the constraints of gravity.

She gasps, and she wraps her little arms around my neck.

And I grab her luscious ass and squeeze, holding her to me as I plunge in again with my cock.

I flap my wings languidly at first, but in increasing fury as my blood heats with each plunge. She's so tight, the contours of her body squeeze the bulbous head of my cock every time I pull free of her body and push back in again.

It is... the... single most pleasurable thing I've ever felt.

In a life full of pain and disappointment, I'm loath to let the encounter end.

I'm careful to let one wingtip swing around to flutter at her clitoris so that I am not alone in my pleasure.

Tears pour down her eyes when her body begins to shake and shudder in the air, and I know I have brought her to her gush. Again, and again, if the way her bright cheeks and wet eyes count as evidence. And the way she is grabbing at her own teats now, taking over plucking at her nipples once I ceased giving them attention.

But the sight of her doing that to herself is my undoing.

My wings fly outwards to their full extension, and I roar.

Then spend my full gush inside her as we fly to the ceiling. Suspended, I fuck her there. Using the ceiling as a wall to fuck her against for the fullest friction possible, my wings blur into a black halo around us.

I continue thrusting until her cunt catches every last drop of my gush.

So that if the Fates are kind, and my fortunes have truly turned, a kit will have caught life inside her this day.

HANNAH

CHAPTER TWELVE

I'm surprised when he actually *leaves* me in the bathroom this time to clean up.

It's becoming obvious to me that every time after sex with this guy I'm gonna need a full-body hose-off. There's just so much—

My face heats in the cold room, and I sink lower in the water. I can't even stop the water at first in these baths, I have to do an initial wash-off of my body to remove the glowing liquid. Only then, once most of it is gone, do I put in the plug and take the rest of my bath. Good lord. I bring a shaky hand to my forehead and look around the medieval room where the basic fixtures of sink, toilet, and tub seem out of place.

They are obviously human-sized fixtures.

This is the first time he's left me alone.

I don't trust it.

I'm sure he's waiting just outside the door for me, ready to pounce on me if I try to make a run for it.

I sink lower in the bath.

God, how long has it been since I had a good soak? Before this morning, obviously. I'm talking about the before times. Before my life went off a cliff into this recent insanity.

Life wasn't all non-stop monster sex and leisurely bath times.

Ha. Nope. Not quite.

I had a job, just like everyone else. Sure, I painted whenever I could on the weekend, but during the week, it was a nine to five, working in a cubicle. A customer service job, answering technical questions and fixing problems for large orders... of post-its. Well, more than that. The company that makes post-its makes many other products, but those were what kept us in business.

And there I was, living in St. Paul before I met Drew, just cozied away in a little house with my mother that she refused to let me move out of, fixing everyone else's problems except the ones in my own life.

I could *absolutely* find out where your pallet of post-its got lost. Oh no, did your shipment arrive damaged? I'm the customer service rep to help you solve your problem!

I've always been cheerful to a fault, even when I've been cursed out for several hours straight. Nothing can get me down.

And then, when I get home to find my mother in a fret about the messy house, I just keep that bright smile on my face. After all, she's done so *much* for me my whole life. Which, when she's tired, she'll remind me about.

"You know, I'm on my feet *all day*," she'll complain, then shoot a dismissive glance my way. "Not that you'd know what that's about. So can you please just do the dishes? For once?" And then sometimes she sighs and looks up at the ceiling. "I always thought I'd be able to retire at this age." A shake of the head usually follows. "But I guess we don't always get what we want."

I was never sure how I was supposed to respond to that. Obviously, *I* am not what she wanted since I am the reason she is still working at this age and not able to live out her trophy-wife dreams. All my surgeries added up, and insurance only covered so much.

Almost all my paychecks I have given over to her for rent, groceries, and everything else. I only kept a couple hundred for myself, to put into a little savings account I was trying to build up.

It always feels like I have been walking around on eggshells around her. So, I thought she'd be over the moon when I came home and told her I'd met someone at the office and that we were dating.

But it was absolutely the opposite.

She freaked out.

She was sure Drew was just using me.

"For what?" I asked, bewildered.

Her face had scrunched up and her voice lowered while she rolled her eyes. "What do you think for? For *s-e-x*."

I laughed in her face. We weren't doing that yet. We'd only shared a couple innocent kisses at that point.

He'd been nothing but a gentleman. And to be honest, I sort of thought of him as my knight in shining armor. I imagined him rescuing me from that old house I'd lived in for most of what I could remember of my life, where I felt more and more like an old maid with my mother and her multiplying cats. She has five now, plus Mittens is pregnant.

Looking up at the cold stone above me, I imagine them now. Mittens has probably had her kittens by now. Mittens and her kittens. I laugh a little hysterically.

That world feels so far away, as if it exists in a different realm.

But I suppose I'm the one who's been whisked off through a fairy gate. Except unlike children's stories, there aren't fey princes here.

Just monsters with even bigger cocks—

I reach for the soap.

The thought makes me feel disloyal to Drew. And yes, I've had passing moments of guilt since I've been here, but I haven't really been alone long enough to think it all the way through. There's no going back now, and I'm finally feeling it.

He was my knight in shining armor... Right?

So why don't I miss him more?

Okay, so no, he isn't perfect. While at first, moving into his place instead of staying at Mom's did feel *amazing*, not to mention he was new, in a life of so much *sameness*.

And he didn't seem bothered by it like others had in my brief dating history.

I was shy, and he was outgoing. So, there were never

any awkward silences between us, because he would always fill it with chatter.

Drew *loved* to talk.

And I *loved* to listen to him. I enjoyed just watching him while he talked. The shape of his jaw. The way his brown eyes glistened when we sat on the balcony off his den as the Minnesota sun set that first summer we started dating, before it was too cold to sit out there anymore.

He isn't like Mom, either.

Sometimes he asked me questions, too, and not just ones about my medical condition. After it was clear it didn't keep me from having sex, he wasn't too curious about it.

He was really excited to hear about my college experience at U of Minn.

He hadn't been able to finish college and was always nervous it would be held against him. About a month later he was up for a promotion.

I was up for the same promotion since we worked in the same division.

He got it.

He told me how relieved he was that his lack of college degree hadn't been held against him. Or apparently the fact that he'd only been working at the company six months to my five years.

But like he said, if I'd got it, it would have just looked like a diversity-hire thing. You know, because of my disability.

When I got my promotion, we wanted people to know it was really because I was the best candidate so there wouldn't be any questions from the other workers, or jealousy, that sort of thing, *he* said. He liked to say things that way—to state things in terms of *we* without ever asking me what I thought about it.

But secretly...

Secretly I thought I already was the best person for the job. And not just because of my college degree.

Drew didn't always do so well, though, when it was suggested that I, or anyone really, might— I swallow and frown at the thought, afraid to even *think* even if not say out loud my deep-down secret thought.

Drew didn't do well if there was even a whisper that I might be better at something than him.

Everything was fine between us as long as we agreed.

Well, as long as *I* agreed with *him*.

But if I *didn't* happen to think something was the right idea, or move, or—

I close my eyes and sink down in the steaming water.

None of it matters anymore.

Drew is back home in Minneapolis in a slightly *bigger* cubicle, with everyone else thinking what a hero he is to have been left by that crazy, disabled girlfriend that he was an absolute *saint* to have not only dated but *proposed to* in the first place. And then she just up and left him!

I doubt the office gossip has slowed down, even though I left two months ago.

And I should do better to believe that fairy tales are real.

Whatever overwhelming feelings I might be have now when my beast makes love to me—

I cut the thought off in its tracks.

This is not making love. No matter how much my naïve little brain wants to protect itself.

This is fucking.

I'm being fucked by a monster who's only happy when I'm on my knees.

I'm being used.

Just like always.

There aren't happy endings. Not in this life, anyway.

I get up out of the bath and haul my foot over the side of the claw-foot tub. I shake my head in wonder at the strength in my legs as I step onto the cold stone floor.

Again, it's a shocking cold after the bath's heat, but I welcome it, as well as the strong flex of my calf as I shift my weight to stand up.

So maybe it's only the romantic happy endings that are hopeless, because this miracle I've all but given up hope on... I stand straight, without pain, and feel my shoulders square up.

When I breathe in and out, there's no obstruction. No pain.

And a tear falls down my cheek. I still can't believe it. To be healed, after all this time. A lifetime. Too many feelings are battling in my chest. Too many thoughts at once.

The tears are indistinguishable from the bathwater running down from my wet hair.

I stand there until my skin is pricked with goosebumps from the cold, feeling whole and strong in my own skin for maybe the first time in my life.

I feel like I could run a marathon.

I hurry over to a shelf with towels on it, grab one, and bend over to twist up my hair. Then, grabbing one more to wrap around my body, I head to the bedroom's open window.

Icy wind blasts in through the open space, but I find it a little less intolerable than I did this morning. Still, I can't just go around naked all the time. I look around for last night's discarded clothes. Maybe I can clean them and sew them back together?

But when I look behind me on the floor, all I see are snow gusts and stray black feathers. I turn back to the window, holding tightly to the wall and leaning out a little to inhale the bracing, frigid air.

Did the monster leave this way? He just closed the door to the bathroom and said he'd be gone for a while. "Don't leave the bedroom," was the last thing he growled to me before he left.

The window opens at my knees and is almost as wide as it is tall. From here I can see some glass panes that might be able to be closed by a series of cranks, but I can't begin to understand how they work. Plus, if the monster left that way, he probably won't be too pleased to fly back only to find sheets of glass blocking his return.

I'm sure he'd just break on through, and then I'd never have hope of a warm night's sleep.

Though, actually, last night *was* actually pretty toasty, with those huge wings of his surrounding us. I shake my head and decide not to think about it. I'll ask about closing the window tonight, though.

I'm about to turn away so I don't turn into a popsicle, clutching the towel around myself, when a glint on the very tip of the horizon catches my eye.

I pause where I stand and squint.

Is that just more ice and snow?

I squint harder, grip the window frame more tightly, and lean a little further out.

I catch the glint again. And blink. Then squint even more, wishing I had a telescope.

Wait, is that a—

I slip, and my top-heavy momentum wrenches me forward. I screech and manage to just barely for a better hold on the frame before tumbling out.

But the towel that was on my head flutters out into the wind. Caught and whipped around violently, the wind tears at it as it falls toward the dark lake below.

"Shit!" I breathe out, my heart rate all but doubling.

But then I scramble back from the window and, instead of staying far, far away, like a sane girl would, I run back for the bathroom.

I grab the thick-bottomed glass cup that the monster let me bring up from our meal so I can drink water.

I want to rush back to the window because the light is slipping. Here in winter, the days are frustratingly short. I walk carefully on the blown in snow and feathers back to the window and hold the glass up. Tilting it this way and that until it provides the slightest bit of magnification I'm looking for.

And holy shit!

My eyes aren't tricking me.

There, in the furthest distance, maybe even on the opposite shore of the lake... is a *manmade* light.

My heart leaps with excitement.

We *aren't* the only ones alone out here, after all.

What if it is possible to escape back to civilization?

MONSTER

CHAPTER THIRTEEN

I slam the dungeon door shut to the screams and animal grunts behind me, my large bullwhip bloody at my side.

With a growl of my own, I hang it on the hook beside the dungeon door and start up the stairs toward the human side of the castle.

"What is done in darkness will come to light," Creator-Father used to always quote. But then he would curse. "Except in this instance. Pray with me, Beast, that none of this ever sees the light of mankind. Or it will be the End of Days."

Creator-Father liked to talk like that.

Talk-talk-talk, that's all he could do when he wasn't putting on his inventor's cap and pretending he was a god himself. He did so like to pretend.

And now it is left to me to pick up his pieces.

A particularly piercing howl comes from down in the hole, and I bang my knuckles against the iron door to silence them.

They know better than to get rowdy after a visit.

Yes, they met the lash of my whip today. So they ought to know better. I could go right back in there, and I rattle the heavy door on its hinges to let them know it.

The screaming settles down some.

Good.

I'm heading back up the steps when I hear a noise up above. This castle should be full of only the howling wind and the occasional cry from the dungeon. But that is all.

I know its sounds intimately.

So that *patter-patter-patter-patter* that I suddenly hear from up above is distinctive.

It's a mortal sound.

It is the sound of her tiny feet on the stairs. She is running down them.

Of course the reason why is obvious.

She's making another attempt to flee.

Anger rises in my chest, making it glow slightly in the dark of the underground stairwell. I disappear in the dungeon for a few turns of the clock hour and she suddenly thinks in the quiet she can steal away?

I shake my head in disappointment, though not surprise.

If anything, I am angry only at my inability to make her obey.

You have been going too easy on her. Too delighted at your cock's gush to do the work you know must be done.

I want to growl at the thought, but unlike my foolish consort, I know how to be quiet.

Onward her steps come toward me.

That's right. Come to me, little consort. Find out what happens when you disobey.

I draw my wings close to me. Even so, the confines of this stairwell are tight, built for mortals. My wings drag against the walls, tearing feathers loose. Still, I make no noise.

Patter-patter-patter-patter.

Still she comes, heedless of the danger lurking below.

I allow my fury to feed me. I breathe it in, along with her scent.

She is near now.

Almost to me.

I crouch low, ready to spring at her once she reaches the ground floor.

But— She doesn't.

Wait, what?

Instead of reaching the ground floor and sprinting for freedom, instead, she turns around and heads right back up the stairs.

I look up into the darkness above me as her footsteps recede.

Has she forgotten something? Some bauble so precious she would actually risk the extra time to go back for it? I am disappointed in my consort's intellect if she is so foolish. Her escape was near... at least I was allowing her to think so.

Or maybe...

I frown, then bend my long neck down to smell myself under my arms. I pull away sharply. Especially after my little visit to the dungeon, I am... ripe.

It is time for another plunge into the icy lake to clean myself—certainly if my prey can smell me and flee danger before I can capture *her*.

Her footsteps are so faint, I can tell she is almost back to her tower where she ought to be. Good. I will go douse myself in the lake and then we can continue our little farce, except I will keep a closer eye on her now that I know she has attempted escape again—

Except my eyes widen again when I hear her coming back *down* the stairwell!

Have I indeed overestimated her? Is she *actually* going back for a forgotten treasure she could not leave without?

I blink in the darkness, shaking my head at her foolishness. And I crouch low.

Oh I will enjoy punishing her.

It is not such a bad thing to have a foolish consort after all, I suppose. She will be easy to keep in line. Likely easier to train in obedience. If I am a little disappointed, well, she is wonderful in almost every other way.

I crouch low as I listen to her delicate footsteps on the spiral stairs.

Patter-patter-patter-patter.

There is no shortage of stairs, but she makes it back down sooner than I might have expected.

I stretch my jaw.

Ready to pounce.

Ready for the punishment that will follow.

HANNAH

CHAPTER FOURTEEN

God, I'm still amazed at these new legs and what feels like a new body, even if it still looks like the old one from the outside.

And my balance!

It's bananas that I'm flying down these stairs without even holding onto a banister.

It's a miracle, even if in the end it comes from a most decidedly unholy source. Even though I'm running stairs, something that's been historically a dangerous activity for me, I start going faster.

Pumping my arms, I glory in the icy wind gust from the completely open windows against my sweat-slicked body.

We're really gonna have to do something about this no-clothes situation if I'm gonna stay much longer... And if I'm gonna ever face that snow outside for very long if I try to escape...

I bite my lip and run harder.

At least the stones underfoot are well worn, so they're smooth under my bare feet. And now on my second way down the stairs, my internal heat has warmed me enough that I don't feel like I'm freezing anymore. For once.

Where on earth *is* this castle, anyway? If, by some miracle, I do make it out, how will I even begin to get home? Either way, the first step is endurance. Hence, running stairs.

I'm almost down to the ground floor again. I can tell because even though I can't see far down because of the staircase's tight spiral, I've started counting windows, and this is the last one before the stairs continue underground.

I shudder to think of what lives down there.

I jog down the last few stairs, about to turn around in the only area where the stairwell widens slightly at the ground floor foyer, before the stairs continue on into the dark shadows below.

Just as I slow—

The shadows suddenly come alive.

Some huge *thing* leaps at me, and I scream my head off.

"Beast!" I fling my arms up over my head as my life flashes before my eyes. "Save me!"

Abruptly, like being yanked back by invisible strings, the attacking shadow stops.

Whereas before I only saw it from the corner of my eye, now I look at it full on.

And see that it's *him*. He pulls back, looking confused, retracting his extended claws.

I stand up straight. "What the hell do you think you're

doing?" I yell at him. "You just scared the shit out of me!" I'm livid. What the actual hell?

He's silent for a moment, as if taken aback by my anger, but it passes quickly enough. "What am I doing?" he asks sarcastically, something I haven't been sure he is capable of. In fact, the more we've communicated, the more eloquent his speech has become, as if he simply has to remind himself of human speech patterns after a long spell of not speaking.

But the sarcasm drips off his lips as he leans forward. "What are *you* doing? Did you think I would not catch you trying to flee?"

"I'm not trying to *flee*, you big oaf!" Only a small twinge of guilt hits after I say the words, but I push them away. Because I wasn't trying to flee right *now,* anyway.

"I'm jogging. Running stairs!" I gesture behind me, as if that will make it more obvious.

His eyes follow where my hand gestures, then narrows back at me.

"Yes, I see you were running down the stairs. *Fleeing.*"

I roll my eyes. Then put my hands on my hips. "I'm sorry, am I a prisoner here? Or did I get the wrong impression when you unlocked those chains around my neck? I thought I was free to walk around. Or *jog.* You know, for fitness?" And so I can build up stamina. Not that he needs to know *why* I want stamina.

His eyes narrow even more. "Fitness? What is fitness? I healed you. You are fit."

Again, my eyes roll. "Jesus, is this about the size of your dick? Not everything's about your ego."

He looks baffled by my words. Maybe he's not familiar

with the saying, because he just looks down at his own member swinging freely between his legs. Even when it's not engorged, the damn thing is huge. I really need to introduce the concept of clothing.

I shift my thighs, feeling a little sore though not nearly as I ought to be, really, considering the size. I shift my eyes away and fight the heat in my cheeks.

Jesus, I'm mad at him right now. *So* not thinking about how that thing was rock hard and somehow *inside* me last night. Nope. Not thinking about it at all.

Right. I'm pissed off.

I fix my gaze back on his face. He looks curious now instead of angry. He didn't miss where my eyes were just focused. Dammit. I'm losing the upper hand. It is *not cool* the way he just jumped out at me, even if he does think I was trying to run away again.

"So am I? A prisoner?"

The furry eyebrows go up, and then he glares at me as if considering.

Then, even more terrifying, he smiles at me.

My, what sharp teeth you have.

I stand taller, keeping my shoulders square. Now that I can.

The terror of a predator appearing suddenly from the shadow and leaping at me is still fresh. What would he have done if I *had* been running away, for real? Except for real this time. I gulp. Hard.

"No." His word growls out low. "Of course you are not a prisoner. As long as you obey and keep your word. You promised me *forever.*"

Those terrified screams from the basement. Are those his former consorts? The ones who *didn't* obey? Did they promise him forever, too? Is that what their forever looks like now?

Instead of calling him Beast, should I call him Bluebeard? One day, will I join the rest of his... collection?

I stiffen my spine then jerk a thumb over my shoulder. "I'm going to continue my jog." If my voice comes out a little strained, well, who can blame me?

"I will hunt and return after sunset. Do not test me by trying to flee."

I want to snap at him again that I *wasn't* fleeing but hold my tongue when he narrows his eyes at me again.

"You will meet me at moon's rise in the Great Hall at the dining table. On your knees. Waiting like the obedient consort you claim to be."

I arch an eyebrow and flash my own toothy smile. "Sounds great. See you then."

I almost wish him *happy hunting*, but after being his prey myself, I can't really wish that upon any poor creature out there.

His narrowed eyes stay locked on mine as he stalks forward toward the open window. His wings flatten against his body then he leaps straight out of the tall, slim window.

I can't help but gasp, my breath taken away by the sight of his bulky body suddenly turning smooth and alkaline as his black wings flare out and he takes flight.

Instead of continuing to watch, I turn my back to him, suck in a deep, icy breath, and head back up the stairs.

HANNAH

CHAPTER FIFTEEN

A bear.

He has killed a frickin' *bear*. And it's one of the grizzliest of grizzlies, if the gigantic pelt he's decided to stretch and cure on the opposite end of the great room is any indication. Why he's decided to do this in the same room in which we're eating, I cannot *begin* to fathom.

Not wanting to get on his bad side, though, I'm here, on my knees by the side of his giant, throne-like chair.

Dear Lord, he was still working on the pelt when I got in, large sacks of salt at his side.

I couldn't look.

I mean, I *try* not to look, but I can't help but glance a few times.

Why in the same room where we *eat*? Why?

Is this some sort of like, warning to me? Look and see.

I can take down this giant, fearsome beast with apparent ease.

After he finishes with the pelt, then he goes straight to the opposite end of the room where a large fire finally blazes and then he starts cooking the bear's meat.

That's when my stomach starts roiling.

I mean, *no*. Just no.

I'm not a country girl. I didn't grow up in places where you go back and forth from prepping the thing you just skinned to cooking the meat you... what? Just tore flesh from bone mere hours earlier?

Also, where, oh where, is the freaking *soap*?

When he finally comes to the table, I keep my eyes downcast.

It's not from submission or anything.

More from trying to keep my stomach under control.

The beast settles into his chair. A bang follows as the cooking pot lands on the table.

"Consort," he demands in his characteristic brutish way. "Eat."

I lift my gaze ever so slightly. Only to see him proffering down a claw with juicy, dripping meat. Only for the wind to blow, bringing the smell of the curing hide right to my nose.

I shake my head firmly, keeping my eyes downcast. "No, thank you."

"Eat!" he demands.

I lift my eyes only so I can glare at him. "Wash your hands!" He's not the only one who can prowl around demanding things.

His eyebrows rise in surprise.

Then he looks down at his hands in confusion. Only to glare back down at me. "I submerged in the lake after butchering the beast. My fur was quite bloody after I separated his shank from his pelvis for the meat. And skinning him was also quite mess—"

I shake my head and lift a hand.

I suppose it is considerate of him to not show up bloody from head to... claw. Except, sorry to say, his vivid visuals only make my stomach turn worse.

"I don't need to know all the details."

A low growl comes from deep in his chest. "Do you shun the food I provide for you, consort? Or the warmth you will gather from the bear's fur?"

I glare at him, furious. I don't care if he can't understand normal human ways. He's an insensitive brute who's not making any attempt to understand what it's like for me here. The way he jumped out at me earlier. God, I'm still pissed about that. "I'd rather starve!"

"Then starve!" he roars at me, baring all his teeth.

"Fine!" I scream back at him, baring all *my* teeth back at him.

He stares at me, obviously discomfited that I don't appear frightened by him. It's clear he usually gets more of a response when he does this. Or are my tiny nubby little teeth confusing him?

I don't back down. Neither does he.

Until, finally, he does, shaking his head like he's a dog shaking off water droplets. "Fine," he half-growls, half-mutters. "More for me."

And then he scarfs down the steaming meat in the pot that he's cut into neat little cubes. He devours it within minutes.

I cross my arms over my chest and look away.

MONSTER

CHAPTER SIXTEEN

"She is not like what I thought she'd be," I say.

"What did you think a consort would be like?" Not a chain rattles as Romulus speaks. He is calm now, after having eaten. For once, the dungeon is also quiet.

So I relax as I pause and consider. "Well, I did not have much time to think it over. She appeared at my cave, and I meant to rid myself of her like I had all the rest."

"But you did not. Why?"

I heave out a breath. "She was so... small."

"Most are, compared to you."

I blink, considering his words. "She was not like the others. I could tell her intent was not..." I struggle for the right word. Words are not my specialty. Since I killed Creator-Father, I seldom use them. Finally, I find the correct one. "... malicious. She was seeking help."

"Help?" Romulus chuckles at this. "From *you*?"

I shrug.

"And you *chose to*?" Romulus is the one who sounds surprised now.

I grunt out my assent. "Others had come to that cave demanding things. But she was the first to offer... kindness in return. So I did not think. As price for the help, she became my consort. Then we came here. And now I..."

"Now you have a consort you don't know what to do with."

"I know what to do with a consort," I bite back.

Romulus snorts. "I was not questioning if your member is in working order. I meant when you are not fucking her."

I am not so quick to respond this time, because he is right. I cannot fuck her all the time. Though it is an interesting thought. Perhaps I could try keeping her in bed longer. I have never tested how quickly it takes for my gush to refill. There has never been any reason. Until now.

"I feed her." Though she would not eat the bear. I frown.

"Feeding and fucking can only take up so much of a day," Romulus observes. Annoyingly wise. As always.

I grunt in agreement.

"Have you tried talking to her?" he asks.

I frown at him. "Talk?"

He rolls his eyes at me. I've always considered it just a strange muscle tic of his, but my consort does it, too. I point at his face, one claw extended. "What does that motion mean?"

"What?"

"That motion with your eyes. My consort does that. I thought it was a malfunction of yours."

He repeats the eye-motion, and I nod. "Yes. That!"

He mutters something under his breath I do not catch, and I lean in further. Perhaps not the wisest decision, considering he is in chains, and I hold the key. I pull back again.

But he does not jerk the chains taut or make a grab for the key. His voice remains patient. "You are a fool. It is a crime of the universe and our Creator-Father that I am strapped with this parasite and you are free."

The anger in his voice is obvious. I feel a pang, but mostly I just shudder. I would not exchange places with him for anything in the whole world. Especially now that I have a soft consort to fuck, and he remains chained in this dungeon.

"I am sorry, brother."

He clenches his teeth and stretches his neck. The "parasite" slumbers now but will not for much longer.

"I abhor pity," he grinds out through his teeth.

I straighten. "Then I will give you none. But please, I beg of you, brother. Give me advice. This consort—" I cast my gaze toward the roughhewn wall. "She is unlike anyone I have ever met before. She does not run from me. Or scream at the sight of me."

No, she just screams in my face and challenges me, baring her tiny kit's teeth at me that look as if they have all been filed down to little nubs.

"Talk," Romulus repeats. "Ask her questions. Listen to

the answers. Then ask her more. It's called conversation. Like we're doing here right now."

I laugh out loud at that. "But you are my brother. And she is…"

His eyes again move upwards and to the right. "I know, I know, she's your consort. Talk to her. If you've found a woman who doesn't cringe at the sight of you, then enjoy her warmth, you lucky bastard."

I frown at him and rise. The parasite is growing restless. I will leave before it wakes. "You are wise in many things, brother, but in this I think you are mistaken. Consorts must be trained. Not talked to."

"Says who?" Romulus bites back. "Creator-Father?" His eyes darken as he strains his neck again. His teeth clench. He is fighting for control. "Because that worked out so well for him."

I bare my teeth at him for daring to make such a comparison. "I am nothing like Creator-Father."

Romulus grimaces at me then holds up his forearms, covered elbow to wrist in hell-metal chains. "Are you so sure?"

With a furious growl, I spin and turn away from him, storming out of the dungeon. I make sure to slam the door behind me in a way that is sure to wake the parasite.

Cruel, perhaps.

But I have never pretended to be anything more or less than the monster I am.

MONSTER

CHAPTER SEVENTEEN

I storm back up the stairs. Talking to my brother has not made anything better. I am more... agitated, if anything. My mind turns and trips over thoughts of her.

My world was orderly before she stumbled into my life. Not easy. Never easy. But orderly.

My body gives signals, and I fulfill them.

A dumb beast, like my Creator-Father called me enough times. I am hungry, I feed. I need to piss, I piss. I need to sleep, I sleep.

I take care of what needs caretaking in the dungeon.

It was only this spring I became... restless.

I abandoned my dungeon duties for weeks at a time after slaughtering large game for food and leaving it for my brothers. I sought out the solitude of the cave halfway across the world where, for the most part, except for the occasional pest, I was left alone.

I followed the cardinal rule.

I stayed away from the mortals.

I suppose even in the lonely mountain encampment, I was still too close to them.

Creator-Father would not have approved.

Then again, Creator-Father is no longer here.

It was such freedom to take my little rebellions. To shirk duty and brotherhood so I might... *escape*.

Escape this castle and its memories and the *smell* of Creator-Father that still lingers in the corners and cobbles of this ancient snow palace.

For a while, to forget.

I was always going to come home to my responsibilities and duties and—

And I never intended on bringing a consort home with me.

But now that I have her here...

When she is near, her scent eclipses all else. I cannot hear the memories of Creator-Father because she seems to fill every available space in my brain.

And my body is mad with fire for her.

I am not a fire-breather, but I may as well be for as much as my body wants to fuck her. I restrain myself only because I fear I might break her. And the thought of breaking the pleasure-vessel I have only just found... No. No, I will be careful with my new precious cargo.

As Romulus reminded me, she is soft.

And so, so small.

The thought reminds me of the tight grip of her incredibly tight pussy.

And thinking about *that* makes my cock harden. It is hot in the castle, usually only bearable on the coldest of winter mornings.

But my consort has no fur, I consider, as my heavy footfalls land on the stairs while I make my way back to her. Is she comfortable here?

I cannot help but think of her as a prize granted by the heavens after my long toil of hardship. She is *so* satisfying.

The thought has my member hardening fully as I climb the stairs back to her room.

But when I push the door open, I find her not stretched out on the bed waiting for me in an alluring pose.

No.

She is... scrubbing the walls?

"What are you doing?" I bark, slamming the door shut behind me.

She jumps, obviously surprised by my appearance.

And then her eyes widen even further. "You're covered in blood." Her face goes white, and she takes a step back from me.

"Answer me," I snarl. "No consort of mine will be a washerwoman."

Her gaze moves away from my chest to my eyes, then her eyes harden with anger. A familiar emotion from her that puts me on more even footing.

"This castle is filthy. If you don't want me to be a," she makes the rolling-eye motion, "*washerwoman*, then somebody needs to be. I'm not going to live like an animal."

Her choice of words makes my lion's ears flick in

annoyance. I charge several steps forward. "An animal like me?"

She does not scurry away, though her gaze does return to my chest. I look down to see the blood she mentioned.

I suppose things were a little... more energetic in the dungeon tonight than usual. The parasite was... rowdy before he slept.

This unexpected confrontation has deflated my cock, so I decide to try Romulus's suggestion.

"Talk," I bark.

My consort's eyes go wide again. "Talk?" She laughs then she blinks, her impossibly thin eyelids fluttering as fast as a bird's wings.

"Fine." She drops a dirty rag in a bucket I'm not sure where she found. Then she brings her hands to her hips. My fur stiffens. I do not know much of her, but I recognize that when she does that, it is rarely good for me.

"What's downstairs?" she asks. "In the basement."

"Talk of something else," I growl.

She lets out a huff. "Okaaaaay. I'm hungry. Not just for meat."

I slam my hand on the door behind me. "Consorts should be grateful for what I provide!"

She takes a step back, and then her cheeks get red, right on the top, two little rosy spots. "Obviously, you don't want to talk if you can't stand anything I say!"

"Say better things," I demand.

When she remains pointedly silent, moving her hands from her hips to cross her arms stubbornly over her chest.

This hides her teats from me, and those two points of color are still high on her cheeks. My cock refills and comes back to life.

"Fine," I growl. "We will not talk."

I stride toward her. "I will make every part of *your* body hungry for my every twitch until you obey me."

"How can you be so full of yourself?" She throws her hands in the air even as she backs warily away from me.

I grin. I like this dance. "Soon you will be full of me. So you can tell me what it feels like."

HANNAH

CHAPTER EIGHTEEN

My mouth drops open at his audacity. "Did you really just say that to me?"

I want to slap him for his insolence. So, it is inconvenient that I feel tingles between my legs, and my stomach swoops in that way that is becoming familiar whenever he gets that lusty glint in his lion's eye.

I put up a hand to stop him. "Are you doing that to me?" Enough. I have to know if he's… magically manipulating my body to respond to him like this.

He stops, bushy eyebrows dropping. "Doing what?"

I get frustrated. "You know what." But he doesn't give anything away… Either that, or his confusion is genuine.

I stomp my foot. "This!" I gesture down at myself. "When you healed me, did you—" I am so frustrated, I feel tears gathering. "Did you do something to make me—" My face heats like a boiling kettle.

"Did you do something to make me get turned on for you?" I finally blurt. "Like magically?"

His eyes widen with surprise.

And then his nostrils flare.

And then he gets that damnable grin on his face again.

"You think I magically make you gush for me?" He steps forward, but again I hold up a hand.

"Do you?" I demand.

He takes another step forward. "Because you cannot imagine gushing all on your own for a monster like me?" This question has a dangerous edge.

"I— I—" My voice, and my body, tremble.

"Even now I can smell you," he says. "Your gush is such a sweet, salty scent."

I gulp. He's so indecent.

And then he gives me the answer that damns me to hell.

"And it is all your own. What you feel is your body's own reaction to me."

He says it he reaches down one of his monstrous, clawed hands between my legs. I feel only the pad of his palm.

How can such a brutal being be gentle enough not to break me?

The tears crest and fall down my cheeks. Oh God. Is he telling the truth?

"But I—" I try to deny. "Before, I never—"

"There is no before!" he barks. "There is only me."

He bears me down to the bed I haven't realized I've backed up so close to.

"But it is good to hear you have not gushed like this before. Is it because I disgust and excite you in equal measure?"

"No!" I say, shocked. He can barely bark monosyllables at me the rest of the time, but now he is so articulate?

His dark, demonic wings flare out behind him. He lands a fist on the bed beside my shoulder, looming above my body as he climbs on top of me.

"Does this monstrous cock make you gush at the mere thought of it?"

"No!" But the word's just a gasp.

He bends me over, so I feel his cock pressing against my stomach. Huge. Immovable. Except my flesh yields to him.

Grows wet.

Gush. The obscene way he speaks—!

"Admit it," he hisses. "It excites you. I excite you."

"You are a brute! I pound him on the chest, even as my legs fall open for him.

"A brute you gush for. And I will fuck you in such unusual ways, you will gush more still."

"Unusual—" I start, bewildered. Afraid.

And excited.

His cock gets stiffer, and he readjusts so that it is lodged at my opening.

"My Creator-Father was bad both at being a father and a creator. But while he was a poor constructor of bodies, at least he did not skimp on the nerve centers. I can feel *everything*." He hisses the last word. "It was meant to be a curse, I think. So I could feel each excruciating lash of his bullwhip on my every feather as if it was a nerve-center."

He thrusts in. Only an inch, but I feel it everywhere because he is so huge—so *wide*.

I let out a small scream. And I gush for him.

He either feels it or... oh god, or he smells it. Or both. For his smile grows. "But now I consider it a blessing. For when I fuck you here, and fill you in your every orifice, I can feel it so good."

He thrusts forward, driving me into the mattress, and my small body receives him. Oh god. Every time I'm sure I won't survive it.

And yet every time my body stretches and makes way. Receiving him.

Oh God, how can any of this be? How can he fit? And how can I—

"You love fucking a monster," he growls, leaning down to my ear. And then his long, long tongue flips out of his dangerous mouth and licks up my throat. Lingering on my pulse-point.

And then he continues licking me. Grooming me like a cat might their mate.

He only pauses to hiss, "And you love being fucked by a monster." Before he continues to lick me. "Your body will bend and sssqueal for me," he says. "And become an obedient little consssort."

My fury flashes despite my body's confusing signals. "Never."

His lion's nostrils flare. "All I have to do"—he grins—

"is press the correct ..." His dark wing whips around and slips between us. Oh God, he is about to—

"... button." The most delicate of feathers begins to strum at my clitoris.

"Oh!" I cry, as I press my face into his neck while he continues to lick, and now suckle at my throat with his long tongue.

There are simply too many sensations at once.

His monstrous cock alone penetrating me, plus his mouth, and his devilishness—it's so much all at once. I can't—how can I—

He's a demon.

He's a miracle.

I reach my arms around his waist and clench him to me. But before I can enclose him, he pulls back and spins me around so that I'm face down on the bed.

"You will be my obedient consort."

The absence of his cock is a shock, but not for long.

"Oh!" I cry as he pushes in again. I'm stretched and he goes in... not easily, but *ohhhhhhhhh*. I wail as he begins to fuck me again.

He grasps my hands and holds them behind my back.

Which makes me... oh god it makes me *gush*.

Why does everything he does to me make me feel so *much*? Is he telling the truth about not influencing me? God, what does it say about me if he's not? If this is all... just... *me*?

Oh fuck, the tip of his wing is at it again. At least, one wing is. Because just when I think there can't be any more assault on my senses, his other wing—

My brain blanks out for a moment when I feel the tip of his other wing firm and strong first a flutter, and then more of an intentional thrust... Pushing its way into my ass.

Oh.

Fuck.

Me.

I gush.

HANNAH

CHAPTER NINETEEN

"It needs to be wet." Oh god, how can I explain human anatomy to him at a time like this? "You can't stick it in dry."

Even as I say it, I wonder what the hell I'm saying. Am I really trying to instruct him how to fuck my ass with his *wing*?

What am I even talking about? Am I even thinking about letting him do this?

It's so wrong.

Filthy. Dirty. The wrongest of wrong.

My hips spasm back against his huge cock breeching me.

Then he lifts his wing, spits on it, and then the feathers are back. And they're just moist enough against the hot flesh of my ass.

At that point, my brain short circuits as those feathers

start fluttering as they work their way into my tight little asshole, vibrating like the freakiest vibrator.

"All your orifices are so hot." He grunts. "The feeling against my wingtst is an excruciating pleasure."

Oh my God, he can feel that?

Because *I* can certainly feel it. It's like the most insane toy. Soft and wet, fluttering at my little anus.

And pushing in.

I cry, tears rolling down my cheeks. I swallow over and over against the pleasure, grabbing at the furs on the bed.

This is an unholy pleasure.

"Oh how you gush for me."

More feathers swipe where his giant cock is pushing into me—his other wingtip. "Extra gush to smooth my way, little consort who cannot help how much her body weeps for me."

A hand comes down at my spine. "Bend and receive all the ways I fuck you."

My back arches all on its own.

I don't want to obey him.

My body, though? His wing is not all feathers. There's some sort of spine that runs along it, and I feel the hardness beneath the soft. It's pushing in my ass.

I cry out, but not from pain.

I bite my lip against the *yes* that almost came out. I don't want to let him know just how good it feels. I've given him too many admissions tonight.

"If only you could see yourself." His voice is thick. "The sight of my dark wing penetrating your ass cheeks." He lets out not a growl but a roar and pulls his cock out before thrusting back in, pinning me to the mattress.

And I gush. Perhaps spurt.

It feels too good.

I look over my shoulder. I'm not sure why, but immediately I know it's a mistake.

His chest is glowing with that light from within, and his golden eyes reflect it. He almost looks like an angel.

Except for his dark wing, curved artfully around— And embedded up my ass. I turn my head, and I thrash in the furs, my body going into some sort of pleasure spasm I don't understand.

But I give into it. Oh, fuck do I give in.

I rut back against him, both the unfathomable fullness in my pussy—and the dark, indescribable feeling of his feathered wing up my ass.

He reaches down with both hands to pry my ass cheeks further apart so that he plunges deeper and my back arches further. He's splitting me in two. Oh God, I'm going to be fucked to death. He made me whole only for this. So that *he* could be the one to kill me with his cock and with his—

I scream out as his other wing curves flutters at my clit. I am encased in the darkness of his wings now.

The darkest of ecstasies overtaking me.

"Gush for your monster," he roars.

And I do.

I come.

And come and come.

He doesn't leave it alone at one orgasm. I'm weeping with pleasure, but he doesn't leave it alone.

His wing at my ass moves in and out, and all around. Like he's loving the feel of every inch of my back cavity as he fucks me. And the feathers. I gasp for air that almost won't come, I'm heaving so hard with pleasure—

The feathers— Oh, god, the feathers—

They find spots in my ass I didn't know could be pleasurable. And he presses them all. Or maybe he's pressing through the wall of my ass to my vagina. I don't know.

I don't know anything anymore except pleasure.

He's destroying me.

My sanity is gone.

Anything I ever knew or thought I knew before this moment.

Was there anything before this moment?

No. There's only him. Only our bodies intertwined. Only the roaring flutter of his dark wings and his guttural lion's roar echoing off the stone. Echoing off the world.

The golden-white light is everywhere.

I can't breathe, but I don't care.

I'll disappear into the light of pleasure and walk straight into heaven.

Or hell.

I don't care. I don't care.

More.

I just want more. And then more still.

I fuck him until the dark spots overtake my vision, vying with the light.

HANNAH

CHAPTER TWENTY

Okay, this is officially too intense. I wake this morning, to find myself covered in the beast's glowing, sticky—

I passed out last night from coming so hard. And then apparently just slept the rest of the night.

What. The. Fuck.

I have never been a vulgar girl. Or one who cares that much about sex.

This is not like me.

None of this is...

After an *extensive* bath, scrubbing myself clean and then scrubbing myself again. And then abruptly stopping because I started getting tingles as too-vivid memories of last night and all that happened *before* I passed out—

He's not even *here*, and yet I'm still feeling—

I stop the running water. I haven't stoppered the

bathwater because I don't trust the water not to be full of... well, whatever was left of his... glowing essence. His *gush*.

After this, I'll have to try to wash the sheets and furs, though I'm not sure that's even possible.

Because there was so much *gush*. I sit in the bath, wringing out my hair and trying not to think of the word he seems so fond of.

Dear *Lord*. What have I gotten myself into?

Certainly nothing that has to do with the Lord, that's for sure. I remember the whisper of his dark wings wrapping around me. And the unforgettable noise of those same wings starting to flutter, flutter, *flutter*.

I get up and step out of the bath.

I still don't know if he was telling the truth about not doing something to my body to make me— Because this is not—

None of this is—

Normal.

No. Definitely not normal.

Normal had left the building.

So what now?

I sit on the edge of the bathtub, water dripping from my body onto the stone. My whole body steams in the cold air, but I'm cold. At least not as cold as I ought to be. I remember non-stop shivering the first few times I got out of this bath.

Maybe I'm coming down with something, and I have some sort of fever. Maybe that explains... whatever the *hell* last night was.

Jesus, I let him put his— Up my—

My face flushes even hotter, and when I put my hands to my cheeks, they, too, are warm.

Am I seriously gonna just stay here waiting around for him to come back and fuck my brains out again?

I've never been a girl who sits around and waits for anything.

Growing up when Mom tried to tell me I couldn't do things because of my disability, it just made me mad. And ten times more determined to prove her wrong and do them anyway.

While no, I was never gonna run a five-minute mile like the other kids... or even a twenty-five-minute mile, I have proved to her I can travel on my own. I can hold a job just fine. I can move around in the world like any able-bodied person, even if a little slower. I find ways around things.

I narrow my eyes.

Where does he disappear to when he's not with me, anyway? Then I remember the blood on his chest last night. And finally I shiver, except it's not from cold. What's wrong with me that I have forgotten about all that blood enough to actually let him—

I shake my head.

He overwhelms me, even if not physically. Either I'm a kinky little deviant who has fantasies I just *really* never unearthed before... I put my hands to both cheeks.

Can a person really discover something like that about themselves at the age of twenty-five? Wouldn't I have known?

Then I shake my head.

The far more likely answer is that he lied last night. He *is* doing something to me. I look over at the sink. Or maybe there's something in the water.

Either way, I need to know more about him. I don't have enough information in this scenario. I'm so blind.

Where does he even come from? Will he give me a straight answer if I ask?

Ha. Fat chance. Look how fast he shut down my questions last night.

Plus, he's obviously sensitive about whatever's in that basement.

Dungeon, you mean.

Again, I shiver.

Then, mind made up to do something—*anything*—I hurry out of the bathroom. And by anything, I don't mean cleaning up this pigsty of a bedroom. That's obviously pointless.

And even though I don't feel as cold today, I grab one of the smaller furs from the bottom of the bed, that still looks somewhat clean, and wrap it around myself.

A glance out the window tells me it seems just as blustery as always, and the snow is thick on the ground. I can't see the glint in the distance around the lake I spotted the other day, but it's not dark out, so I probably shouldn't expect to. I try not to second guess what I saw the other day. I can't lose hope.

After last night…

My chest clenches. After things getting so out of control…

If there's one thing I've always prized about myself, it's my control. If he can make me so out of my mind...

I shudder and pull the small fur tighter, even though it's little more than a cape. It doesn't really cover anything.

And I get hot anyway as I hurry into the great room.

My sudden impulse to leave the room feels reckless. I don't even know where he is. I keep every sense alert as I go.

I stop in the great room only long enough to pause by the fire. It's always roaring.

Who keeps it stoked? The beast? What seems like an endless supply of firewood is stacked almost to the ceiling in a small inset in the stone wall a few feet from the hearth. Is that where he goes when he disappears? To hunt and gather more wood?

How long will he be gone? Other than the wind, I don't hear a thing.

No screams from below.

Nothing.

The castle is quiet, apart from me rustling around as I grab one of the thinner pieces of wood from the stack.

I did a little exploring yesterday before I started washing the room. In fact, I only grabbed the bucket so I'd have an excuse in case the beast found me wandering. But he stayed away for so long. Most of the daylight hours.

This is something I'm counting on today as I nudge the end of my stick of firewood into the blaze at the hearth.

The castle does have more furnishings in some of

the many stories below. Because of the vaulted ceilings on each floor, the main part of the castle is only eight stories tall. This is apart from the tower turret where the beast keeps me, which extends another six stories into the sky.

I can't imagine how old the place is, or where on earth we are for this place to still be standing.

My mind was full of these questions yesterday, but I don't bother with them today.

I'm on a mission for different answers, no matter how doomed it might be.

I might not be in my right mind, but I don't know who would be after last night.

I—

I *felt* things. Yes, obviously I felt the... the sexy things. The orgasms that about popped my head off.

But it was more.

I don't know how to be that intimate with someone and not feel things. I don't know how to receive that much pleasure, to be brought to such heights and not—

I have to know if I can trust him.

I have to know if he's lying.

I'll go crazy if he keeps doing that to me, and I don't know if he's—

So after the end of my long piece of firewood catches light, I don't think. I wrap the base of it with the fur from the bed, then I turn back for the stairwell.

And I start back down the stairs. Down from the first floor into the darkness of the unlit floors below.

Down and down I go as the fire starts burning its way

down the log. Sparks and bits of fire fall onto the pelt I turned inside out to cover my hand holding it.

I jog faster. The flame sways wildly every time as wind from above blows down the spiral stairs.

I focus on my feet and keeping my balance, so I don't tumble into a fiery heap.

The fire quickly consumes the stick as I continue down, but I don't stop. I keep going into the darkness beyond.

I will have my questions answered.

I will find out what secrets the beast keeps in the dungeon.

HANNAH

CHAPTER TWENTY-ONE

The dark is intimidating. Colder than upstairs somehow, even without the icy gusts.

Maybe it's my fear of what I'll find here. Or maybe it's everything else finally catching up with me. My feet feel like lead blocks the more steps I run down.

So many floors up top. How many stories *down* does it go?

Dear God, why did whoever built this place dig so deep? What did they need to bury down here?

I'm all-out shivering, the fire burning perilously down the wood. It's almost licking the hide now, and my hand underneath.

I'll have to cast it aside soon.

How far down?

It's quiet. No screams.

I wish I could pretend I'd never heard them. And never seen the blood on the beast's chest.

But down below, fire aflame on the whole stick of firewood now, I see the bottom floor.

I don't let my steps slow. Now that I'm here, there's no turning back. Even though obviously there is.

Throw the damn stick away and get your ass back upstairs!

I ignore my flight response.

But the little voice in my head continues. *Why do I have to know, anyway? The Beast is gone. I could flee for the light around the lake right now!*

I clench my teeth. I don't have enough stamina to make it there yet, I don't think. I need answers.

Finally, I reach the bottom—a little square foyer, barely big enough for the stairs to empty into.

The dirt is so thick on the floor here, my bare feet immediately become filthy.

But that's not what concerns me.

No, the large, iron door, with three heavy bars locking it captures my attention. And the filthy, bloody bullwhip looped over and over on a hook right beside it.

My heart skips a beat as I freeze.

At least until the fire finally makes the leap to the hide and the flame dances even higher. I screech a little and finally fling it away from me to the corner of the landing.

For a second, I'm afraid the dirt will put it out.

But there's still enough wood to fuel the flame. And now the fire has caught the outside of the fur, which burns with a foul odor.

Well, shit.

I'm here.

Am I going to look behind Door Number One, or not?

I study the three heavy iron bars that are obviously the only locks barring the door. Each has a crude handle.

I might as well try. I've come this far.

I put both hands on the long handle sticking out from the first crossbar and shove.

The track isn't rusted, but it isn't oiled either. And it's so, so heavy.

At first, it doesn't budge.

Did Beast build it? Can only someone like him, with his strength, move it?

Sweat breaks out on my brow. I'm so small in comparison. Even with my restored body and muscles, I have nothing in comparison to his brute strength.

Still, I push with all my strength, even putting a foot against the far wall.

It doesn't move.

I'm about to give up.

And there's relief in my heart that I won't be able to solve this mystery after all... when suddenly the damn bar gives and starts to move along what feels like an ancient track.

Dammit.

I put my other foot against the wall and grunt as I keep shoving.

The bar moves all the way free, clearing the door.

I'm covered in sweat now, and there are still two bars to go.

I hop back to the floor once it's clear and the flame from my firestick flickers, burning down.

There's not much time if I want to see this through.

It's probably that and not me thinking things through that has me grabbing the second bar and repeating the process.

The whole time I pray that this one will get stuck and keep me from being able to open the damn door.

But this one moves much more easily. I only have to put one foot against the wall for leverage to move it.

And the third moves even easier still.

Sweat is pouring into my eyes by the time all the bars are free.

All that remains is to open the door and see what's inside.

Well, fuck. What have you gotten yourself into this time?

I swipe my forehead impatiently.

In for a penny, in for a pound? I need to know if there are other past *consorts* chained up down here. I need to find out if this is my fate.

I.

Need.

Answers.

So, I grab the handle of the door.

And I pull.

CHAPTER TWENTY-TWO

Oh God, the stench.

That's the first thing that hits me as I pull open the door.

If I thought the castle upstairs was dirty, I had no damn clue.

It's dim, dark because there's no light except the light I brought with me, and that's burning down.

I pinch my nose and stay on the threshold, too afraid to at first step inside.

"H-h-hello?" My voice is shaking. "Is there anyone here?"

A rattle of chains greets my question. Oh shit. There's *something* down here. Maybe I'm totally wrong. Maybe this is just where Beast keeps his… pets or something.

But then *eyes* blink at me. A shocking white in the dark.

I stumble backward.

And I'm more shocked than I can say when a light turns on. An electric one, up high in the ceiling. I don't look at it, though, because there's too much else to take in.

Mainly the man who seems to have flicked on the lamp.

The eyes that blink at me in the darkness.

I'm so confused.

He looks—

He's—

Just a man.

A handsome man, if a little filthy. Though he has taken pains to wipe his face and keep it clean. But the rest of him...

His arms are chained from elbow to wrist, and it's the same with his legs. From knee to ankle, heavy, heavy chains are wrapped—double wrapped even. And at wrist and ankle, heavy iron shackles are secured, like the one the Beast first put around my neck.

He's wearing tattered clothing that's so filthy, I have no idea what its original color might have been.

"Oh my God," I step forward despite the filthy stone floor beneath my bare feet.

He holds up one of his bound hands. The metal links rattle horribly, and I follow the length of chain to see where they are affixed to the wall.

He is standing, but I see a bench, and in the corner, what looks like a rudimentary bathroom—essentially a seat with a hole in it that leads to God knows where.

"You must be the consort," he says in slightly accented English. His facial features remain so calm, his hand still extended in a *stop* motion.

And then he stretches and clenches his teeth like he has a pain in his neck. His eyes bulge a little and flick toward the corner.

He sighs as if inconvenienced by something, still clenching his teeth, and then looks back at me.

"You should run. Now."

"What?" I ask, not sure I heard him right.

His neck bulges as he continues to stretch it, now at what looks like an almost inhuman angle. His eyes bulge more.

"Run!" he screams.

I stumble backward a few steps.

Just as his head twists round like something out of that old *The Exorcist* movie.

And there's *another* goddamn face on the other side!

I take a step backward so fast I fall on my ass.

Except this face isn't genteel or clean. It still looks human, but the glint in the eyes is... maniacal. Evil, I swear. Behind him a tail rises, whipping back and forth in the air.

I scream. I can't help it. I've never seen anything like—

But my scream wakens something else in the darkness I didn't see until now.

In the corner I hadn't been looking at until now because there hadn't been moving now is another... another... creature.

At first, when it lifts its head, I think maybe it's like Beast. It has some sort of animal-like head. Eyes that blink at me.

And the arms of a man.

But then there's another set of arms.

And another set.

Each with heavy chains around them, like the... other one.

It opens its maw and screams, and I know this is the creature whose screams and howls have been caught on the wind and come up to my tower apartment.

When I scream, unable to keep it in, the many-armed one comes leaping at me. Running on legs and one of its sets of arms.

And the two-faced one starts to laugh, and then, faster than any natural creature, also leaps at me.

I screech, to my feet, and flee up the dark stairs.

Snapping chains, wet snarls, and the screams of hell follow at my heels.

And all I can think is, oh God, oh God, oh God!

There isn't time to close the door.

HANNAH

CHAPTER TWENTY-THREE

I run, and I run, and I run.

I don't go back up the stairs.

I mean I do, but only to the ground floor.

And then, I don't care about my lack of stamina, or scouting things out, or any other damn thing.

I'm buzzed with adrenaline and terror and—

And my new legs take me tearing through that ground floor of the castle.

Anything to get me away from those goddamn hell-beasts that are only a chain's-snap away from chasing me.

I'm fully naked as I sprint out into the snow. It's not safe, but I don't care.

I meant to find or make shoes before I fled. I have some calluses on my feet that built up because of the way I used to walk. But only on the outsides of my feet. I barely feel the snow's icy coldness, my feet are already so numb from walking around the cold castle.

Does that mean I'm already near frostbitten?

These are just some of the millions of thoughts blazing a mile a minute through my head as I sprint away.

The sun is shining as I head toward the lake, but that's almost worse. Snow-blindness is a thing, and I'm sweating as the icy wind slices through me.

This is unwise.

But then so is every single choice I've made today.

The voice in my head is cackling wildly. *So is every choice you've made since you went in search of miracles. And found a devil instead. In a house of demons.*

But still, I run. I reach the lake and start running across the hard-packed snow around its circumference toward that glint I hope I didn't hallucinate the other day.

I'm shocked I'm not already winded.

Just a few days ago I was getting winded on the stairs, and god knows it takes more than one day of training to gain stamina.

If anything, I should be a ball of strained muscles today.

Especially after last night.

But thinking about last night right now will pretty much make my head explode.

So I just put one foot in front of the other. I pump my arms. Something I do more because I've watched other people do it my whole life than because it's familiar.

I've never run full-out like this in my entire life.

A wild elation hits me.

I'm giddy as I run for my life.

I feel like I could leap right off the ground and take flight.

This is either a runner's high, adrenaline flooding me from all the shit I just saw, a combination of both, or like my life sort-of flying before my eyes before my heart explodes from pushing it too hard and I drop dead.

Either way, I keep pumping my arms and kicking my legs forward, numb stumps of my feet digging into the snow with step after step.

The bank of the iced-over lake is thankfully clear of brush.

And so, I run.

And run and run.

My little rabbit's heart keeps beating, somehow, as I push myself harder than I ever imagined a body *could* be pushed. Much less *my* broken body.

I glance about everywhere. I should watch the snow below my feet. No, if I do that, I'll go snow-blind. So, I look over at the lake.

But if I don't watch where I'm putting my feet, I'll trip!

I try to shake off that thought. That's old thinking. Old-body thinking. I don't trip every other step anymore without my crutches. And it's more important to keep tabs on my surroundings right now.

Especially the sky.

I immediately look up, expecting the beast to be flying overhead.

There's nothing but a heavy overlay of gray clouds, though.

It doesn't help my thumping heart.

I look ahead. Keep pumping my arms.

Then glance over my shoulder to see if the creature that ran on all fours with its knuckles somehow got free of the chains and is chasing me from behind.

But no, there's just the castle further and further in the distance, the turret disappearing in the low-hanging fog.

Jesus, it hardly looks real.

I face forward again and run.

I'm only a little tired. My adrenaline supply isn't running out, somehow. Thank God. I won't question it. I won't question anything ever again, so long as I can get away.

Of course... I might just be running into a wilderness of snow, the glint I thought I saw only something in my imagination.

And I'll run until my adrenaline hits its dead end, and I die quickly of frostbite.

Unless *he* finds me first.

A fresh burst of adrenaline hits, which seems impossible considering how little I've eaten lately.

I don't know how long I run.

Hope dwindles the further I go, and still, nothing.

Nothing but white, endless wilderness, trees further away from the lake blanketed with so much snow...

And just when I feel my eyes start to ache from all the white, the endless, endless white, it starts to snow.

My nose runs as tears hit my eyes and it all freezes right there on my face. I can't feel my toes. Or my feet. My breasts have gone numb. My hands that chop through the air as I run feel like spikes.

I feel delirious.

I want to fall over and die.

But as soon as I think that, my fury against death that drove me in search of a miracle in the first place—ha! some miracle—keeps driving me forward.

The adrenaline must finally be wearing off because my sprint is more like a jog now. The internal heat that was keeping me going isn't enough against the searing, icy wind that cuts through me. My sweat has frozen on my brow.

Giving up means dying, but I don't know how much longer I can go.

When I look up again at the sky, suddenly I'm flying forward. I must have tripped over something, is all I can think as my wan body dives forward into the unforgiving, hard-packed snow.

I'm crying useless tears as I try to push myself up using my aching arms and frozen-block hands.

I won't die ten years from now after all.

I'll die here.

Today.

God, will you forgive my hubris, thinking *I* of all people deserved a miracle? I traveled the world. I saw all the people far needier than me. And still I kept chasing. Chasing life.

And look where it has gotten me.

Frozen tears gather on my cheeks.

I crawl a few inches forward in the snow but now that the cold has got me...

I.

Will...

Die.

HANNAH

CHAPTER TWENTY-FOUR

Drew is by my side as we approach the table full of our colleagues for dinner. They all stand up when I get closer even though they didn't do that when another couple sat down just moments before. I'm using my walker, though, and I can already see everyone's eyes on it.

"Don't. Get up. I'm o-kay," I say, my characteristic slow speech pattern even more apparent when I'm nervous, which just puts me more on edge.

Drew is holding the crook of my arm, and when we reach the table, he rushes ahead to pull out my chair for me. Everyone realizes too late they haven't left an open chair in an accessible space, so they all hurriedly start to scoot over a couple chairs to the left around the large corner table to make space for me.

Their gazes flick back and forth between Drew—

always so handsome—and me, asking the unspoken question: what is *he* doing with... *her?*

Drew puts his hands on my waist from behind to steady me in case I fall as I transfer from my walker to the chair, and I clutch onto the tabletop to ensure that doesn't happen as I shift my weight forward on my awkward, unsteady colt-like legs.

Drew presses a kiss to my temple as soon as I make it to a seated position without any catastrophes. And I swear, from the other end of the table, a few of the associates' wives swoon with how sweet Drew is being.

They're right. I really do have the best boyfriend in the world. I cringe in shame for ever thinking anything different. I'm ungrateful for what I have, and if I'm not careful, one day I'll look back at this moment and regret not appreciating him more.

Suddenly, I shiver.

Cold.

I'm so, so cold.

And then Drew is tugging on my arm to get my attention.

"What?" I try to ask him, but it's like my mouth won't move. And then I am blinking awake as the dining room disappears into a dream.

And instead I'm surrounded by white. So much white, everywhere.

"Devochka!"

I blink against the blinding white, struggling to remember where I am. "What's happening?" Hallucination? Does that happen when you freeze to death?

But again comes the voice. "Devochka!" Then a stream

of words in a language I can't understand. I try to pry my eyes open one more time, so frozen, I barely understand what's happening.

But then I see a pair of... boots?

Big boots frosted with snow.

And I'm so confused. Where am I? I'm so tired. Was I asleep? Did I actually fall asleep in the middle of the Arctic? How am I not dead already?

But now there's a face above me. Not the beast's lion face either. Or another terrifying monster.

It's just a man—a very old man, his beard encrusted with ice and snow. His eyes are wide as he looks down at me and another stream of words bursts from his mouth. I don't understand a single one of them except something that sounds vaguely like *angel*.

Which makes me laugh.

And that hurts. My whole chest hurts.

The man bends over and lifts me in his arms. I'm quite small, I suppose. Maybe he's only sort of old. It's just that his beard is halfway down his chest and white.

I giggle again. Have I found Santa? Am I at the North Pole?

I glance around. The way he's holding me, I can see the sky. And I scan, searching for the beast. It'll be my luck if he swoops in now, kills my good Samaritan, and drags me back anyway.

But the sky remains clear.

And when I focus on the ground, my heart leaps because there, in front of us, half covered by ice and snow— is a house!

More tears come, though I didn't think I had any left.

I didn't imagine it. I *did* see something.

This light in the darkness. My salvation.

The man kicks open his door and immediately heads for a roaring fire. I weep to see it. The air is so much warmer here already.

He takes me near the fire and lays me on a couch that's like a futon, then shoves that closer to the fire. All the time muttering over me. Immediately, he pulls several blankets that were in a pile right in front of the fire— warming I guess, likely for him when he came back in. But he piles them one after the other on top of me, covering my nakedness and warming me at the same time.

I blink, the ice on my lashes melting and turning wet, along with the ice on my face. My icy tears finally turn wet again and slide down my cheeks.

He piles blankets on top of me more and more until the weight of them swallows and presses down on me. They smell musty and comforting, like my grandmother's attic.

Only then does the man start to take off some of his own snow coverings.

He is old, but not as ancient as I first thought. Maybe in his sixties? Skinny as a rail, though. If he is Santa, he needs to work on his belly full of jelly.

God, I feel delirious.

And sleepy.

My eyes start to fall closed, but he snaps gnarled fingers in front of my face. "Nyet, doch'. *Nyet.*"

I feel numb all over, and now with the warm weight of the blankets and the fire...

He holds a finger in front of my face in warning. I blink, exhausted.

Somewhere in the back of my mind swims a warning that I suppose it *is* bad to fall asleep when you're in danger of hypothermia, and I've fought so hard to get this far.

So I fight to hold my eyes open.

Then the old man disappears from in front of me, and I hear pots and pans bang around, then a kettle whistling.

Several minutes later, he returns. I've managed to keep my eyes open, but barely.

He says something, repeating it a few times, and it sounds like *"chocolate coffee,"* as he holds out a steaming mug to me. Or maybe I just get that from the smell. It certainly looks like hot cocoa, but I can also smell a coffee scent.

He sets the mug on a rough-hewn wooden coffee table strewn with paperback books and grabs some dusty pillows he's shoved off the couch.

He's gentle as he helps me lean slightly against one arm of the couch, pushing the pillows behind my head. But he doesn't bother unburying my arms from the blankets. He just lifts what looks like a heavy mug to my lips. I open my mouth tiredly.

But as soon as the warm but not-too-hot chocolate hits my tongue, I blink, a little more invigorated. These are the first calories I've had in a while, and the heated liquid is welcome as it slips down my throat.

My body is so cold, I can feel the path the hot mocha takes into my belly. It's an unsettling but welcome feeling.

Like liquid strength.

I bring my arms out from beneath the blankets, still carefully keeping my breasts covered, and I take the mug from him. The chocolate is bitter, dark, barely sweet at all, especially combined with the coffee. But I don't care. It's life.

I drink more, and more life seeps into me. My chest warms even more.

I cry as for the first time in an hour, I think I might actually survive this.

The old man smiles at me.

Then he starts to chatter at me again in his language. Now that my head is a little clearer, I try to parse out what I'm hearing.

I listen as I swallow the entire cup of hot mocha. I'm not sure if it's having the heat in my belly, the sustenance, or the caffeine, but I feel about a thousand times better than I did even being dragged in here.

I think he's speaking a Slavic language. Which I guess makes sense considering the snow.

I'd been hoping I was still in North America, but I think that's out of the picture now.

"Where am I?" I try.

He just looks at me blankly.

My arm is still weak as I gesture around. "Where?"

He chatters at me again.

I sigh and look back to the blazing fire. Then wince, because my eyes hurt from the snow.

But then, to my everlasting shock, he disappears for a second, and then comes back with a satellite phone.

This place looks like little more than a fortified shack

in the middle of *nowhere*, and he has a freaking sat phone?

"Politsiya?" he asks, looking ready to dial.

My mouth drops open. Do I want him to call the police? In some Slavic country? Jesus, what if I'm in Russia? We're all but in another Cold War with them now.

But if he has a sat phone, I can call anywhere in the whole world.

I reach for it, and he hands it over easily.

MONSTER

CHAPTER TWENTY-FIVE

My little consort was... *perfect* last night. I feel my lips curve upwards as I fly back home, my arms full.

The feeling inside my chest is such a foreign one at first, I don't know how to name it. And then it strikes me.

Happiness.

Fuck. She's making me *happy*.

A century ago, I wouldn't have thought such a thing was ever a possibility for one such as me. Creator-Father cursed me the day I was born. Said I was useless. Nothing. Even as he tried to discipline me day after day into being something he could—

I shake my head and let my smile overtake my face instead.

There is no point in memories anymore.

There is only the future now.

I let myself spiral in the air, simply for the joy of feeling the wind in my feathers. It's almost a giddiness.

I chuckle. Romulus would surely not believe it if he could see me now. But she has made me so happy.

She is my...

Miracle.

I grin wider, feeling the wind in my teeth. Last night was the culmination of all I could not hope to dream for. When I brought her to such climax, and I implanted my gush in her, and felt my seed spurt—

My chest fills with such— such—

The angel spark within me starts to glow, a danger as I fly for it breaks through my normal cloak of darkness. But I'm close to home now so I don't even care. Close to her. My grin grows wider.

I think I will fuck her first thing. Yes, my cock aches at the thought. She will probably have cleansed herself. She is quite peculiar about her cleanliness.

I will delight in dirtying her again.

The castle comes into view, and my glow grows brighter. I must look like a shooting star, for the winter sun set a while ago.

I spiral down toward my home, the bizarre happiness growing in my heart at the thought of seeing her. At wondering if she will hold her hands on her hips again and challenge me with that fire in her eyes. She challenges like a petulant kit with tiny claws. And then when she gives in, that fire is passion between her legs.

I am so happy.

All the way until—

Why the fuck is the door to the castle open like that?

Icy dread slams me, a shock like a punch to the face of my happiness.

I hit the ground with a loud thump and immediately drop the load of fancy mortal food I went far away to find for her to the snow. Green, leafy things and red and orange fruits roll into the snowbank.

What the fuck has happened in my absence?

Snow has built up against the door. I do not want to believe what my eyes are seeing.

I do not want to believe that my consort has betrayed me.

Even as the obviousness of it makes me want to slam my face against that self-same door. *Go get me different food, she says. Yes, go far, far away.* And she fucks me so well, even makes me—

The roar finally reaches my throat and comes out through my wide-open mouth.

And then she runs.

And the light in my chest is all gone. No, I am very, very cold now.

I should have expected betrayal. I am a fool not to.

As I turn to fly after her and chase down what is mine, a roar answers me from within the castle. It is Thing, but it is wrong.

Too near. Far, far too near.

What. Has. She. Done?

With a growl of pure, animal fury, I enter the castle

and yank the door shut behind me. It takes some doing, the snow drift has grown so high.

And then I go down to deal with the mess I was too foolish and blinded by cunt not to foresee.

HANNAH

CHAPTER TWENTY-SIX

I stare at the phone and want to laugh. Who can I call? Whose number do I even know?

I know exactly two numbers by heart. And calling my mother certainly won't do any good. She's no good in a crisis. She flaps her hands and starts to cry. Even when I would fall as a child. Which I did a lot. She hates the sight of blood. After my surgeries, she would stay in the hospital with me, but sometimes… okay, a lot of the time, she made it more about *her* trauma of having a sick child than about me who was actually going through it.

And there's only one other number I know…

So I dial it.

I half don't expect him to answer. And when he does, I'm still not sure exactly what to say.

"Hello?" Drew's voice comes over the phone, far clearer than I was expecting. It's so strange to hear his voice again.

Especially here, after all that's happened. "Look, if this is a telemarketer, I'm hanging up."

"No!" I say quickly.

There's a pause, and then, "Hannah?"

I suck in a breath at hearing him say my name.

"Hannah, is that you? Hannah?"

"Yes." I exhale even as my chest clenches at the admission. "It's me."

"Jesus, your mother and I have been so worried about you. Tell me where you are so I can come get you. This has gone on long enough. You need to come home. Look, I forgive you, okay?"

I frown. "Well, I—" I start to speak.

"It's okay," he says. "I know you haven't been in your right mind lately, but I forgive you, and we can go back to the way things were. Just tell me where you are, and I'll fly there and take care of everything."

My hand clutching the phone starts to feel numb again. Drinking the hot coffee had made some feeling start to come back, but now everything inside me just starts to feel... numb.

"Hannah? Hannah, tell me where you are."

I look over at the kindly old man, eyes blinking out from underneath bushy eyebrows.

"I— I don't know. Siberia, maybe."

"What do you mean, you don't know?" Drew sounds irritated. "Siberia? That doesn't make any sense. Hannah, what have you gotten yourself into?" Then he lets out an impatient breath. "You know what, never mind. Can you hand the phone to someone else more— Just hand the phone to someone else who knows what's going on. You're not in your right mind."

I yank the phone away from my ear and push the button to hang up. I'm breathing hard, which hurts my chest. And then I push the phone back at my rescuer and pull my arms back underneath the warm blankets.

I don't like the tears that crest my eyes any more than I like the thoughts running through my head: *what an asshole.*

I turn away from my rescuer, face to the couch, and curl into the covers.

The heat of the fire feels good against my back. And a thousand scenes with Drew race through my head. Him reaching over impatiently when I wasn't cutting my meat fast enough and cutting it for me. His constant litany of, "Hannah, no, not like that," when we were out in public together. Chastising me like I was a child who embarrassed him. Whether I wasn't using a napkin correctly—it was meant to go in one's lap when you weren't using it.

I had terrible table manners, apparently. My laugh was too loud in movie theaters. My crutches were *always* in the way of things when I wasn't using them. I could never stow them in a place that wasn't a problem for him, though he swore he wasn't embarrassed of me when I was using them.

But he was. I could tell he was by the way he was always apologizing for me when we were around other people. Like in this cringey way. *Oh sorry*, he would say, his cheeks coloring a little if I knocked into something in a crowded restaurant, *she's disabled.*

Like it isn't fucking obvious.

And like it is anything to fucking apologize for.

I don't know why it has taken me this long to get so furious about it, but sudden, white-hot rage fills my chest.

I'm not even that angry at him. I mean, I am. He's a prick. A pretentious, privileged, ableist bastard for whom I was always way too good for. But it's me I'm really furious at. For putting up with that. For believing for a fucking second he was all I deserved.

As absurd as it is, the monster has treated me better.

Yes, he wants me on my knees while he feeds me, but at least it is out in the open. He calls me his consort to my face. Even the queen of England called her husband her consort.

And in the bedroom, unlike Drew, the beast gives as much as he takes. God, does he give. My cheeks heat with the memories even as tears fall down my cheeks.

And he is the one who gave me my miracle. Even if I haven't kept up *my* side of the bargain.

Because I've run away, like a scared, selfish little girl. And now I am here, with nowhere else to go.

Shit.

What if... I've made a mistake?

But those monsters in the basement!

Now that I'm finally not running, though, I think through what happened. One of them spoke to me. The handsome one... well, before his head twisted around, anyway. I shiver and clutch the blanket tighter.

Before he turned, though, he spoken to me. He called me *consort*. He knows who I am, and told me to run.

What if they are locked up down there for a reason? Or was I just trying to justify *my* monster's bad behavior?

They were terrifying, that was sure. But did any creature deserve to live down there chained up like that? Could anything justify this?

Running is the right decision, I try to tell myself. At least after I opened that door, anyway. But did I really need to go down there and open it in the first place? I shake my head. I'd needed answers...

I shove my face into the musty couch pillow. I don't know what's right or wrong anymore, though I'm starting to have a sneaking suspicion deep in my guts that I... that I've done wrong.

MONSTER

CHAPTER TWENTY-SEVEN

I stomp through the ground floor of the castle. Apparently, I've arrived here right on time, because Thing is just crawling up from the staircase from the dungeon below, chains still rattling from around his arms. He obviously finally broke chains from the wall but hasn't bothered to shake them free.

And by the way his eyes have gone full red, he's pissed.

Well shit.

But it turns out that's not even half the problem.

Because right behind him comes Remus. Romulus is sleeping. Remus is in full control, looking maniacal as ever. He pets Thing's head as he grins, smile stretching too wide for his human-shaped lips. *His* eyes burn red with angel-spark, too.

Fuck. My hackles rise, and my claws sharpen.

"Consort decided to come play," Remus taunts.

Thing opens his jaws and roars. His face is human but the proportions are slightly wrong. And then there're the fangs. Plus, his blue skin is so caked with filth now, he looks more monstrous than me, even without considering his multiple, huge arms.

"If you touched her, I'll—" I start.

Remus cackles. "Oh, she ran away before we got free. She was just a curious kitten, come to see what lurked in the big, bad dungeon, but she left the door open." Again the grin splits his face almost from ear to ear.

Creepy fucker.

"And now that I'm home, you'll go straight back where you belong," I growl.

"To hell?" Remus says with an arch of his eyebrow. "Too late, brother. We already live here."

"You'll have to get past me," I growl.

"I've been looking forward to this." His tail rises behind him and his wings flare out. But then he stretches his neck with clenched teeth.

I smile at that. With all my teeth.

It's a tell. Romulus is waking, and he's fighting him. Always an eternal battle within themselves.

Remus grimaces in fury, knowing that I know. And then he yells, "Attack!"

Thing launches forward, and I crouch, ready for it.

I haven't full-out fought my brother in many years now, but we were often set against each other in the past by

Creator-Father. I only hope the time in the dungeon has made him weaker instead of more vicious.

I run on my powerful legs straight toward him, opening my mouth to let out a powerful lion's roar.

Thing is fast, and we collide in the center of the grand room. We clash with an explosive *thud*, tangling claws, and snarls.

Thing has so many arms and a multiplicity of claws tearing at me, but I have wings and I rise from the ground above him. He rears on his legs, but he cannot stand like a man for long, and he falls back onto his knuckles. Still, he has two pairs of arms that reach up for me.

But I have another target.

I fly straight at Remus, whose own wings have flared out, ready for me. His teeth clench, neck veins straining. He holds out his arms, and his hands begin to glow blue with angel spark.

Fuck. I can't let him gather too much. I fly faster.

The Great Hall is as big is the castle is wide, but I still reach him before he can complete the rune-lights.

What he has gathered is still enough that when he forces his hands outward and the rune-lights fly at my chest, I'm knocked backward, all the way to the wall.

Where Thing is waiting to pounce. All six hands full of claws dig into my chest and tear across my face.

I roar and snap back with my teeth, flipping us so that Thing and I roll across the floor. Muscles and bodies and wings and claws and teeth—

He's on top.

And then I'm on top.

He rolls us again, and his fangs aim for my throat, but I have more teeth, and I snap back, then use my wings to fling myself again so we roll. I roar, "Submit!" as he lands below.

I pin him beneath me, holding two pairs of arms to the ground with my forearms and the last pair with my dexterous wings. Thing roars in fury below me, but I finally have him in a submissive hold as his eyes glow red.

At least until another blue blast of runes comes from Remus, knocking me clear away from Thing, almost all the way back to the door where I started.

My wings smoke, the smell of seared feathers raw in my nose as I immediately flip back upright to charge Remus again. I leap into the air, flying over Thing's head.

Remus is in the air, and we collide near the ceiling, arms locking as we try to force the other backward. His tail whips around my waist, adding to the force trying to drag me down. I regret keeping him so well fed, because for several moments, it's a true contest.

And then he clenches his teeth and strains his neck.

I grin. "Fighting two battles?" I hiss. "There's a reason Creator-Father chose me as favorite."

Remus howls in fury at me, hands clenching at my biceps. Except he doesn't have claws. "You can't even keep hold of your consort!" he seethes. "And we both know you were not the favorite. That was Layd—"

I do have claws, and I dig them into his shoulders where I'm holding him back.

He screams in pain even as his neck veins strain further. The red fire drains from his eyes the next moment, even as neck begins to contort, his head spinning.

Below us, Thing howls.

I laugh as Remus's grip on my biceps loosen.

Moments later, I'm looking into Romulus's cool gaze. "Well, brother. What have you gotten us into now?"

CHAPTER TWENTY-EIGHT

It's dark out. Nighttime.

And I'm finally warm again. I'm not quite sure how.

I should have frostbite on at least some of my toes from that exposure, but when I finally pull them out of the blankets to stuff them in some thick socks the old man presents for me, I'm able to wiggle all my toes. And fingers, and my nose. My host also offers me an oversized flannel shirt, sweater, and corduroy pants I'm only able to keep up with a belt that we have to bore some new notches in to fit around my much smaller waist.

Sure, he fed me soup and more hot-chocolate-coffee until I felt all of it sloshing around steamy in my tummy but still...

I don't know much about how to convert temperature into Celsius, but I do know that 0 degrees means freezing.

And the thermometer stuck to the outside of the window of his small kitchenette read -40 degrees.

Maybe I avoided frostbite because I was moving constantly?

Or... far more likely, it's because of something the Beast did when he healed me.

Apparently, he performed more miracles than one.

Am I... superhuman now or something? Or just able to withstand cold? Did he do it just so I'd be able to parade more comfortably around naked in his freezing castle or is it an unintentional side effect?

I went down to that dungeon looking for answers, and all I managed to do was unleash chaos and a thousand more questions.

Did the Beast get home and find... the others?

I shiver even though I'm finally warm in my new clothes. The old man misunderstands and lays an extra blanket around my shoulders, but I shake my head and stand up.

I feel remarkably strong for as weak as I was only hours ago, collapsing in the snow like that. I should be far more sore, too, considering how far I ran. I didn't even stretch.

A month ago, after a few hours just *standing* on these legs of mine, not even walking, would have had my muscles in spasms all night.

Fresh tears come to my eyes. Unexpected tears of gratitude. To the Beast.

The past few years, I swore I would pay any price, do *anything*, if only—

You said that before you knew what the price was.

So what if I made a pact with the devil? I went in with my eyes open. Mostly open, anyway.

And then I ran away like a coward, the first chance I got.

"Thank you," I say to the man, taking off the blanket from around my shoulders and handing it back to him. "I don't even know your name." I put my hand to my chest. "I'm Hannah."

He smiles. "Hannah."

"What's your name?" At the confusion in his eyes, I repeat more slowly, "Name?" and gesture at him. I pat my chest and say, "Hannah," then gesture back at him.

He smiles again with understanding. "Mikhail."

"Well, thank you, Mikhail." Recalling something I'd heard from movies, I try, "*Spasibo.*"

His eyes flare a little. With recognition? Or anger? Am I not in Russia after all?

But he just pats me on my back and spits out another torrent of words I can't understand.

And then I start toward the front door. Which has him talking again, this time in alarm. This I get, not the actual words he's saying, but the gist of it, He doesn't think it's a good idea to head out into the cold darkness, when there's not a thing around for miles. Again he mentions *politsiya*.

I shake my head because I know something he doesn't.

If the Beast isn't already looking for me, he will be soon. He won't let go of his consort so easily, I don't imagine.

You run, I will chase.

Yes, he will be looking for me, and I don't want him to find the kindly old Mikhail. While the Beast hasn't been violent toward *me*, I still remember the stories of the missing hikers.

"No, Mikhail." I put out a hand to stop him. "I'll be fine."

He tries to step in front of me, but I push him out of the way. If he tries to keep me here, I'll get more than upset. I won't hurt him, but I won't be kept, either.

Luckily, though, he moves out of my way, his face bewildered.

Right before I get to the door, he shoves something toward me. I grab the heavy object, looking down to find a flashlight.

The next moment, he's spun away and then returns with a knit hat and scarf. I'm so moved by his thoughtfulness, I have to fight back tears.

"Thank you," I say in English, not wanting to try Russian again. And I mean it. Even if he won't understand my words, I hope he'll feel the earnest tone to them. "Thank you for everything. You've been a lifesaver today, and I'm so grateful for your kindness."

I bend forward and hug the man's small, wiry frame. And then I turn, yank open the door, and head out into the blisteringly cold night, my flashlight beam the only light in the dark.

I'm glad to get away from Mikhail's small shack. I really don't want Beast to find him.

But it's also lonely as soon as the light of the shack is behind me.

The whipping wind is the only sound in the otherwise quiet night.

It's so, so silent out here in the wintery-est winter I've ever seen in my whole life. And that's saying something for a girl who grew up in Minnesota. But this snow is *intense.*

If it hadn't melted some and then repacked itself, I wouldn't have been able to run on it like I did today. And the fresh fall from today is so deep, each step I take lands me up to my calves. Mikhail gave me a pair of too-large boots, as well, that we used an extra pair of shoestrings to wrap around the ankles to hold them on my feet. They're heavy but not impossible.

Well, they ought to be impossible to keep lifting after the day I've had, but I continue to have a miraculously endless well of strength.

Because of the beast.

Every single new feat of strength my body can do makes me giddy, confused, and grateful. Now I understand why people run marathons and climb mountains.

Because they *can.* Because they want to push these beautiful machines the gods have given them to their fullest capacity, and then a little bit further. Because it is glorious to breathe air, even when it's cold as knives, into your lungs, and then back out again, and then back in.

Even now, walking toward a castle full of monsters, there's peace in my heart.

And it's not only because of this new strength in my body. Well, that's obviously the impetus, but really, it's the change in perspective it's all given me.

I let the people in my life walk all over me.

My mother. Drew. I let him treat me like crap. I made myself small for him. Not small in stature, I don't mean. Small as in… I let him be the big man because it was what he needed. It was the only way he could go through life. I let him talk down to me and pretend like he was the only one who could take care of things. I let him take over when the whole time I was perfectly capable.

I made myself small. For a man, of all things.

But then, I'd grown up that way. Making myself small for my mother, who fretted over so many things about my illness and how it impacted *her* life, without it feeling like she was ever connecting to *me*.

Me going off on in search of a miracle, even when some part of me deep down had never really believed I'd find one… That had been more about me taking back control of my life. I'd been saying *no*, for once.

No, I wouldn't let them control me anymore.

No, I wouldn't let my mother suffocate me.

No, I wouldn't marry Drew and make myself small for the rest of my *life* so he could feel like such a big man. Sometimes, I wonder if he cared more about what being with me *looked like* to our colleagues than he ever cared about me as a person.

Maybe it's not fair to say. It was just a suspicion. But there were a thousand ways he made me small. In his glances. In the way he ignored me when we were at parties, stowing me in a corner except when he needed to show me off.

In the selfish way he fucked me, only ever caring about his own pleasure.

Even if the Beast takes away everything he gave me for breaking my promise and leaving, and my time on this earth is limited, after all. I'll never forget the freedom I've felt this past week.

And I'll never accept less ever again.

I'll make myself small for no anyone. *Anyone.*

That's the last thought I have before the whoosh of rushing wings and the lion's roar from overhead alerts me that I've been found.

Startled, I aim my flashlight into the dark sky.

Just in time to see the Beast's furious face as he descends upon me. Glorious black wings flare. His chest burns with light from within. And his sharp teeth are bared.

MONSTER

CHAPTER TWENTY-NINE

"Where were you?" I growl.

I have my consort back in the castle. My brothers are locked back where they belong. My feathers are only minimally singed, and the ache from Thing's bite already fading.

Considering the chaos that met me when I arrived home earlier, it's not too bad.

But my rage, oh, that has not abated one bit.

Especially considering my consort's obstinate silence.

I slam the wall above her head with my clawed hand as soon as we are back in the castle and roar in her face. "Tell me where you were and where you obtained these coverings!"

She winces at the volume of my question then glares at me. As if *I* am the one out of line here. When *she* was the one who ran away and let out my brothers. My extremely dangerous brothers.

"You wear nothing but what *I* allow," I roar again, slicing down through the clothing that has an unfamiliar stink on it.

An unfamiliar *male* stink.

"Who were you with?"

Not even the sight of her breasts bared by my slicing the clothes down the center can do anything to assuage my anger.

She just continues to glare at me. And say nothing.

"Answer me!" I pound the stone wall above her head again.

"Why?" she finally retorts. "So you can scream at me some more?" Her hands go to her hips. She ignores her clothing gaping open at the front, exposing herself to me.

And I imagine her showing up naked in front of this other male.

I back away from her, my fur bristling up my neck.

There's no one else anywhere around here for fifty miles. For a *hundred* miles. I should know. My *nose* would know.

I fly these skies all the time. This is an empty, abandoned land. There are no roads. No life except that which is wild. Like me and the other beasts that roam.

Which I hunt as prey.

Certainly no filthy *men*.

Yet here my consort shows back up, trudging through

the snow, in the clothes of one. Carrying the objects of one.

And she will not tell me a word of where she has been. Or who she has been with.

"Tell me who you were with!" I roar again.

To which she lowers her fists by her sides and comes up to me. "Stop screaming in my face," she yells at me.

It's loud and hurts my ears. I jerk back from her.

And then decide I'm done once and for all with her insolence.

"You broke your word," I say. I don't roar this time. No, my anger has suddenly gone cold instead of hot, and she will learn this is a different kind of danger.

I see her hesitate. Ah, she is smart enough to sense it.

Too late.

"You will soon learn to obey," I hiss from between my teeth. "If I must teach you the same way I discipline my brothers, so be it."

Her eyes cloud over. "What does that—" she starts.

"You'll find out." And then with one arm, I scoop her up around her middle, trapping her arms against herself.

She squeals and starts to wriggle in defiance. Always defiance with this one.

"You will learn your manners," I say, "and you will learn to obey like a consort ought. You will beg to serve me."

"Ha!" she says, fighting and kicking in my arms. "Never. No man will ever make me small again!"

I leap off the ground and fly across the great room with her, which elicits the predictable screeches from her, then continue dragging her up the stairs. It's a tight fit, but I hold her against my body.

"Ouch!" I roar when she gets a good kick in against my wing.

I'm glad to reach the bed chamber and fling her onto the mattress. I'm only sorry I put fresh furs on it earlier. She deserves to lie in our fuck-mess for her misbehavior.

She bounces on the mattress, then rolls and comes around to face me, her face furious. "Don't you *ever* manhandle me like that again!" she screams.

I just grab her and flip her so that she's face down on the bed. Then I hold her down with my wings and knees while I tear off the rest of her clothing.

"I am no *man*," I say. "I am monster."

She screams furiously as I continue holding her down and use the scraps of her ill-gotten clothing to tie her to the posts of the bed.

Facedown.

So that her cherry little ass is out to me.

She fights all the way until I've tied her last free ankle.

"What the hell do you think you're doing?" she screeches, once I've got all four of her limbs tied to the four corners of the bed.

I move back from the bed and grin at her. With all my teeth, making sure she can see me.

"Obedience training, little consort."

"You son of a bitch!" she howls. "If you come near me, I swear I'll—"

"You'll what?" I ask, teasing her maliciously as I pull

out the implement I readied before I went in search of her. "Run away? I'll just chase and catch you again."

I make sure she gets a good look at it, too.

Her eyes widen in shock when she sees the smaller replica of the whip from the basement dungeon.

She grinds her teeth while watching me with so much hatred in her eyes that I laugh out loud. Oh this *is* going to be fun, isn't it?

"Time to play, little bunny." I crack the whip, and the noise of it echoes wickedly in the otherwise empty room.

She flinches.

I hold the leather of the whip to my nose and inhale. *Ahhhhhh*. The scent of so many memories.

I approach and put a knee on the bed, ignoring her string of curses. She was such a docile thing when she first approached me at the cave.

I retract my claws and run a hand down her warm spine. Such soft flesh.

"I'm going to enjoy marking you."

"Go to hell," she spits. "I can't believe I thought you were better than any other man."

I chuckle at that. "Oh I'm much, much better than any man. Haven't you learned that yet?"

I continue to trace my hand down from her ass to her tailbone, and then down to the lush, plump flesh of her ass cheeks. I give them a light tap with my hand, enjoying the slight jiggle.

What she doesn't know but will soon learn is that this whip is not *exactly* like the one downstairs.

My dungeon whip has stinging nettles at the end, with

big chunks of metal woven into the leather twine. It's the only thing Thing can even feel anymore, his hide has grown so tough.

So no, with my little consort, I've planned a much sweeter torture.

I give her ass one more little *smack* with my palm, reach down between her legs to rub at the spot that makes her gush, and then I back up to the appropriate distance.

And then I inhale deeply, smile wide, and say, "Let the obedience training begin."

Then and only then do I let the whip fly.

CHAPTER THIRTY

I expect searing pain.

I expect tearing flesh.

I expect something out of a horror movie with medieval torture.

Instead...

There's a searing *sting* on my ass. Along with the imposing *crack* noise of the whip.

I turned my head away from him, not able to watch my own whipping, but now I spin my head around quickly to see what happened. Did he... *miss*? Oh God, oh God, he's already rearing back again, and I watch in horror as the whip arcs through the air toward me again—

Only for another hot little *sting* to sear my ass cheek. The opposite of the one from the first time.

My mouth drops open. No noise comes out.

There's only the noise of the whip flying through the air.

The *crack*.

And then the sharp *sting* against my ass. My whole body jumps. That one smarts more.

But it isn't... I try to look over my shoulder at my ass, but the angle is impossible with how he's got me tied up.

And again he lands another strike, and a little yelp comes out of me this time at the sting.

But it's only ever a sting.

He's not even breaking skin.

Which is when I realize... dammit, he knows what he's doing. He's in control of the thing.

Which is when I start breathing funny.

Little stings hit all up and down my ass cheeks. Expertly, and never in the same place twice.

He moves around the bottom of the bed so the wicked little tip of the damn whip can hit—

"Oh!" I cry out in surprise when he gets—

Shit, did he intend to whip between my legs and get my— Fuck, of course he did. I blink rapidly, not sure what I'm feeling anymore.

Except that... oh fuck, I think I'm starting to get *wet*.

It's just, I was expecting brutality, and then he does this super-expert stinging sensation thing, and I— I'm so confused about everything again, just when I've decided he's a bastard.

He *is* a bastard. *He tied you to a bed and he's* whipping *you!*

"You understand, yes? Your body bends to me."

Somehow, he's snuck up on me because his voice is right behind my ear.

I startle and look over my shoulder only to find him

hovering right above me, one knee bent on the mattress. The tips of his wings have flared outward like they do sometimes when he's—

When he's aroused.

"You *will* submit to me," he says, and then that long, wicked tongue of his is on my neck. "One way or another."

I tremble beneath him.

He's again tracing down my back, but it doesn't feel like his hand. I try to look, but he grasps the back of my hair to hold me still, facing the mattress.

"I don't know if you deserve my cock after the stunt you pulled. Maybe I'll fuck you with the handle of this whip. Bad consorts don't deserve their master's cock or to feel the light of their master's gush."

"You aren't my master," I hiss, still furious.

"Ah-ah-ah," he says. And this time, when he smacks my ass, after the whipping, it more than stings.

I yelp.

"You'll learn, little consort. I can be a very patient teacher."

And then I feel an object between my legs. Is it his hand? It doesn't feel like his—

"That's the handle of the very whip I just punished you with. And you're going to take it up your pussy and thank me for it."

All the air in my chest huffs out.

"No I won't." I glare while he continues grasping my head firmly.

"But my hand is here, too," he says, and I feel it. "And I can smell you. Your gush has already begun."

He rubs the hand not holding the whip down my hip.

"Such a shapely little consort I have. So ready to gush for me at all the dirty things I do to you."

I try to shake my head in denial, but then his thumb is strumming against my clit and his hips lean in. All the stimulation has primed me.

And isn't this exactly what I was thinking about when I hung up on Drew earlier?

This is the kinky shit I'm just learning that I'm actually... into?

I don't fight the moan coming up my throat when his strumming becomes more intentional. Isn't this the wildness inside me I've been yearning to discover my whole life? So what if it starts with sex? So what if it starts with a kinky whipping, tied to a bed by a self-described monster?

"I'm going to fuck you with this whip now," he hisses in my ear. "And you're going to squeal and gush for me."

I can only moan and wiggle my hips slightly. Arching my ass upwards. Making myself ready for whatever he'll do next.

Because goddamn it, I *will* gush for it. I am already. I want to see what comes next as much as I can hear how excited he is for it. My body will admit what my mouth doesn't have to.

I want this.

"You won't get my cock again until you earn it," he continues to whisper, his voice low and guttural. And then he starts to push the leather-wrapped end of the whip inside my pussy.

It's far smaller than his monster's cock, so I don't know why I get so tense around it and it feels so—

Intrusive.

"I'll fuck you with all kinds of things," he growls. "I love seeing the end of my implement disappear inside my naughty consort's cunt."

A little spasm goes through my body which lubricates the damn whip handle.

Beast takes advantage and pushes in ruthlessly. My legs are spread, and there's nothing I can do, oh God, nothing I can do.

It shouldn't turn me on. Nothing about this should. I should be screaming at him.

But that's not what my body says as it clenches deliciously around everything he feeds inside me. Especially with the hard pad of his fingers stroking at my—

"You'll love everything I give you. You'll beg me for more." His voice is so low. So gruff. It takes on a certain edge when he's aroused. Like when he's angry but different. Huskier.

"You'll make that high-pitched noise in the back of your throat that you're struggling not to make right now."

I shake my head in denial but then he starts to rub the swollen flesh of my pussy and clit down against the wet handle inside me. Goddammit, how does he know how to do that?

A little wanting grunt escapes my throat. I clench my eyes shut, determined not to make any other noises of pleasure. I won't give him an inch. I'm still pissed at him... Aren't I?

He twists the handle around inside me, and I blink. I

can't help grabbing hold of the torn clothing he tied me up with. I've got to hold onto something or I'm going to combust.

Because that wicked whip handle has a bulbus thingy on one side and the way he just twisted it—it's right up against my G-spot. Does he know about G-spots? How could he?

And then it hits me. Am I not his first consort? That thought floods me with a sweep of ludicrous jealousy, which washes me with a thousand other questions, mainly: what the hell happened to the others?

He's not gripping my hair to hold me in place anymore, he has had to let me go so he can start playing with my clit. I swing my head around to glare at him. "What did you do with the other consorts?"

I can barely see him since he's perched at my ass. Mainly, all I can see is wings, but his body goes a little rigid at my question.

"What consorts?"

"I'm obviously not your first," I spit. Even as I feel ridiculous with the handle of a whip half inside me. What, am I jealous?

I'm only met with a chuckle, and then both his hands are back. One tapping the bottom of the whip handle so that the end buried inside me rubs and drags against my G-spot, all but blinding me with pleasure as he starts really massaging my clit.

And then he's bent over my back, sudden warmth from the cold room.

His wings are surrounding me. Dark blotting out the

single electric light overhead. "You are my first consort. My only ever consort. Forever."

And then he bends over even more, his lion's mane falling and tickling as not just his tongue, but his whole mouth lands on the back of my neck.

Teeth prick my skin as he really begins to work that whip handle. In and out, and with every *in*, against my pulsing G-spot. His other hungry fingers working my clit.

Meanwhile I'm struggling to grasp what he's just said. I'm his first? His *only*? Me?

My chest spasms against the bed as I start coming.

"That's my good girl," he whispers darkly in my ear as breaks from my neck. And then he goes back to kissing and nibbling.

I come so, so hard.

I don't black out.

I'm terribly, terribly awake for the pleasure that hits like shock waves of electricity up from my pussy, through my chest, out, out—

I keen a high-pitched wail.

And in my ear, his husky voice. "That's right. Keep giving it to me. That's my good, good girl."

CHAPTER THIRTY-ONE

When I wake, for once, I'm not alone.

The beast is with me, asleep at my back, one heavy arm slung low over my waist. To make sure I don't run again? Or just because he fell asleep this way?

He untied me after fucking me with the whip but didn't seek his own pleasure. He just wrapped himself around me in the bed, and we... slept. I was starting to think he never sleeps.

I exhale heavily. It's still dark out, all but pitch black in the room.

Welcome to the rest of my life?

Because if I'm not trying to run away anymore, if I accept that in return for what he has given me, I'm really going to... stay...

Well hell.

I sink into the pillow and blink against the darkness.

I really work better when I have goals. Stomping through the snow last night, everything seemed so clear. But now... what comes next?

Because despite the sex, I can't imagine it's as simple as happily ever after.

I roll over in bed toward him, a little panicked.

He's a light sleeper, and he immediately wakens, his wings lifting out behind him. His chest flares with light, illuminating his golden-colored cat's eyes.

I thought they were creepy when I first met him.

But now... well, they're actually kinda beautiful. Not that I'm going to let him know I think that.

"Trying to run again, little consort?" he growls.

I roll my eyes. "Please. If I was trying to run, I'd be much sneakier."

A growl comes from low in his chest which glows brighter.

"Oh please." I smack his shoulder lightly. His eyes dart to where I just touched him, then back to my face.

"I'm not trying to run," I say softly. "I just thought..." I lower my eyes. "Since it seems like this is gonna be, ya know, a long-term kinda thing—"

"Forever," he interjects.

I roll my eyes again. "Would you let me finish?"

He just lets out one of those little snuffling huffs he does.

I raise my eyes to his again. "Then I thought maybe we should actually know each other's names."

This time *he's* the one who blinks in surprise. Ha. For once I've caught *him* off guard.

I suck in a breath, surprised at the nervousness that's suddenly hit my chest. I say it in a rush. "I'll start. My name's Hannah. What's yours?"

"Han-nah," he tries it out, putting emphasis on both syllables like they're two separate words. I can't help but smile.

"Now yours," I urge.

"Abaddon," he says. "The Destroyer."

"Oh." I nod, trying not to show any alarm. "Nice."

"Creator-Father said it was a good name for a chimera demon."

"A what?" I try not to choke, my voice going high-pitched. He did *not* just say what I think he did. Did he? *Did he?* I've been having sex with a freaking demon?

Abaddon sighs. "Not that I'm a real demon."

"Oh," I nod, trying to look as non-judgmental as possible while my sky-rocketing heartbeat slows. A little, anyway. Now that I've finally got him talking—who knew all it took was sleepy morning-after running away and kinky sex that was the trick? Okay, I'm still only feeling slightly hysterical. "From everything you've said, I take it you and... Creator-Father didn't get along?"

He huffs out a bitter laugh. "No. I wasn't a real angel. I'd come out a demon instead, and he'd tried so hard."

His wings flare out behind him. They usually only do that when he's turned on or angry. I'm taking that it's anger this time.

"He stole the angel-spark from the Great Hall when he left. He thought he could take it and recreate more like himself." He shakes his head, a grimace turning his mouth down. "But all he could find on earth was... bits and pieces. Like your Frankenstein story. He tried to stitch things together and infuse us with angel spark."

He stares at the dark ceiling, his chest glowing brighter still. "He hoped to create a great army to follow him. Thinking that one day we might even retake the Great Hall on the plane of light."

"Like... Heaven?" I ask, my voice an octave higher than normal.

He waves a hand dismissively. "Not like you mortals think of it. But yes, there are great beings of light there. Others like Creator-Father's forebearers were once was before they fell. Anyway—"

I want to protest. Uh, can we go back to the part where Heaven, or something like it, might be *real*?

But he's already moving on. "Creator-Father failed at his every attempt. First came Thing."

"Thing?"

"My brother with many arms and the wicked tail."

Oh. Yes, I remember Thing quite well.

"Then he reached in the forge and tried again to create me, Abaddon, who might be his great Destroyer after all. But I was only another disappointment, having nowhere near the beauty of the angels he sought to recreate. Not that it deterred Creator-Father. He simply tried again. Thus came Romulus and Remus, and... other experiments gone awry." His eyes go distant.

It feels like I'm hearing some sort of new mythology being read out of a book. And I've always loved a good story.

"What happened then?" I ask.

He looks back at me. "You really want to know?"

"Are you kidding? You can't stop now! What happened?"

He blinks, those cat's eyes of his sliding sideways. "Well, for a time, though he was disappointed by our ugliness, we still tried to be all that Creator-Father hoped. My brothers and I were... good at destruction. But we were unruly, too, and the world was changing, no longer welcoming gods among them..."

He is slow to speak, and I get the sense that for every bit that he is telling me, there is a mountain he is leaving out, like I'm getting only a glimpse of the iceberg visible above the surface. But I'm grateful for even scraps of information, so I listen avidly as he continues.

"And while our Creator-Father may have originally had visions of taking back the heavens, he became consumed with the glory to be found in the petty wars of men. He desired power, above all else, and for that, he needed more warrior children."

"Warrior *children*? That's awful."

"We come out of the forge fully formed. I told you that already. We were never children as you think of them."

"Well yeah, but still. You might be... grown on the outside, but that doesn't mean you weren't..." I struggle to find the right words. "You still had to develop. In your minds. And you had to learn how to live and move and *be* in the world."

He pauses, then shrugs. "Perhaps. Some of us were better at it than others. And Creator-Father did not have much patience for us... learning."

"You said he created more. But there's only Remus, Romulus, and... really couldn't you come up with a better name than Thing?"

Abaddon shrugs. "It is what we have always called him since it is what Creator-Father called him. And yes, we had one more brother. Layden." Again his eyes move away from me. "Creator-Father used the last of the angel-spark to create our youngest brother, certain he had finally figured out the recipe for strength, indestructability, obedience, and above all, beauty."

Ugh, *recipe*, really? Creator-Father sounds like a mad-scientist. And a dick. I go up on one elbow, still entranced by everything I'm hearing. "So what happened? Where's Layden? And your father? Where's he?"

But all of the sudden the light goes out of Abaddon's chest, and we're once more engulfed in darkness. There's only the wan light of the dawn beginning to come through the window.

"Talk, talk, talk. You are like Romulus. Talk is useless." He leaps out of bed, wings outspread fully either in a stretch or because he's been upset by the last of my questions. "I am hungry. I will find food."

ABBADON

CHAPTER THIRTY-TWO

My consort—no, my *Hannah-consort*—my chest glows a little at having her name. At her *giving me* her name.

Hannah-consort frowns. "Awesome. Bear meat for breakfast. Yum."

I sense she is not speaking truthfully, because the frown remains on her face.

But then her stomach rumbles. She *is* hungry, but perhaps not for bear meat. Ludicrous since bear meat truly is the choicest. But who knows how these mortal stomachs work? I have not spent time among them in many centuries. These days, instead of seeing me as a god, they tend to look at me, point, and scream. Then either flee or shoot at me if they have a weapon.

"Come." I draw my wings back in tightly to my side so I can fit through the narrow doorway.

I hear her little feet on the stone floor behind me as she follows.

It pleases me every time she obeys, and I like that she is again naked for me. Then again, perhaps she is just trying to get on my good side after running away yesterday. I barely keep the growl in my throat at the memory of arriving home only to find her gone.

I will not forget so easily. She has betrayed me once, well, twice, if I count her pitiful attempt to run away by the lake the first time I bathed.

I will not be made a fool a third time.

Still, I take her down the many stairs to the ground floor where I abandoned the bags of food I gathered for her yesterday. They remain by the door where I dropped them to do battle with my brothers.

"Whoa, what happened here?" She looks around at the table and chair that our battle knocked sideways.

"What do you think?" I bite out. "I had to get my brothers back in line. You set them free."

Beside me, she at least has the grace to look ashamed, but then she spots the food. She rushes forward, her bosoms bouncing in a way that makes my cock harden as her face transforms with delight. "Oh my God, where did you get this?"

She drops to her knees and starts sorting through the bags. It is cold enough in the castle to have kept the food fresh, at least.

"Cheese!" she exclaims, holding up a mottled yellow-and-white block.

"Is it meant to be that color?" I ask, distastefully.

She just laughs at me and keeps pulling items out of the bag. "And lettuce." She holds a leafy green plant to her chest like it's the best present.

I thought consorts only delighted over shiny gemstones, but this one looks like a little tree is giving her spasms of joy.

"And broccoli and onions and peppers!" Then she looks up at me. "Tell me there's a kitchen somewhere in this drafty old place, and I don't just have to cook over the fire."

I grunt. Then nod for her to follow me. The word she said is an old one to me. I have not heard it in many, many years. Not since Creator-Father walked these stones. He liked to keep delicacies in such a place.

"Come," I say.

She shoves everything back in the bags then picks them up. They are nothing to me, but she struggles to carry them.

I both want to go over to her and ease her of her burden, at the same time disliking myself for the thought.

I cannot trust her. She still has not told me where she disappeared to. Or where the strange male's clothing came from.

Even the thought makes me want to snatch away the food. Not to ease her burden but to say she can only have it back once she tells me all I want to know—

Except my consort... Hannah... I think of her shuddering body last night... Despite her occasionally spiteful tongue, she gives in to me every time.

And she was hiking back *toward* the castle. Though

maybe her foolish mortal senses merely got turned around in the snow, and she still thought she was fleeing.

But I will make her tell me all eventually. And my Hannah-consort must have all the food a mortal body needs so that perhaps my seed might take root inside her and grow. Then she will have no choice but to accept her life here, as mother to my many kits.

So, I take the bags which are a burden to her, but only so that we may move faster.

"Come," I repeat. "Cook."

"Why are you back to monosyllables?" she asks after I snatch the bags from her. She's crossed her arms over her bared bosoms as she walks, but she quickly drops them so she can keep up with my long strides. "You were so talkative this morning."

Too much so, it seems. She is the one meant to be answering questions. Not me.

"What male did you get the clothing from?"

She looks away evasively. "I just found them."

"Where?" I bark.

Her eyes flash angrily. "Somewhere."

I pause. "Do not defy me. I will tie you to the bed again."

"So you'll just starve me?"

I look to the ceiling, wishing I have a magical deity to pray to like she is always doing. But certainly there is no God in the sky to help one such as me. No, starving her will not do well for my new goal of getting her with kit. So I say nothing but continue stalking back to the stairwell, down one flight, through a door, and then charging through the underground.

"Some help here? Can you actually see in the dark? Because I can't."

I look behind me to find her perched on the threshold, still at the door where only a little bit of light from above filters in.

Oh. Right.

"Yes, I see in darkness." I head back and crank the big lever by the door from down to up.

Unnatural electric lights buzz on from overhead. I wince and squint. I hate the unnatural light of mortals.

Creator-Father had no more need of it than I do, but he prized it greatly when it was invented, along with the gas stove he had installed in these prized kitchens. He prized all mortal things, not that he would ever admit it. He was jealous of so much of what the mortals had. Unacknowledged gifts, he said, from *his* Father.

So, he had Romulus, the engineer among us, fashion the castle with electric light and gadgets far beyond what the humans of the time had. This was decades before their mortal inventors as soon as the concepts were discovered. On occasion, over the years, when he is in his right mind—hence, when Remus is not around—I've allowed Romulus out of the dungeon to update the infrastructure and fixtures around the castle so that it does not fall down around us.

Hannah-consort gasps as she enters the kitchen, and now I am glad I allowed Romulus his little projects. She seems especially impressed with the modern-looking stoves. I've never found much use for them, but occasionally Romulus likes to cook a feast using the strange devices.

"Holy crap! All this was down here, and you're only showing it to me now."

She smacks my arm as she passes me. It feels like a caress, and I want to yank her back to me, but she is already headed into the large kitchen area.

Creator-Father rarely allowed me in here when he was alive. He said I was too big and too brutish to handle all the delicate implements. Though Romulus has updated everything to be far more sophisticated than anything in Creator-Father's era, and in all that time, never once have I broken a thing.

It's true, though, I did destroy many of Creator-Father's little trinkets and prized human possessions after his death. The castle used to be full of such objects. In celebration, rage, and grief, I destroyed everything, and then burned them in the same pyre we burned his body in.

I approach carefully, assuming Hannah-consort will also think I am too clumsy to be in the space if my horns bump into the many pots and pans hanging from hooks on the ceiling.

Though I crouch over uncomfortably, I still bang into one, which sets it clanging into all the others. Furious, I drop the bags of food on the long, shiny silver countertop.

"Oh, careful!" Hannah-consort says, turning to me in concern. "Are you okay?"

I freeze, fury choked in my throat... Her face... She looks concerned for me, not the cookware. But the space is too— There are too many memories of Creator-Father clouding my mind—

Monsters don't belong here! You'll never fit in, I don't know what I was thinking making one such as you. What good is a warrior who can't slip in and disappear among the mortals? I'll have to try again. But this time to create one who is not a revolting monster! He paced back and forth while I hung my head in shame. And then he glared back up at me in disgust. *You're still here? Out of my sight!*

"Abaddo—" Hannah-consort starts but I spin, my horns knocking and banging against more pots.

I growl in fury. Fine. If she won't tell me where she went while she was gone, I'll just have to find out for myself.

I head for the door, anger lit in my chest again. It is a relief. Anger I know what to do with. Not all these tender feelings.

I will go hunt down the male she received clothing from and take out my anger on *him*.

And then I will come home and breed my newly fed Hannah-consort.

"Abaddon!" Hannah calls again, but I just slam out the door.

HANNAH

CHAPTER THIRTY-THREE

The meal is delicious. The kitchen is state-of-the-art, but old. Maybe forty, fifty years old? Barely used, though. It all works like it has been newly installed after I relight the stove's pilot light. I have no freaking idea how all this modern equipment got shipped all the way here—wherever *here* might be—or how this old castle got wired with enough electricity to run it all.

But it's good enough for a world-class chef, much less little ol' me.

I feel almost silly cooking myself a simple omelet on the giant grill, but it feels like the easiest way to get the -tastiest ingredients in, plus some protein.

I have no idea where Abaddon stormed off to, but if he's not going to demand I sit on the floor on my knees while he feeds me off his questionably clean claws, hey, I'm not gonna fuss about it.

No, I eat off silverware I'm pretty sure is actual silver. And even though I mean to take it slowly, I absolutely scarf down the meal. And there's even orange juice!

Oh my gosh, after barely eating for several days, it feels like heaven. I sit back on a little stool that's beside one of the long, stainless-steel countertops and pat my tummy.

Absolute bliss.

I clean up leisurely. Not like I have anywhere else to be. And then I put away the rest of the food in a huge walk-in refrigerator.

It's empty except for a wall of condiments that look just as old as the appliances in the kitchen. Yikes.

I head back out to the kitchen and find trash bags. And gloves. Then I go back into the walk-in to do a clean-out.

Who on earth did this castle belong to before Abaddon and his brothers got here? Did their father build it? Abaddon cut off so abruptly this morning when I asked questions about the guy. Was he a... ya know, a demon-monster like them? Abaddon said the guy had stolen angel-spark from the Great Hall which wasn't Heaven but was something like it? So was their father an *actual* demon? Fell-from-Heaven like in the stories, kind of demon?

I shake my head as I throw away an ancient bottle of what looks like ketchup. The bottle has Cyrillic writing on it, strengthening my we're-in-Russia theory.

Maybe this Creator-Father guy had just been some mad Cold War-era scientist doing bananas human experimentation who had a god-complex and just told them stories about angels and demons? He told them about Frankenstein, too, so really, there was no telling. Maybe he imagined himself as something between a god and a modern-day Frankenstein.

I toss the ketchup bottle in the trash bag with a grimace. I do *not* want to know what is growing in these bottles after all these years.

The clean-up takes a couple of hours.

But even a good scrub-down doesn't do anything to take care of the sour smell inside. Maybe I can ask Abaddon to get some baking soda next time he's out? Like, ten boxes or something?

I finally stepped out of the fridge and close the door behind me, only to yelp at finding Abaddon standing in the kitchen again.

"You're back!" I say, my heart racing. At his sudden appearance, or the grumpy look on his face, I'm not sure. Or just because... it's him, and every time I'm near him I can't help my mind flashing to intimate things we have done together and the way he has brought my body to life in ways I never imagined—

"I found nothing," he spat. "I scoured my land in all directions and found *nothing*."

"Oh," I say, blinking. I'm glad. Mikhail does not need a ten-foot, angry Abaddon showing up at his door and causing trouble for being nice to a girl who showed up all but dead on his property.

"Oh?" He storms toward me. "That's all you have to say?"

His horns bang into the pots, and he swipes outward

with his wing, knocking the whole rack of them to the floor.

"Hey!" I say, immediately dropping to the floor to start collecting them. "That wasn't necessary."

"What's necessary is for you to tell me where you went yesterday!" he roars.

Ugh, I hate it when he gets like this.

I look up at him from where I'm on my knees. His legs look almost human, except where they jut out backward at the ankles and end in hooves instead of feet.

That is to say, when I look up, I see exceptionally muscled thighs and a shadow hanging low beneath the loincloth he occasionally wears. No clothing for me, but he gets this little cloth, huh?

I abandon the pots on the floor and get back to my feet. My cheeks are hot in a way I can tell means there are bright pink spots on them. I'm only momentarily delighted by how easy it is to pop back up. My whole life getting off the floor has been a whole *thing*. I learned how to do it, of course, using my crutches and grabbing onto something for stability. But this whole just being able to pop up-and-down-thing is still novel.

And it takes away some of my anger, since this big oaf in front of me is my miracle-giver.

So, I just smile at him and say, "I had a lovely breakfast, thank you. Did you get something to eat? Maybe that's why you're so grumpy."

He looks completely taken aback by my sudden topic change.

"I ate some bear jerky on my way out," he snarls.

"Oh," I say brightly. "I'm happy to hear it. An empty stomach is no good. Speaking of..." I'm suddenly struck by a thousand new questions, "I really didn't react well to meeting your brothers. I found this apron in the closet, so I won't be naked when I meet them. It's musty and moth-eaten but should still hides enough. Will you take me down and introduce me properly?"

CHAPTER THIRTY-FOUR

Perhaps there is something faulty with the food I brought. I have heard certain mushrooms can have hallucinogenic properties.

She is making no sense at all.

I bend over in concern to look into her eyes. Creator-Father sometimes liked to take substances. He enjoyed all the mortals' *luxuries*, as he called them.

"What are you—" she starts, but I ignore her, holding her right eye open with two fingers so I can get an appropriate look at her pupils. "Abaddon!"

I like the sound of my name on her lips. I like it very, very much, but I do not let it distract me from my examination.

Her pupils do not look very large or very small, as Creator-Father's would when he took substances. Nor are her eyes red.

I let go of her face, and she scowls at me. "What was that for?"

"I am unsure if you are of sound mind."

At which point she laughs at me. Laughs. At *me*.

"Why? Because I want to meet your brothers?"

I pause a moment, then nod.

"Well, from what you said this morning, they were created just like you, right?"

Again, I nod. I am not sure what she means by this line of thought.

"So why do you treat them like they're monsters?" She sounds exasperated. "How can you lock them in a basement? I mean, yeah, they look a little... um... terrifying."

I nod more vigorously.

She puts her hands on her hips. "But so do you. How would you like it if *you* were put down there and chained up in all that filth?"

A growl emanates from my throat. I spent many, many years chained up exactly as she describes.

"I thought so," she says loftily. Then she leans forward and puts a hand on my arm. "One of them spoke to me, and he seemed in his right mind..." Her eyes drop. "Well, before, ya know, his head spun around."

"Yes. Romulus is quite lucid, but his parasite makes him dangerous. They are all dangerous."

Her eyes flash at me. "So are you. Does that mean you deserve to be locked up like an animal?"

This is not where I intended this day to go. I planned to have my cock inside her sweet cunt by now, working on breeding a kit.

"Hannah," I soften my voice, "there is no hope for them. They are true monsters."

Her eyes flash in a way I am becoming all too familiar with as she steps back from my reach.

"How do you know? Have you even tried to treat them like... *people?*"

I laugh incredulously at her ludicrous proposal. "They have always been what they are, and always shall they be so."

"Why?" she asks, crossing her arms. "Have you ever tried anything different or do you just assume so?"

"I know so."

"Have you ever tried anything different?" she asks.

She is infuriating. "I know my own brothers."

"Have you ever *tried?*" she repeats.

"Creator-Father tried everything!" I explode furiously. "Romulus cannot keep control over his parasite. He *asked* to be locked away down there."

Hannah-consort just shakes her head. "Parasite. You keep calling him that. He seemed like a... like a twin. Maybe he has his own consciousness. Maybe if you treated him like an actual—"

"Parasite is a monster. It only seeks to destroy."

She stamps her foot. "Just like you? *Destroyer?*" Her words stop me short, but only from frustration because I cannot explain better to her.

"You whip them," she says. "I saw the bullwhip. And not like—" Her cheeks go red. "It has blood all over it. If you show them nothing other than violence and cruelty, of course they'll show you nothing else back. And from everything you've told me about your father, he seems like a real asshole. But maybe if we tried gentleness and kindness, it might—"

"Enough!" I roar.

But she will not quit. "At least with Romulus. Let me talk to him. Let me at least *try*—"

"I said no, and that's the end of it!"

Her mouth drops open, and her eyes narrow to such a squint I can barely see any of her pupils. And something happens to her voice when she next speaks. It is low, and dangerous.

"You might be able to order me around in the bedroom. I might even like it there. But you are sadly mistaken if you think this *forever* we're starting now is going to go like this. You ordering me around like an asshole and me just going along like a good little girl. This is my fucking life, too." She stomps right up to my face and sticks her tiny little forefinger in my face. As if I am not four times the size of her. "And I *will not be made small*! Ever again!"

And just like that, she will not speak to me.

A mere consort. Refusing *me*.

I growl.

She is fed now, so I easily lift her off the ground and set her up on the high counter and kick away the pots at my hooves.

When I spread her legs, she is at a perfect height for my cock to penetrate. *Hmph*. So at least this room is good for one thing. My wings flare out. I smile when they knock into more pots and pans. I've decided I like the idea of destroying what Creator-Father always wanted to treat so preciously.

She has managed to cover herself again. It is Creator-Father's kitchen cloth this time.

I delight in piercing it with my claw and shredding it, top to bottom.

She looks like she wants to say something, to scream at me, but she does nothing but hold her mouth stubbornly shut as she grasps at the cloth.

I continue to slice it off her. "The only clothing you wear is what *I* provide."

She rolls her eyes up to heaven. Is she saying inward prayers to her make-believe god when she does that? So much about her is fascinating. And ludicrous. Such as freeing my brothers from the dungeons.

All of it makes my cock hard. Especially when she crosses her arms over her bosoms and defies me.

Which makes no sense. Consorts ought to be obedient.

But Hannah-consort is no regular consort, I am coming to realize.

She goes out in snow, discovers secrets of my land not even *I* can find. She looks into my monster's face and does not flinch. She sees my brothers and wants to *help* them, of all things, not run in fear for her life.

She has the fire in her eyes as she clutches the shreds of her cooking cloth.

My cock is larger and harder than it has ever been.

I will breed her and keep her forever.

I sniff the air. She has only a tiny bit of gush now. That will not do. And despite my cock's pulsing girth, I must remember I am making a point.

She is slow to obey, but she must. She *will*.

I am a patient monster. At least I have always been up until now.

When I reach down between her legs, she turns her head stubbornly away from me, as if she is uninterested in what I am doing.

But her legs remain slack, and I easily work my finger between them, claw retracted.

She is not able to remain unmoved when I find her little bud and begin to work it. After a lifetime without knowing any female bodies, I pay attention now that I have one before me. And I have always been a quick learner.

Her body is so yielding, even if she tries to remain stubborn with her face turned away. And I delight in hearing her soft gasp as the gush begins. The pad of my finger soon turns wet.

My cock pulses, and a small bit of gush gathers at the tip. With my other hand, I reach down and swipe it up with my thumb. Then I rub it all along her bottom lip.

She gasps, and for a moment, her head turns my way and our eyes connect.

I push my thumb inside her little mouth.

"If you are stubborn and will not speak," I growl. "I am happy to keep your mouth otherwise occupied. Now suck."

Her eyes are wide. While she does not suck my thumb as I command, her little mortal tongue does come out to swipe at my thumb as if her curiosity cannot help but taste what I have offered.

Which sets off something in me I do not expect.

Because suddenly I must know.

I have only seen the obscene act in pictures. Moving pictures Creator-Father sometimes allowed me to watch.

I have to know. My wings flare out, and I rise off the ground until my pulsing cock is no longer at the height of her pussy but at her sweet mouth.

My heart is pounding out of control as I bob before her lips.

"Say no," I growl.

But she just arches one of those wicked little eyebrows and reaches up with both hands to grasp me. Her little hands don't have a hope of making it around my wide girth. But oh, *fuck* do they feel good on my shaft. Even though she cannot put even an iota of the pressure I do when I yank myself to relief on occasion.

But then she—

Oh fuck. She pulls me forward to her mouth and opens wide.

At first her little lips are like a kiss, right at my bulbous head's slit. And then she licks like a kitten might.

My head hits the ceiling as I lose control of my wings momentarily. But I don't care. Oh gods and devils and all other deities on this earth and any other— Just let her do that again.

She giggles, and then does as I ask.

Her tongue is like silk. Silk on a monster shaft should feel like nothing. A mere breeze. I shouldn't be able to feel it. But instead, oh fuck, I do feel it. I feel it like every nerve ending is shocked awake with pleasure.

And when she swallows only the bulbous head of my

cock in her mouth, probably the most of me that will ever fit in this particular hole, again my flight goes frantic.

Which makes me pop in and out of her mouth. Effectively fucking it.

She grasps my shaft tighter to hold me in place, and I growl, absolutely losing it between the press of her slight little consort's fingers and the *pop* of re-entering her sweet mouth. For she sucks hard every time I am in her mouth, and her kitten's tongue licks and I—

Oh fuck, I—

My gush explodes into her mouth, the overflow down her chin and breasts a glowing liquid waterfall.

I lose my flight completely and crash onto the counter beside her, no doubt making a dent in the damn thing. But she has so flummoxed me.

She giggles, and I barely have the energy to keep my eyes open as my chest spasms, the aftershocks sending extra gush pulsing out of my cock. I only wish I was able to keep my flight so I could still be in her mouth.

Distantly, I remember I was supposed to be making some point.

I've been trying to teach her obedience of some sort.

So why am I the one curled over and panting on Creator-Father's fancy countertops?

I can't care, I have just been so well fucked. And when I look over at my Hannah-consort, I cannot say I am displeased to see her covered mouth to breasts, dripping to her sweet little cunt in my gush.

ABBADON

CHAPTER THIRTY-FIVE

I *am* displeased, however, when she continues not to speak to me.

She is attempting to bend *me* to *her* will. The mere thought of it is ludicrous.

"Is this about my brothers?" I ask, after two longs days of silence, when we are dining. I have come to like hearing her voice—or any voice other than mine and Romulus's. I feel it deeply now that she has taken it away again, and I am returned to silence.

She looks pointedly at me and nods.

Anger spikes in my chest. "Don't be ridiculous," I roar. That she would be so stubborn over my *brothers*! "I told you everything has been tried with them."

She rises from the table where we have been dining in the Great Hall. I allowed her a chair since I decided she is not like Creator-Father's consort, so I don't have to treat her as such.

But now she is so defiant I wonder if I have made the wrong decision.

"Sit back down," I demand.

She glares at me, and I stand up, my fur bristling.

For a moment it is a stand-off between us. If she continues to defy me, I will have no choice but to tie her to the bed and fuck her into submission. Which cannot help but make me grin. "I *dare you* not to."

She throws her hands up in the air and sits back down. At this point she knows my tactics well.

I'm only a little disappointed she gave in.

I continue to eat my bear meat. In silence. Which grates on me.

"Speak," I demand after another few minutes.

She just looks pointedly at me with one eyebrow lifted. Then she spears a piece of some greenery that looks like a tiny little wilted tree, and shoves it in her mouth, chewing ferociously.

She is obstinate. So fucking obstinate.

It makes me hard.

But still, I must break her of this disobedient streak. "I don't know what this obsession with my brothers is about, anyway!" I slam the table so it rattles her plate. She grasps her water goblet right before it tips over and glares at me. She will not speak, but her face at least is still quite communicative. Mostly to let me know she is displeased with me. Except when I am making her gush.

Yet I have not given her my cock again.

It seems wrong to breed her while she is being disobedient. Last night, I brought her to the point of gush and then withdrew. Over and over, trying to elicit words from her.

And even during denied pleasure, she just kept putting her arms over her chest and denying me her voice.

Eventually, I tied her arms to the bed post, but even then, she would not break and speak. Even when her body cried out with the need to gush. When I kept her on the edge, all but torturing her with it—

I shake my head. No one is as stubborn as she is. Except perhaps my brothers. But theirs is madness, not stubbornness.

Of course!

I see it now.

Hannah-consort is so stubborn, she will not believe unless she is *shown* she is wrong. She is the kind who must see with her own eyes.

Is it infuriating that she does not believe what I tell her without seeing it herself? Yes. But as one who so long believed my Creator-Father's lies without testing him, perhaps some part of me respects her for it. She has got an idea in her mind, and until I prove her wrong, she will continue in obstinacy.

Decision made, I stand up so abruptly my heavy chair scrapes across the stones.

"I understand you must see to believe," I declare, letting her know by my tone I am not happy about it. That I am disappointed by her.

She does not appear to care. She just pops up from her chair. "Really? You're willing to try? Oh thank you! Thank you, Abaddon!"

She bounces over to me and throws her arms around my chest, her smile wide.

I stare down at her in shock and cannot help my chest's glow as she squeezes me. And when she looks up at me, with that happy, genuine expression of delight, it glows brighter. Which is just embarrassing. I try to tamp it down.

"You will be disappointed," I warn, and turn away so my wings will hide the glow. I stride toward the stairs, tossing a fur from near the fireplace at her. "Cover yourself. Your nakedness will only drive them to further frenzy."

"Thank you." She hurries to keep up with me and wraps the fur around herself, holding it down with her arms. "I mean it. We'll never know unless we try."

I only grunt. Right when I feel I have regained the upper hand with her, she tilts me off balance again. I know the outcome of this little experiment of hers, and I am angry that I must go through the farce. Yet it will make her happy, even if the result will be disappointment.

None of this is what gaining a consort is meant to be like.

Except the fucking. That... is better than I ever might have thought.

The light in her eyes, too, and the feel of her taking my arm and squeezing it just now. My whole life I have only ever been... Certainly no one has ever looked at me with the light of joy or happiness in their eyes.

Perhaps she only seeks to free your brothers because she knows they are powerful, a dark voice in my head warns. *They are her only hope of overpowering you. If she can get them free of their chains again, then she hopes to make another escape.*

It is the only thing that makes sense.

My fur stands on end as I head down the spiral stairs into darkness.

It is a fool's errand to expect anything other than treachery.

Will I be a fool tricked by a mortal's flashing eyelashes and her sweet lips on my cock?

You are the one heading down to experiment *with your brothers. Fool.*

I barely keep the growl within my throat.

"Should we have brought some food with us?" she asks from behind me. She had to let go of me as we began to head down the stairs since they are so narrow. "How often do you feed them?"

"Why?" I growl, turning on her in the darkness. Her arms are outstretched to the walls, and her face is startled, momentarily afraid at my loud question. And then she reaches out blindly in the darkness for me, smacking me lightly on the wing.

"Sheesh, don't scare me like that. You know I can't see a damn thing down here. Why do I want to know if you feed them?" she asks. "Uh, cause they're people. Or, well, you know what I mean. Because it's the humane thing to do."

"We aren't human," I growl, turning around and continuing to head down.

"Humane doesn't have to mean— It's not right to starve any living creature."

"I feed them once a day."

"How often do you eat?" she asks.

"Twice a day."

She makes a disgruntled noise. "Well, see? They should eat as often as you do. And there's no reason for them to live in such filth and darkness."

She does not know what she asks. Thing and Remus can be vicious at feeding times. I intentionally did not bring food with us. Though perhaps my point will be better proven if I brought some bear meat, so she can see them descend and fight over it like the animals they are.

Finally, we arrive at the bottom floor. I take the bull-whip in one hand as I begin releasing the bars with the other.

And then I open the door to hell.

HANNAH

CHAPTER THIRTY-SIX

I know Abaddon is reluctant to come down here, and I can't explain to him why I feel certain this is something we have to at least try. By *try*, I mean really try, and find a way to succeed.

In my other life, I used to volunteer at animal shelters, and we dealt with some really mean, really ugly dogs. But I've never been one to care too much about a creature's exterior. None of us can help the body we're born with.

It's the spirit inside that counts.

So I yank the bullwhip out of Abaddon's hands and throw it behind us as he hits a switch and the lights flicker to life.

I study the corner I didn't see notice time until it was too late. Immediately, I see what I assumed was a boulder on my first cursory visit. This time, I detect the quick flash of red blinking eyes.

Thing is awake, and aware, as he likely was before. Romulus and Remus are chained where I last saw them, but they intimidate me.

I will tackle one creature at a time. The fur Abaddon tossed me from upstairs is a large piece, and it covers me well as I hold it around myself like a large, puffy bath towel.

I hum a gentle tune as I enter the room and get down on my knees on the filthy floor in front of Thing, doing my best to ignore the stench.

"Not so close," Abaddon hisses from beside me.

I wave him away. I have my own process. And if I lose a hand, well, then I guess that'll be part of the learning process, won't it? I suspect Abaddon will leap into action before he lets that happen, but I refuse to assume these creatures are killing machines.

How can they be anything else if they are never given a chance?

So I inch a little further toward Thing and hold out a hand, palm up so he can get familiar with my scent.

"Hi there." I allow my voice to be gentle. "Abaddon here thinks you'll hurt me, but I'm wondering if there's a better way. Maybe today we'll start with just getting to know each other. What do you think, buddy?"

Thing raises his head slowly and blinks his bright-red eyes. His shoulders shift as he rises from his haunches.

I make myself breathe calmly as first one set of human-looking arms lift from the darkness, then another, then the third pair. With the bottom pair, he uses his hardened knuckles like an ape might, coming a little nearer.

He's filthy from head to toe and the claws of each pair of hands have grown out, almost to the point of piercing knives at the end of each hand.

When Thing gets close enough for the chains on his wrists to stretch taut and pull from where they're attached to the wall, he hisses, and I see that he has sharp fangs.

I tamp down my fear and take another calming breath. I allow myself to smile. "You're quite fearsome, aren't you? You and your brothers? That's okay. I'd like to get to know you, anyway."

Another hiss meets my words, and Thing scuttles around a little, back and forth along the length of his chains. But his red eyes never leave me.

"My name is Hannah," I say, slowly drawing a hand to my chest. "I'd like to be your friend. What's your name? Can you speak?"

He scuttles backward, his head moving restlessly, a tuft of black hair that's all tangled getting in his eyes.

"It seems like it's been a long time since anyone's brushed out your hair. Maybe I could help you with that," I say softly. "I live here now, too. I'm Abaddon's..."

"Con-sort," says the creature in front of me gruffly, and my chest alights. He talked to me! I turn and grin up at Abaddon, who's scowling down at me.

I ignore him and turn back to Thing. "Yes, that's exactly right."

I give him a glowing smile but make sure not to look him in the eyes in case he considers that a challenge. "I'm Abaddon's consort. Sometimes I hear him calling me

Hannah-consort." I laugh a little, and Thing reacts, startling at the sound.

"Oh, sorry." I quickly cover my mouth.

One of his hands mirrors my actions, covering his mouth. It's sweet.

He reminds me of some of the pit bulls when they first get to the shelter. Vicious-looking and scary, yes, but real sweethearts at heart once you get to know them. A bark that's worse than their bite. Unless you really piss them off or catch them on a bad day, that is.

"I'm hoping I can come and visit you every day," I say. "I'd like to get to know you. We can take it as slow as you need. Or as quickly. Can I ask, do you like it down here in the dungeon?"

This gets a reaction out of him. He snorts loudly and shakes his head. A definitive *no*. My heart squeezes. Of course he doesn't want to be down here. How long has it been? He's an intelligent being, and he's been locked up in this dark, filthy place.

"Okay," I say. "Abaddon worries you won't be able to control yourself."

At Abaddon's name, Thing raises his head and lets out a furious growl. Abaddon roars back and snaps the bullwhip.

Which makes Thing start to go crazy. I barely crabwalk backward in time as Thing gallops forward. He's jerked back harshly by his chains, and he's met by the crack of Abaddon's whip slicing into one of his biceps, which makes him howl.

"Abaddon!" I cry.

"Leave!" Abaddon roars at me. "I told you this was a fool's errand."

From the back wall comes a cackling laugh. Remus has awakened. "Oh, pretty consort is soft-hearted." His head has twisted around, and he grins manically at me with his too-wide mouth from beneath stringy, filthy hair. His tail rises behind him like a snake. I didn't even know he was capable of speech. "Maybe you should let me play with her, brother."

I grimace and back away toward the door.

Thing snarls and lashes out at Abaddon from his chains, which leads to another cruel snap of his bullwhip.

"Stop it!" I yell at Abaddon. Who looks at me like I'm crazy. Remus's cackling and Thing constantly rearing against his chains isn't helping anything, so I head for the stairs.

Abaddon follows. The door to the dungeon slams behind him, and I breathe out to calm my nerves as the iron bars slide back in place. Then I head back up the stairs to the lighted levels. I pause on the ground floor foyer.

"Are you satisfied now?" Abaddon growls at me moments later when he arrives at my side. "I told you it was hopeless."

I turn on him with my mouth open. "Are you kidding? You totally provoked them." I throw my hands out. "And who wouldn't be goaded with you whacking them with that damn whip thing every other second." You made Thing *bleed!*"

Abaddon looks astonished. "He's a monster! He was about to attack you."

"We were having a perfectly nice conversation before you inserted yourself."

"Nice conversat— He said one word to you."

"How many does he usually say to you?" I cock my head. Abaddon's silent.

I exhale furiously. "You saw him shake his head. He hates it down there. Of course he does. He's a thinking, feeling being. And you've got him locked up in the dark. It's atrocious. I can't believe you, of all people, would lock your own *brother* up like that!"

"Me, of all people?" he growls then moves into my space, backing me up against the wall. "Why? Because I'm a monster, too?"

I look up into his intimidating face and the frankly barbaric way he's acting. I put my hands on my hips. Refusing to be intimidating. "Yes," I say right into his lion's face. "Exactly that. And because I've seen the whip marks on your own back underneath your wings."

He roars and turns away from me.

And then he leaps out the window and flies away.

"Fine!" I yell after him, holding onto the window ledge for balance. "Just run away instead of talking it out with me! Because that's real mature!"

Once he's gone, I immediately feel bad. Obviously, bringing up whatever torture he's been through is a sore subject. It had to be inflicted by their father. It's quite evident he was a terrible man. He must have abused them all. So of course Abaddon believes it is the only way.

I sigh, incredibly sad. Because despite it all, Abaddon *isn't* like his father. He might have learned his ways, sure.

But with me, Abaddon's been... well, not gentle, exactly. But he hasn't been cruel, either.

And then I look back down toward the dark stairwell.

He can be taught there's a better way.

Maybe there's a reason I was brought to this strange little family. Maybe there are more miracles to be found here than just in the release of my pain and newfound strength of body. Maybe, just maybe, I can bring some healing, too?

I sigh.

Or maybe nothing so lofty as that will happen if there's been so much damage and trauma done here.

But I do know that even the biggest projects start one step at a time.

So I take the stairs to the kitchen, fill up two big buckets, and head back down to the dungeon.

ABBADON

CHAPTER THIRTY-SEVEN

I tell myself I am out seeking again the male from whom she got the clothing, or to hunt, should I see any prey. I tell myself I am not fleeing from a tiny mortal a fourth of my size, with no wings or claws or fangs. I tell myself I am not afraid of mere *words*.

I scoff at the idea. And fly faster. Harder.

Yes, Creator-Father whipped me. So hard it has left permanent marks upon my back.

Discipline was necessary when I would not listen. I can be obstinate. And he was not—

I roar so loudly I cannot pretend to myself I am hunting anything, for the noise will scare away all prey.

I fly harder. Faster. Higher.

"What a disappointment." His voice rings rancorous in my head. *"You cannot even win a fight against your*

brothers, even though you are the superior destroyer. I should strip you of your name and make you the Thing."

He often set us against each other. Always the two of them against me. And when we tangled too long without a victor, he'd set upon us with the bullwhip to separate us. And then extra lashes to each of us after we were chained up again to punish us for all that we lacked.

The new monsters, he said. They wouldn't have our flaws. They would be *truly* superior.

Ha.

Creator-Father was as flawed a Creator as he was a Father. Our youngest brother, the most beautiful and perfect among us, was tortured by the supposed *gift* our father bestowed upon him and knew not obedience because his constant craving was endless.

But did that make Creator-Father any more grateful for us who had come before?

No.

He despised us all the more for his failures.

His whip grew heavier.

Another roar rips from my chest. I will not, *cannot,* dwell on memories.

I will not give into the madness that took my brothers. It is *not* in me. I am whole in ways they are not.

I am superior.

Creator-Father said so.

If the thought does not give me as much comfort as it once did, what of it?

I torpedo through the sky as I head back toward the

castle. I am furious at Hannah-consort for stirring all these things up in me. My life was peaceful before she came.

Enough.

I will not let her stir my brain into a stew. I will breed her, and draw comfort from my kit, and that will be that. I will be a better Creator-Father and do what he never could. I will create a superior destroyer. Perhaps many.

Yes. My chest warms as the thoughts take seed. I will keep her bred, and she will bear me the army of destroyers that Creator-Father always dreamt of.

Perhaps, someday, my sons and I will even do what he could not. Perhaps we will storm the Great Hall and claim it for ourselves. I will rise higher and farther. Creator-Father will weep, down in whatever Underworld pit he has found himself in, that he ever underestimated my strength and greatness.

I grimace, the light in my chest cooling. Glory, if not happiness, is a future worth seeking. And it will be mine.

I am dreaming of this great future, and of stuffing my consort full of my seed to begin this great conquest, as I fly back toward my home.

I'm dreaming of exactly how I will make her cunt gush for me when I alight on the same window from which I leapt.

My ears perk forward to listen for her movements. I expect to hear pots clanging in that damnable kitchen, where she seems to spend half the time these days.

But instead, I hear something that sets a growl in my chest and my teeth on edge.

She is singing. I have only heard the noise from her

once before. When she was singing for *Thing*. And the noise echoes up from the dark stairs below.

She went back down after I left.

She has opened the door to the dungeon.

And she is singing to Thing again.

Fury almost splits my head in two, straight down the center.

But I don't roar. The seething, writhing thing that has taken root inside me keeps me silent as I stalk down the stairs, all my fur standing straight up.

I cannot believe she is testing me thus. I did not think I had to command her to stay out of the dungeon, but I thought I had made myself quite clear on the issue all the same.

She must know she has disobeyed me.

I have been too soft on her.

Creator-Father was wrong about so much, but when he disciplined me harshly, I listened.

Perhaps I must be harsh with her, too. Mortals are foolish creatures, and if her going back down to play with monsters does not prove it, I do not know what else does.

She is a spoiled child in need of correction.

My head pulses with my anger as I pull my wings tightly to my sides. Still, they scrape the walls as I take the stairs three at a time.

And then I am there, stalking through the dungeon doorway.

And there *she* is, all but sitting in Thing's lap, wearing another of Creator-Father's kitchen-coverings as clothing. She sits within the circle of his many arms, his many sharp claws, his *fangs*.

First is fear for her. Then more fury than I have felt yet as other thoughts stab. Jealous thoughts.

"Here we go," Remus observes dryly from the back wall, alerting everyone to my presence.

My consort looks up at me with a bright smile. "Abaddon! Look, Thing and I—"

She is cut off by my hand closing around her throat. Easily, I lift her off the floor and out of Thing's grasp, turning and holding her high in the air. She looks shocked, her face going white, her feet kicking uselessly in the air.

"You will never come down here again," I warn her, fury in every word.

Too late I realize my mistake.

Remus's tail whips around my throat and jerks me backward before I register what has happened. That I have not moved far enough beyond his chain's length. I'm yanked off kilter and my consort drops to the floor.

They are in mutiny against me. How long? How many times has she come down here and worked her wiles on him the same way she has on me? Is she his consort, too?

Immediately, she scurries back to the wall opposite me, her hands going to her throat, eyes wide with shock and betrayal.

I am confused by the regret stabbing me. But perhaps that is just Thing's claws, which indeed have all come out at once and are stabbing every part of vulnerable skin he can reach.

"No!" my consort yells, and Remus's tail tightens at my throat.

"Why no?" Thing's voice seethes at my ear.

Hannah-consort skitters across the dungeon and hides behind Thing's back. She places a hand on his shoulder.

What the fuck is happening? Fury and confusion war. Everything within me wants to lash out at Thing. At her. At all of them. She looks at me as if I have betrayed her, yet obviously she is the betrayer.

I have been a fool to ever believe a word out of her lying mouth, to ever believe she feels anything for me—

My fury lends me strength. If I bear my wings backward, I can overpower—

"Don't hurt him," she says, her voice quiet.

Then Thing's rough voice. "He hurt you. You bear kit. He deserves death."

Kit? *KIT?*

All strength gives out of my legs, and I fall to my knees.

"Kit?" asks Hannah-consort.

But as Remus's tail releases from my neck, I turn, and I see.

Shackles fall from my eyes, and oh gods of the Great Hall, do I see. Or rather *smell*.

Thing is clean.

His hair is no longer a matted, filthy mess, but clean and combed. His skin is cleaned of filth and even his claws have been cleansed and trimmed. He not only allowed her to touch him, but to bathe, groom, and cover his nakedness. He, who attacks if I ever come within feet of him.

Though I am on my knees now, he has reared up on his legs, all six arms and thirty claws bared and ready should I attack.

He, who has always had a more wickedly acute sense of smell than I, protects my consort from *me*.

For he has scented what I only now catch the barest whiff of—that she is *already* with child.

And I, like my father before me, am the only true monster here.

HANNAH

CHAPTER THIRTY-EIGHT

"Thing," I ask quietly, not wanting to startle the gentle but still volatile many-armed giant who stands in front of me. My valiant protector. "What did you mean when you just said I bear kit?"

I can't look at Abaddon. I can't think about the trust he's just destroyed between us. I also can't stop rubbing my neck where he gripped me and held me in the air.

Obviously, I stirred up something for him earlier when I brought up his father's abuse. I mean, he's done some intense things between us but there's always been a line. And I... I was even starting to—

But now he's gone and stampeded past that line in a way I'm afraid might be unforgiveable.

Focusing on what Thing said is far easier to bear. Even though I'm almost equally terrified of its implications.

Thing doesn't turn his head toward me. He's still

watching Abaddon, who's crumpled on the floor. I'm glad he has eyes on him because I still can't look.

"Kit," Thing says. "Brother's seed planted in belly. Grow now and become kit."

My eyes shut as I feel the weight of his words slam into me.

Oh shit.

My hands drop from my neck to the stiff cloth of the old apron and my stomach beneath. Holy *shit*. "You mean I'm pregnant? How do you—"

"He can scent it," comes Abaddon's broken voice from the floor. "It's one of my imperfections. I cannot scent as well as my brother. Hannah-consort, I did not mean to—"

"You meant exactly what you did." Fury fills my chest. "Your actions have spoken for you." I still can't look at him.

Is this really where my wish for a miracle has brought me? To the doorstep of a demon who will lash out at me when he cannot handle his own feelings?

"Give me the keys to Thing's chains," I say quietly.

"You cannot—" Abaddon starts.

I just fucking lose it. "You're the only one who's ever hurt me in this place!" My scream echoes off the filthy walls. "He has only protected me! So I choose him as my protector for now. Now give me the goddamned key!"

My anguished words echo around and back again in the stone of the dungeon.

There is silence after the echo finishes.

And then the sound of Abaddon getting off the floor. Still, I keep my face averted. Even when he says, "I will go get them."

He's only gone a short time.

"I am sorry," comes Romulus's voice at the back of the dungeon. "He will not know how to ask for forgiveness."

"I don't fucking care about that right now," I spit.

"No," Thing says. "No forgive."

"I said I don't care!" I'm biting back tears that are about a second from turning into sobs. I don't know for whose sake I'm trying to hold them in, but I bite the inside of my cheek hard rather than showing weakness, and I'm glad, because moments later, Abaddon returns with keys clanking on a ring.

"Please take them from him, and I'll free you. We can go upstairs and find a more comfortable room for you."

A hum of agreement comes from Thing's wide barrel chest. Eyes still averted, all I see is Romulus's tail whip around forward. And then the dexterous tail comes around before me, a large circle of ancient looking keys hung carefully on the strange leathery tuft at the end.

"T-thank you," I say to Romulus. I hate the tremulousness of my voice. I hate Abaddon getting to see how much he's shaken me.

Then I step close to Thing and put the key in the first of the eight cuffs securing Thing's limbs to the wall, six for his arms, two for his legs. The lock is difficult to turn, but I manage it. These look like new locks, huge and brutal.

It takes both my small hands to slide the arched shackle up and free of the loops of chain. The cuff comes free of Thing's forearm with a rusty *crack,* and clatters to the floor. But finally, one by one, I begin to free him.

He shakes one wrist free and then another, and another.

Finally, I kneel at his feet in supplication. I ignore Abaddon's grumbling growl, only a little bit away from us.

"Please don't attack him once you're free," I murmur to Thing, looking up into his red eyes. He only offers me the quickest of glances. Evidently, he doesn't want to take his eye off Abaddon.

I'm probably being just as foolish to put my hope in him as I was to put my trust in Abaddon. I mean, look where that got me. Maybe Thing's just manipulating me so he can get free because I'm the first fool willing to come along and undo his chains.

But no, I refuse to judge someone by what they look like on the outside.

Usually, I consider myself a good judge of character. I can always sense a volatility and woundedness in Abaddon. I'm horrified and saddened by what he has done today, but... well, I haven't known him all that long.

Thing has a similar history of violent trauma, and I should be careful with him. But I sense his desire to nurture and protect is genuine.

For now, I'll work with what I'm given and go forward less naïve, with eyes open wider. Maybe a little less hopeful.

Unconsciously, I bring my hand back to my stomach. Thing calling it a *kit* hasn't made me feel much better.

I never even thought about getting pregnant. I just assumed because we were obviously different... *species,* that we couldn't... well, you know.

You know what they say when you assume things, idiot. It just makes an ass *out of* u *and* me.

Yeah, yeah. Cause now's the time for jokes.

I squeeze my eyes shut, but just for a moment. Because before I quite realize what's going on, I'm being swept off my feet.

I snap open my eyes, ready to yell at Abaddon to keep his grubby paws off me.

But it's Thing.

He's lifted me in his middle pair of arms and raised me high into the air as he starts loping on his legs and bottom set of knuckles toward the still-open door and the freedom that awaits beyond.

"Thing!" Abaddon calls out.

Thing's body vibrates as he turns around to look behind us. "What?" he barks.

Silence for a moment, followed by a, "Thank you, brother."

Thing lets out a noncommittal grunt then lopes with me in his arms out the door and up the stairwell.

HANNAH

CHAPTER THIRTY-NINE

Thing chooses the second story for his floor.

And it's quickly apparent he does need the entire floor. I can't imagine how he lived being locked in one place for... I shudder... however many *years* he's been down there because now that he's free, he's a whirl of non-stop movement. He doesn't just want one bedroom. He wants *all* the bedrooms.

Remus has followed us, hanging back and watching his brother with that uncanny Cheshire's cat grin of his. Abaddon remains absent, and I'm grateful. I stay near Thing, following him from room to room, chattering and encouraging him if only so I don't have to think about the state of my own life.

After a few hours of bounding around, Thing finally turns toward his brother.

"Why are you still here?" Thing asks Remus. Like

Abaddon, when I first arrived, his speech has grown more and more confident and expansive the more he's practiced with me the past few hours. As if he's remembering how to communicate. "You swore if ever free you never look back. Leaving us in your dust."

Remus grins that uncanny grin that shows all his teeth. "It's suddenly gotten interesting here."

He flicks his gaze past Thing so it lands on me. The hairs on my arm prick up. Despite my humanitarian efforts here, I'm not an idiot. Well, okay, considering I'm voluntarily standing in a castle full of monsters with some sort of monster-hybrid baby in my belly, maybe that's debatable. But even I can sense the predator in Remus's eyes. Thing obviously can, too, because he steps between Remus and me, and a low rattle comes from his throat.

Remus's grin sharpens, and he runs his tongue along his incisors which seem just a tad too sharp for my peace of mind. They don't have any kind of vampiric thing going in addition to all the... wings and teeth and claws stuff, right?

Maybe Thing will be a little more direct about where it is they all come from. I mean, obviously I've gleaned from Abaddon there is some mysterious *father* involved, but who was he, and what *really* happened that brought them all here?

I might have been fine with nebulous information before but dear God, now—

I bring my hand to my stomach again. I need concrete answers now. For one, is this pregnancy something I can even survive?

"Has this ever happened before?" My voice is sharp and high-pitched, bouncing off the cobblestones.

Thing swings back around from where he's facing off with Remus, eyes wide. Remus's eyes are wide, too, but whereas Thing looks cautious and unsure, Remus exudes excitement.

"Never," Remus answers. "We didn't think it was possible."

Great. I swallow hard. "Why not?"

Remus sidesteps Thing in a single fluid motion, and comes right up into my face, startling me to step backward. Remus just follows, obviously caring not one iota about personal space. He crowds up in my face, as if he wants to examine me from close, like one might an animal at a zoo, or a specimen in a lab.

"It's truly magnificent," Remus says, about an inch away from my face as he stares at my nose, then shifts to look at my mouth. He reaches out and pries up my lip to examine my teeth.

"Hey!" I yank back from him, and he looks at Thing.

"It's the obvious solution to our dilemma. A consort to not only slake our sexual thirsts but bear us offspring as well."

My mouth drops open. "Women aren't just pieces of meat, pal. We're not just here to, to, to be"—I sputter, my hands waving—"solutions to your dilemmas, sexual or otherwise!"

Remus merely peers at me peculiarly for a moment then turns back to Thing. "I want one."

"Did you hear a thing I just said?" I sputter.

"Well you can't have this one," comes a sudden response from the corridor, and I spin just in time to see Abaddon's hulking shape as he enters the room. The gold in his eyes is all but gone as the pitch-black slits of his pupils are so large, they absorb his eyes as he stares Remus down.

My chest clenches with rage at the sight of him. I'm so infuriated by what he did earlier. Too many emotions are choking me. I was starting to— And then for him to betray my trust like that—

"Why not?" Remus circles me. "I like the smell of her, and she doesn't seem very fond of you at the moment."

"Back off. She made a deal with *me*. She's mine. For forever."

His words only send the red-hot anger inside me burning white.

"I belong to no one." I push past Remus so I can barge up to Abaddon. Thing steps between us at the last minute, and I try to push him away, too. He doesn't budge.

Which makes Abaddon start to do the throat-growl thing he so loves to do. Except unlike when he's making love to me, this sounds like he's about three seconds from tearing off one of Thing's arms.

"Stop it!" I yell, if only because the pressure valve inside me needs some sort of relief. At the silence that ensues, all I want to do is yell some more. And actually, now that I've finally let up a little of the roar that's been building up inside me all this time, I want to scream and scream and maybe never stop. Because it's not just these three infuriating idiots who are lighting my wick on fire.

I point my index finger in Abaddon's face. Even though

he's a full four feet taller than me, I don't back down. "My whole life people took one look at me and thought they could tell me how to live. They assumed they knew what I could, and more importantly, what I couldn't do. Along with *who* I was allowed to be and what I was worth. So don't you think for one goddamn minute that just because I made a deal with you for my health and my life that I *ever* agreed to exchange *myself* or my freedom. You *do not* and you *will not* ever own me."

His mouth drops open, lion's teeth glistening, but I cut him off before he can get a word out. "And if you think different, you might as well have killed me the day you met me because I was already living a life of hellish captivity. I refuse to exchange one cage for another."

Abaddon lowers himself to his forearms, crouching as he sometimes does to come down to my level—or when he's feeling especially dangerous. "So you mean to leave me? You never intended to honor the contract? Is that what you are saying? You plan to leave me with my kit in your belly?"

"I'm saying exactly the opposite." I throw my hands up in the air in exasperation. "I won't leave unless you make it impossible for me to stay."

Abaddon pulls back from me with a roar. "Stop speaking in riddles!" He turns and bashes the wall with his fist.

Thing immediately leaps between us again, but I stand my ground and glare past him at Abaddon, who scowls at Thing.

"There's a child between us now," I say, my back stiff as

I glare him down, "And regardless of what came before—your deal or contract or whatever, I don't care if I made it with the devil himself—if you ever lay a hand on me again, I'll have Thing saw it off, and leave you for good."

The shame hits him at my reminder. *Good.*

Then I turn away because I can't look at him anymore. Also, am I a fool for not leaving now? A man lifts you up by the throat, you leave. Even if that "man" is a demonic monster creature who doesn't exactly know his own strength? Do the extenuating circumstances count enough in this case to make an exception?

Fool me once, shame on you. I look over my shoulder at Abaddon as he stands, guilt warring with confusion on his face. Fool me twice...

But it hasn't been twice. He's only broken my trust once.

So far, anyway...

All of the sudden, I feel so tired, which surprises me because I haven't felt tired in days. Not since Abaddon healed me. Which just reminds me of how complicated the knot I'm caught in really is. Especially when it's followed by the question: am I tired now because of the pregnancy? When will I start to feel symptoms?

And what the *hell* can I expect with a hybrid monster-human baby pregnancy? Where's the *What to Expect When You're Expecting* demon-monster baby edition?

"See?" Remus chimes in. "She doesn't like you, but maybe she'll like me."

My mouth drops open. Is he kidding? "You're a sociopath," I say to him.

"I don't know what that means," Remus says with a charming grin, "but I'm very good at what I do, and I always get what I want."

I roll my eyes at that. "What do you do?" I ask, while Abaddon starts making the angry throat-growl noises again. Thing is again standing between me and him, or rather him and Remus more likely, in this case. Thing, my unofficial bodyguard.

Remus's grin sharpens again. "Why, I make War, my dear. Don't tell me brother dearest didn't tell you. You didn't stumble into the lair of just any old monsters." He holds out his arms. "We're famous. I'm War, that's Death," he points at Thing. "Our other brother Famine died the day we killed our father, and the one whose kit is in your belly is—"

"Don't!" Abaddon roars.

"Who?" I ask, my gaze ping-ponging between Abaddon and Remus. "Who is he?"

Remus just grins wider, showing all his sharp, white teeth. "Why, he's Pestilence, of course. We're the Four Horseman. So apt because he really is a pest. He's been up my ass for about a millennium, but I gotta say, locking me up in a dungeon for the last two hundred years. New low. Even for you."

Abaddon roars his full lion's roar in response, and Thing is using all six of his arms to hold him back now.

"Pestilence," I whisper, and again my hands go to my belly. I blink rapidly but I just can't take in what I've just heard. This is officially *too much*.

"Try not to tear each other's heads off," I whisper to the room at large, then turn and walk out, leaving them all behind.

I need a fucking bath.

ABBADON

CHAPTER FORTY

I stare after my consort. I am not to be walked away from. I should tie her to the bed again and make her shiver and tremble. Then not allow her to gush until she speaks to me and promises she will never leave.

But what good is a promise when I have heard her just now say that she *will* leave, no matter our deal? Especially now that Remus has told her what I am.

Fury flares in my chest. She will not find leaving so easy. I will hunt her to the ends of the earth anyway, and that was before she had my kit in her belly.

Yet even just now she has just walked away from me.

I want to charge after her, but as if sensing my impulse, Thing blocks the doorway.

"Let her go, brother," he cautions.

The fire in my belly burns brighter. "You are a mad

beast for millennia, and *now* you decide to speak like a civilized person?"

Thing huffs at me, his shoulders hulking even larger as tension gathers. "You treat me as a beast, you will get a beast."

"You slaughtered whole armies. Entire cities. You *are* a beast!" I roar in his face.

Thing straightens, all his arms going out in attack mode. "I was *instrument* of slaughter."

"And if anyone's gonna go on about taking out whole cities," Remus chimes in with a dark laugh, "I mean, that's rich coming from you, brother." He stares me down. "All fear the mighty Pest if he but passes by the threshold of your door."

I bare my teeth at him. "You killed more than any of us, inciting war in their puny hearts. Father just had us there to pluck at the carcasses and finish carrying them off. Or don't you remember the Battle of Borodino?"

But foolish of me to forget, Remus feels no shame. He smiles warmly as his eyes go to the ceiling in remembrance. "Ah, the bloodiest day of all of Napoleon's wars. How could I ever forget? The sky was ablaze with cannon fire and the ground six feet deep with bodies and entrails." His eyes glisten. "That was a good day for all of us."

Thing turns away in disgust, and my stomach sours. Father always thought his Horseman—for that's truly what he thought of us as—just calvary to be brought out to win his secret wars, would never fail him. That we would go on fighting for him for eternity as his loyal soldiers, even though he treated us—

...like mere beasts.

I turn away from all of them and stalk toward the window. The air is stuffy and unbreathable here.

Father's ambition knew no bounds. Like Napoleon, he wanted to take over the entire world, but we were an unruly lot. Remus only wanted to tear apart the world—he knew no sides, only chaos and war. Famine fed off all the starving soldiers, as did I, who swept relentlessly among their ranks.

And Thing... well, he was mindless and blood-engorged, just fury and madness as infantryman slaughtered one another by the tens of thousands, and he carried them off to the deathly planes.

It just wouldn't stop. One battle, and then another, armies chasing each other uselessly across the countryside on horses barely standing up, they were rotting through their saddles.

Who would have hope for this foolish humankind after that? Who would bother?

They called me Pestilence, but I saw with clear eyes who were the pests upon this earth. And for so many years I fought at my father's side to rid the earth of them.

I believed blindly in our father's mission for endless power... I was his truest disciple.

Until the day I became his greatest enemy.

Perhaps it would have gone better for him had I believed in him with less fealty. Had I had a ninety-nine percent belief in him, or the lackluster disillusionment of my brothers. Anything other than my absolutist devotion.

Because when I hit my breaking point, I shattered completely, and in my rage, destroyed my Creator in the way none of his adversaries, seen and unseen, ever could.

The world would know war and destruction again, but by then it was either driven by humankind bent on their own destruction or other monsters. For my brothers and I never rode again after our father and brother were put in the ground.

"That was the last day," Thing says.

Remus just tosses a grape in his mouth—part of the food I got for Hannah-consort—eyelids fluttering with pleasure as it pops in his mouth. I'm about to growl and go wrench the rest of the cluster of stolen fruits not meant for him from his hand when he speaks up. "That day was just the beginning of the end."

"It was the last battle."

Remus grins. "But there was still Moscow to burn to the ground before we were through."

"Father was so proud," Thing remembers grimly.

I scoff at that. "Father was never proud. Out of all of the emotions that were foreign to the man, that one he understood least of all."

"He was a terrible father," Remus agrees, "but he made us great."

"How can you say that?" I challenge. "You know what he was. You were never deceived. He created us, his children, and despised us even as he was happy to use us as if we were nothing more than dogs. And when we were of no more use to him, he put us down with as little thought. We all watched him murder Layden right in front of our eyes. As if it was a lesson to us."

"I've seen humans with their dogs," Thing murmurs. "I do not think we were thought of so highly to him."

"You think you are so much better?" Remus laughs at me. "As Thing reminded you not five minutes ago, you did the same to us the second you had the chance. You chained us to the wall like animals for two hundred years. At least with Father, we were free to wander and slake our appetites."

"Your mean your appetite for war, slaughter, and destruction? Would there be anything left of this earth had I let you continue on in your bloodlust?" I bare my teeth at him. "You forget I wasn't your only jailer. Seems like you need to take up your disputes with your own twin, who voluntarily walked into that basement to save the world from you."

For a second the genteel smirk disappears from Remus's face as absolute rage takes over. If there's any-one on this earth he hates more than me, it's Romulus. No contest. They share one body, and sometimes I wonder, one mind?

While I stand here and talk to Remus, on the oppo-site side of his body, Romulus's face lies sleeping. One always sleeps while the other is awake, and whoever is awake gets to face forward. For centuries the two worked together toward one purpose—the tactician and the madman. While one slept the other would continue the work, an unstoppable machine of war. Until the rift between them, when Romulus turned on Remus, and agreed to help me confine him to the wall with the hell-metal chains.

"What will you do now, brother?" Thing asks. "You have consort and kit to think of."

What does he mean, what will I do now? I can only glare at him, still furious for his calm, rational speech when he would only snarl at me like a mindless beast for two centuries. "I will do as I have always done."

Thing shakes his head, as if disappointed in my answer. Which is even more infuriating. "You must go gently with your consort. She is small and these humans, easily damaged. She carries your kit, who is the hope of a future. If you cannot learn to be gentle, you will not be allowed to be in her presence."

Behind Thing, Remus grins and rubs his hands together in anticipation of a fight.

He is not wrong. I want to rip into Thing for his words and insinuations. "I would not hurt my consort!"

"Perhaps that is what Creator-Father thought, too," Thing says gravely. "And yet we all know how that turned out."

His words slice like a knife, cutting off my retort at the knees.

Ah yes.

That which we don't speak of. Not that we've spoken of much in the last two centuries since we lit our father's dead body aflame and buried the ashes ten feet deep in the earth. Something we ought to have done about a millennium earlier.

Perhaps then our youngest brother would still be

among us. He who always felt so much, the emptiness inside him as great as the starvation he inflicted on those doomed humans our Father set him upon. He'd connected to the consort our father brought home more than any of us, finding in her the gentling mother's presence none of us had ever known.

And so when the day came that my father lost his temper—as he was prone to do—and he shoved her down the stairs...

We all who were so familiar with bloodshed came home from stalking the fire-choked Moscow streets, the Russian army recently fled and the French about to capture and loot, to find her bled out and our father commanding us to clean it up and get rid of her body—

Layden lost it.

He attacked our father. But, the youngest of us, he was best as a weapon of mass destruction, not hand-to-hand combat. He could weaken our father, but that was nothing to the Creator. Father had fought through hunger before. He toyed with our brother, torturing him before death by first slicing off his glorious wings and pouring burning hot hell-metal over his back so they would never grow back. We thought it would end there.

But when Layden continued calling our father a murderer, enraged, he turned and plunged a hell-metal sword through Layden's too-soft heart.

While we all did nothing, staring on in bewildered shock.

HANNAH

CHAPTER FORTY-ONE

I wake after a deep night's sleep, breathing out in relief as I sit up and looking toward the door. I barred the door last night to keep Abaddon out. I was afraid as I climbed into bed that he'd simply break it down or fly in through the window. Frowning now, I think in my drowsy dreaming state I heard the loud thumping of him discovering the locked door, but he didn't break it down.

For once, he has respected a boundary.

It's too soon to really call it progress, but at least it's something.

My stomach rumbles and, as the morning sun blazes in through the window, I know I can't hide away in here forever. I need to go down to breakfast.

Half of me wants to climb back under the covers and pull them over my head. But my stomach gurgles again, reminding me that damn, I really am hungry. Like, starving. When did I last eat? Did I skip dinner last night? I can't remember. Everything was just such a shock. Abaddon acting out like that. I skim my fingers over my neck.

And then finding out about the—

I shoot my other hand to my belly.

Jesus. I've forgotten, but now that I've remembered, it all seems so absurd.

I'm pregnant. Dear God. What am I going to do? What *is* there to do? Go down and have breakfast, I guess.

Then, like a knee-jerk reaction, I think of Drew's voice on the sat phone. He has this thing where he would pull me into a hug after a long day and say, "Now you don't have to worry about a thing anymore—you have me. I'll take care of everything."

And if I let him, he really would just sort of... take over.

It was such a relief at the beginning. He just barged right in and moved me out of Mom's house, taking care of all the details of the move.

Then little by little, he took on more and more.

Small stuff at first. After all, it only made sense to share a cell phone plan. And after we moved in together, well, he really did have a better head for math... so it just made sense for him to take care of the bills. And since he was paying the bills, well, wasn't it only logical to get a joint bank account so my paycheck could get directly deposited into it, so he could pay everything from there? We were about to get married anyway.

And when he suggested we get rid of my hand-drive car because we could commute to work together since we worked in the same building—well that was really the financially responsible thing to do, wasn't it? Everyone in my department at work thought it was so romantic how he came in at the end of every day to help carry my bag.

I never heard the end of how lucky I was to have a man like Drew—only once had a coworker slipped and said out loud what I always suspected they all thought, while staring at Drew's taut ass as he walked out after dropping me off one morning: "You must feel so lucky. You know, especially considering..." Her words trailed off as her eyes dropped to my legs. It had been a bad week, and I was in my wheelchair that day.

I was too stunned and hurt to say anything in the moment, only thinking up a million cutting comebacks hours later when I was crying in the bathtub.

But it did make me more determined than ever to be *useful*, even as Drew made that more and more impossible with his constant helpfulness and determination to make life *easier* for me, always with a logic I couldn't deny.

Yes, he was right, it was really stressful, I supposed, to work all day, then try to make it to book club on Tuesday nights. And my body was always so extra tired after craft circle with my friends on Saturdays, which made me especially cranky. Which I did, undeniably, tend to take out on Drew, and he didn't deserve that. He was *so good* to me, after all.

So little by little, my world got safer and safer.

Smaller and smaller.

But small was cozy when you were with the love of your life... right?

So how could you just up and leave him like that? Not even a word of goodbye—just a note? If it was such true love?

He was such a good man.

He gave and gave.

I was selfish. It was so obvious to everyone that looked at us that I didn't deserve him. Even those who didn't come out and say it. I saw it in their eyes. The thing was... sometimes on the bad days, I was terrified I saw it in Drew's eyes, too.

But why would he be with me if he thought that? So I told myself it was my own insecurity. I told myself not to sabotage a perfectly good relationship. No, a *great* relationship. The love of my life!

I sigh, a hand on my belly.

It seems so useless now—those silly old dramas I wasted so much time torturing myself because they seemed so dreadfully important at the time. Considering my present circumstances, though, it all seems quite foolish. Like someone else's life, or a dream.

Then I look out the castle window. Okay, so maybe it's more like *this* feels like the dream. Except that I feel like I've been more of the real *me* since I've been here, and it has nothing to do with my health or my outer body.

Then again, all dreams feel real when you're in them.

I slap myself hard across the face.

"Ow!" I blink away the sting. Then look around again. Still in a castle. Well. It was worth a try.

Then I stand up, straighten, and exhale. As much as

I might want to hide away here forever, I have a feeling Abaddon will eventually come hunting me down.

Plus, this new, real version of me isn't in the mood to hide or avoid my life anymore. Ever since the day I decided to take my life by the horns... well I guess I'm ready to see where this ride takes me. Again I bring my hand to my belly. Especially since if this is all real, and there really is a *baby* growing inside me now, I don't see what other option there is anyway.

So I stride first for the bathroom, to shake out one of the old aprons I washed in the bathwater after bathing myself. It's a little crackly with ice, and I'm not sure it's exactly *dry,* but I put it on over my head anyway.

It should feel freezing—I should be shivering with my teeth chattering, considering the snow drifts I still see on the floor in the sides of the room—but it barely bothers me as I pull on the garment over my head. I frown. I swear, it's like my internal temperature has changed from ninety-eight point six to... something much higher.

I turn and head for the door, disconcerted, but as I do, I notice something else that feels different. I pause and stretch my arms over my head. My back cracks. My eyes pop open because, all things considered, that's usually a disastrous noise for me.

But I just feel looser, and as I extend my hands high, toward the ceiling, I realize—holy shit! Am I taller than I was yesterday? Because that's when it hits—my back isn't as humped over as it was. I'm standing up fully straight.

I blink in shock and try to look over my own shoulder at my back, a hopeless endeavor that just sends me spinning in circles. I start for the bathroom, again, halfway there before remembering there are no mirrors anywhere in the castle.

Son of a—

I thought Abaddon said he wouldn't heal me any further. Has he changed his mind? As some sort of peace offering?

I unbar the door hastily and head for the stairs, all but flying down them toward the kitchen, driven both by my hunger and my need to know if Abaddon is the reason for these new changes in my body. But I don't make it all the way there. As I'm passing the ground floor, I see the brothers all seated around the large dining room table. I pause and slowing, head into the room.

"You're late," Abaddon growls from where he sits at the head of the table. Remus and Thing sit on a long, heavy wooden bench to one side. That's new. I guess they unearthed the bench from some room I haven't seen yet.

Abaddon's eyes are dark as he glances my way. "I was about to send Thing to fetch you."

Then he snaps his fingers and points to a plate of food at his hooved feet.

Right. I laugh to myself at the naiveté of thinking he would have given me any more healing without demanding something in return.

"Yeah," I say, "We're through with that." I swoop down in a graceful motion like a dancer, snatch the plate off the ground, and bound away with it before he can snatch for me, still seated like he is. I'm shocked and delighted at how easy the movements are after a lifetime of stumbling and feeling dizzy on my feet.

Breakfast is fried eggs, a slab of meat, and a big, uncut tree of broccoli. It all looks absolutely delicious, and I'm even more ravenous now that I see and smell the food.

I plop myself down between Remus and Thing because I think it will keep Abaddon at bay.

Naturally, it instead only seems to set him off, but I'm too busy digging into my eggs and tearing at the meat with my teeth to care. Forks and knives have been neglected from the table settings, but human utensils are still a concept I'm working on getting Abaddon used to. I'm too hungry now to bother with decorum, so I don't go get them. My teeth might not be as sharp as theirs, but they get the job done.

I can't help but moan in delight as I chew. "Oh my God, this is so good. What is this?" I shove another bite of meat in my mouth. Then I hold up a hand as Abaddon starts to answer. "No, don't tell me," I say, a little garbled with my mouth half-full. "Don't ruin it. It's too delicious for you to tell me I'm eating horse or something awful." I moan again as I chomp on an especially succulent piece.

"Does she make noises like this all the time?" Remus asks from beside me, food abandoned on his plate as he watches me in fascination.

I wave grease-covered fingers at him for him to stop, but it's too late. Abaddon's truly pissed now.

"Don't speak to my Hannah-consort."

So I turn to Thing. "Will you please tell your brother that he doesn't get to tell me who I can talk to?"

Thing looks to Abaddon. "Hannah-consort says that—"

Abaddon roars in fury, sweeping his plate to the floor. I can't help but gasp as I shove the last of my eggs in my mouth. The waste! All that delicious food, on the ground!

"You will speak to *me*!" Abaddon demands.

I turn to Thing again. "Thing, will you politely remind your brother of what I told him yesterday? He does not own me. I am not a dog to bark when he commands it."

Remus chuckles from my other side. "Told you, brother. Just think. Father would be so proud. You're a chip off the old block after all, treating us like dogs."

Abaddon leaps to his feet, a growl emanating from his throat.

I continue to eat my food calmly. Well, rather, I continue to scarf down my food. Dear God, food has never tasted so good. And I've never been able to shove it in my face fast enough. Is this a pregnancy side-effect? I'm munching on the broccoli as I turn to Remus curiously.

"So how do you two decide which of you gets to eat?" I nod toward Romulus's sleeping face on the other side of his head. "Do you share a stomach or have two of those, too? Do you just take turns, or what?"

Remus's eyes sparkle as he looks back at me, grin widening. "You ready to ditch that animal yet?" He jerks a thumb over his shoulder toward Abaddon, Remus's tail lifting to twitch in the air like an animated cat's. "He's a child, can't you see? You need a man."

I choke on the bite of food I've just swallowed, and Abaddon is on his feet again.

I put the rest of my broccoli down on my plate with the

last of my meat and sigh in exasperation. I have a feeling if I stay here much longer, one way or another, the rest of my meal is going to be ruined. "I think I'm going to finish my food back up in my room."

I hop up off the bench and slip out of the room. Behind me, the brothers erupt at each other. Oh well. Instead of heading up to my room, though, I aim downstairs toward the kitchen. I'm still hungry.

I think I'll just go cook myself several more eggs and eat them in *peace.*

ABBADON

CHAPTER FORTY-TWO

I am angry that my brothers have driven Hannah-consort from the room. I want her back. I want to roar at her to return. Or better yet, chase her to her bedroom, tie her to the bed, and feed her the last bits of food from the edge of my claw.

She does not look back at me as she leaves.

The fury that burns low in my belly feels like hellfire, not that of the angels. But for once in my damned life, I manage to stay still.

I swallow my rage. For as much of a fool as I am beginning to realize that I am, I do see this: I am pushing her away even as I aim to draw her near.

But the fury bubbles nearer the surface because I do not know how to change it.

I am a monster. I was built to conquer through destruction, pestilence, and death. I am a despicable creature. There is no solace to be found in my arms, and yet I cannot—*will* not—give her up.

Even as I watch her walk away from me.

As soon as I hear her small feet pattering on the stairs, I turn on my brothers. On them, at least, I will not hold back.

"You," I bark, aiming a clawed finger at Remus. "Give me your twin. Now. I need the tactician to scry for me."

Fire burns in Remus's eyes, as it always does when I tell him to relinquish control to his brother.

But I have no time for his petty ego. "Do you want to lose her?" I snap. "Then let Romulus take the reins. She ran into someone that day she left the dungeon door open."

Remus shrugs. "What's it to me?"

I charge toward him. "Did you hear what I just fucking said? She encountered someone. She was naked, and this man gave her clothing. When I questioned her further, she said he took her inside his cottage."

"So?"

"So?" I mock. "Thing all but razed the village to the ground, if you'll remember."

"That was two hundred years ago."

"I remind them of the danger if anyone comes sniffing around," I growl. "The locals consider the whole forest cursed, and I did my part to reinforce the belief by giving the plague to anyone who came near for the first hundred years."

Remus shrugs. "So you have become lax."

I speak through my teeth. "That is what I'm telling you. I have not. I fly patrol regularly, and there is no one.

No shack or hut or even a fishing lean-to. There's no one in a hundred-mile radius except us. That's why I need Romulus to scry."

Remus's jaw works. Then he rolls his eyes, just a moment before his face goes completely blank—the only warning we get before his head swivels on his neck. Even though I've been seeing him do this my entire life, it's still disconcerting.

Romulus blinks awake.

"Lovely to finally have you at the fucking party, brother," I growl. "Catch up quick."

Romulus's eyes go up and to the right—doing that weird thing where he's accessing their shared memory. Fucking creepy, if you ask me. Not having your own brain to yourself.

"All caught up? Fucking lovely. Now call the angel runes."

Romulus heaves out a breath, yanking on the edges of his long sleeves as he reaccustoms himself to control of his body. "Good morning to you, too. I haven't called the runes in over two centuries."

I clap him on the back. "It's like riding a bike. It'll come right back."

He frowns at me.

"Just do it," I growl. "Hannah-consort was right about one thing at least—too long you have moldered in that basement. It is time for us all to live again. Even your twin is learning to be civilized. It is truly the dawn of a new era."

I put a hand on his shoulder again, but instead, this

time, I squeeze. "Which is exactly why we need to be aware of any potential threats out there."

Romulus pulls away from me, but slowly. Like all his movements, he does so with calculation, while staring me in the eye. "Do not pretend you do this for all our sakes. I see that, like always, you are simply taking the path most expedient to your own desires. You and my twin have that in common. You are both utterly predictable. Also, you are a fool if you think he is becoming civilized."

I narrow my eyes at him, but this time he reaches out to clap me on the back. "But your predictability is one of the things I like most about you, brother. And I agree, if there is anything out there that might be coming at us, we must be ready now that there is something precious to protect. I will scry for you."

We move away from the dining table toward the empty half of the large hall, so that nothing obstructs Romulus as he spreads his wings to their full span and lifts his hands. His leonine tail whips furiously behind him as the air begins to stir with his chanting in the bell-like angelic language.

Theoretically, all of us should be able to scry since we carry the spark, but Romulus is the only one with the patience to sit down and learn the language of angels.

I was there the day Father poured the angel-fire into clay and created the twins. Each experiment was more disastrous than the last, and yet he would not be dissuaded. And at first, when he looked upon the beautiful, winged creature that was left in the basin of his creation chamber, he laughed with such joy.

Because Romulus is indeed as handsome as any of the heavenly host. Our father had come *so* close to perfection.

But how he did howl with fury when their head spun on its axis and he first met Remus. Creator-Father immediately began to strike Remus across his equally handsome face, and that was the first memory my brother awoke to in this world: being beaten by his Creator-Father for daring to exist.

When our father recovered from his fury, he bestowed a "gift" on them as he did each of us at our birth once he saw what his creation had wrought—they would thereafter carry the spirit of War. Warring always for control of a single body and bringing spite and enmity wherever our spiteful father would send us out as his soldiers.

It has not been an easy path for any of us, perhaps, though like my father, it was easy to blame Remus when he was a wrathful and unruly youth.

Romulus bore the brunt of it, and as I look upon him now, almost a millennium later, for the first time, in shame, I acknowledge my part in it all.

I am the eldest. It is an unkind world, and if not each other, who else do we have in this cold universe?

I ought to have protected them. Too long I believed our Creator-Father's lies that his way is the *only* way.

I was weak to be so deceived.

Young perhaps, but also weak.

And I despise nothing else more than weakness.

In front of me, Romulus's brow furrows and wind

sweeps through the hall, whipping in a circle around him and his outspread, dark grey wings.

It is beginning.

The white-blue runes begin to glow in the whirring air, arcing between his outspread hands, cutting through the other realm to this one.

But almost as soon as the runes begin to appear, Romulus's eyes widen in shock.

And then he's blasted backward as if shot by cannon fire. I struggle to stay on my feet as the wind disbands like a whipping tornado, runes disappearing almost as soon as they appeared.

Thing lopes across the floor to where Romulus lies in the blasted-apart dining room table, which is now just kindling.

"Brother!" Thing pulls Romulus back to his feet and helps to clear wood chips from his wing feathers.

"What the hell was that?" I bark.

Romulus's eyes are wide as he coughs and sputters, looking around as if trying to get his bearings.

"An angel," he whispers.

"That's not possible," I spit. "They retreated behind the gates to retire in the Great Hall."

"Well obviously not all of them," Romulus says heatedly. It's so out of character for him to seem ruffled, but I cover my surprise.

"We should never have become so lax," he snaps.

I get in his face, furious at the challenge in his words. "None of us knew we would ever have something that would be worth protecting."

I leave it unsaid that before now I may not have cared if this fortress was breeched, or that if after all this time I have finally met a foe strong enough to defeat me. I've continued my existence for so long now more from habit and sheer stubbornness than out of any desire to live for so long...

Until her.

And now... the kit. The possibility of a future.

"What did you see?" I demand of Romulus, who still seems dazed. I can't lose them now that I have just gained them.

This all feels like history cruelly repeating itself. My father's consort was also a fleeting light of kindness in our long darkness. But like delicate candle flame, she flickered only briefly before being snuffed out.

I will *not* let the same happen to Hannah-consort.

"What did you see? Tell me!" I grab him by the shoulders but Romulus's eyes remain wide, and if I didn't know him better, I'd say, *panicked.*

That is, before they go completely blank, and then his head spins a one-eighty, and I'm met with Remus grinning at me. "Trouble in paradise, brother?"

Roaring in fury, I toss him away from me. All things considered it's the less-violent option. "Bring your twin back. I have questions for him."

But Remus just makes a *tut-tut-tut* noise. "You know we share memories, fool. Just lemme take a peek." His eyes tilt sideways, widening slightly. "No shit. An angel, huh? One of those fuckers escaped the pearly gates?"

"What do you see?" I ask. "What does it want with us?"

Remus shrugs, plucking small wood splinters from the table off his shirt. "How should I know? Like Romulus said, he didn't get a good look before the motherfucker blasted us with angelfire through the runes. But he was already looking our way, that was for damn sure. It didn't feel like an accidental rune-cross. And he was shielding himself. Rom's rusty. He hasn't scried for centuries. He wasn't careful enough."

"Fuck, so it already knew about us, is that what you're saying? Is it coming? You don't think—"

"What?" This from Thing, who's been loping nervously in the open space beside us like an animal with barely leashed energy.

"It couldn't have been him who Hannah-consort met that day in the woods, right?"

"Of course not," Remus barks out a laugh. "Else why would it ever let her go?" He looks my way. "Your scent was *all* over her. Any worthy adversary would have kidnapped her and held her for ransom."

A growl comes from low in my throat even at the thought. "She is not to be left alone for a moment."

Remus grins. "I'm happy to take first watch."

My growl grows to a roar. "Don't make me rip out your throat, brother, just when we've started getting along so well."

He leans in, teeth in something between a smile and a menacing warning. "I'd love to see you try." His eyes glitter with mania.

"Stop being fools, both of you." Thing gets off his

knuckles and rises to his full height. "Must stop fighting each other if the threat to Hannah-consort is real."

"Oh it's real," Remus says. "That angel rune-fire knocked me across the damn room, and you know how difficult any matter manipulation usually is through scrying. I'd hate to see what the motherfucker could do in person."

I swear. Angels quit this world many millennia ago. It's why our father thought that if he could steal enough angel-fire to recreate some, he'd be able to rule over this world of mere humankind.

I glare at Remus. "I'll be the only one watching *my* consort." But then I look over at Thing. "Well, Thing can take watches while we sleep. No one rests until we find out more. Whenever Romulus comes back, tell him to get back in practice warding himself until he can scry again without getting knocked on his ass!"

With that, I storm out of the room and head up to the bedroom because I don't intend to let my consort go another moment without my eyes on her at all times.

HANNAH

CHAPTER FORTY-THREE

I'm in the bedroom, polishing off my food and thinking about returning to the kitchen to rustle up some more when the door bangs open. Thankfully, I've just put down the plate or I might have dropped it.

I didn't think of barring the door, and I immediately go on the alert as Abaddon's hulking shape fills the space after he ducks past the threshold and shuts it behind him.

"You go nowhere without me by your side," he barks.

I cross my arms over my chest. How many times are we going to have to have the conversation explaining that I'm not a dog? Obviously, he doesn't listen. So why am I wasting my breath? In fact, not talking seems like an excellent idea.

There's no point in talking to a person who doesn't see me as an equal, so I won't. I just stare at him pointedly, my arms crossed tightly, and then I turn away from him without a word and start to make the bed.

"Hannah-consort," he says.

I ignore him and continue to tidy the bed linens. I once had a really temperamental friend who loved to give me the silent treatment if I ever committed what she considered the least slight against her, so I am familiar with the tactic. Briefly, I consider how this did not go well for me when I tried it with him last time, but I'm feeling stubborn.

"Hannah-consort," he repeats, louder this time.

I continue to ignore him, and even start to hum lightly under my breath as I continue my task.

"Hannah-consort," he roars. "Pay attention to me."

Or what? I think, but do not say. And perhaps it is the devil in me, testing him like this, when I know how volatile his temper is.

But he is not the only one who can get angry. Maybe I haven't even known it till now, how deep the well of anger inside me goes. A lifetime of slights, degradation, either being treated as if I were invisible or as if I were a burden—

My movements become sharper. I yank the bearskin bedcovering taut, and it snaps with the quick movement.

I have as much rage as he has, and yet I do not strike out at all those dear to me.

I hear his hoof-steps on the cobblestones, and I swear, if he explodes at me, this will be it. I will leave him for good. Forever. Somehow, I will find a way. I have done impossible things before, and I will do them again.

But when he speaks again, his voice is low, and it is controlled. "Hannah-consort will go nowhere without me at her side. And if she will not agree to these terms, then she will go nowhere."

What does that m—

But stubbornly, I will not ask.

And as it turns out, the answer is quickly provided.

For the next moment, Abaddon pounces on me and bears me down to the bed I have just made.

Had he been rough with me, I would have attacked him and fought like a wildcat. But his claws are carefully retracted, and I know he is taking the utmost care to be gentle with me as I land on my back on the bearskin.

He comes on top of me, but not with his weight. He bears his knee between my legs, and his ink-black wings flare out behind him, darkening the daylight coming in through windows.

Still, stubbornly, I don't make a sound, only staring at him furiously for a moment before averting even my eyes from his. Denying him even the communication of eye contact.

"Hannah-consort will be safe." He breathes out, and then he takes my wrist, easily overpowering any resistance I might have made—and I'm not sure that I do try to resist, which feels fucked up even as my chest starts fluttering—as he bears it to the mattress up above my head. Then, still keeping me pinned beneath him, he brings out a length of rope from underneath the bed.

I want to demand to know what he's doing. But well, it's fairly obvious as he loops the rope around my wrist and then shifts to tie it to the bedpost. I adjust beneath him, stubbornly staying silent as he easily pins me down with his wings while he works, quickly tying one wrist, and then another.

He's tying me to the bed again.

I won't speak to him, but I let out an outraged noise from the back of my throat. Things are different now. He can't just—

"Yes," he says, more a purr, "you will scream for me soon enough."

Which suddenly makes all the moisture in my mouth go dry. And, as if it's transferred directly to another part of my body, my legs began to squirm.

But Abaddon isn't nearly done, yet.

He moves down my body, his wings beginning to flutter all around me. I recognize that flutter.

And then he grabs my left ankle. I'm not sure if I'm anticipating or dreading being completely stuck in place. Last time I was face down, but now I'm on my back, which means I can see everything he's doing.

I kick out with my right leg, the last limb left free, but he only snatches it out of the air, always careful to retract his claws like always when he interacts with me. It doesn't lessen the strength of his grip, though, as he forces my leg back to the bed and then loops yet another rope around it.

Where the hell are these ropes coming from anyway? Were they there just waiting under the bed all along? Jesus, he's obviously prepared for this.

Alarm spikes through my chest.

But if I'm being entirely honest... there's excitement

mixed in with it. *What is* wrong *with you?* I ask myself, squeezing my eyes shut.

That helps nothing, though, because then I'm completely unprepared for when Abaddon moves back up my body.

My sex contracts and gets so wet, I'm startled. And really, really excited for what comes next.

Which is, apparently, Abaddon's hands squeezing my thighs as he bends over my sex. I'm not even sure when he rucked up my apron skirt, but my legs are stretched open by the way they're tied to the bed. And when he breathes out over my sex, I almost break my own vow of silence.

Because holy Mary mother of God!

That. Feels. *So. Good.*

And you know what? These past few days have been stressful. And maybe it's screwed up because *he's* the one who made them so stressful. And I haven't forgotten what he did—

But him eating me out in that amazing way I know he can, might just go a long way toward healing the gulf that's opened up between us.

My hips buck up toward his mouth on his next heavy exhalation.

And then he's on me. Like a voracious... well, beast.

Unlike me, his hands are most definitely *not* leashed. And he grabs my ass and drags my entire body up and into his mouth as he all but unhinges his jaw to begin devouring me. His inhumanly long tongue slips into my channel while he covers his long teeth with his lips and then bites down, putting pressure on my clit with his bite while he tongues straight to my G-spot.

Oh sweet baby Jesus, it's like the world's most insane head anyone could ever dream up.

And that's all before he starts to *suckle*. A whine comes from my throat. I've forgotten how good this feels.

He mauls, sucks, and licks with that infuriatingly textured tongue until I'm arching my back in futility trying to get closer to him but unable to because of my tied limbs.

It's so good, and still I want *more*.

I can't even tell when I start to come, because the pleasure launches so high from the very start, as soon as he got his mouth on me. It's like I've been coming the entire time.

Except wait, no, oh God, I think I'm coming now. I think this is— Oh my Jesus *fuck*, I think *this* is the orgasm that's about to hit—

I and grip around the rope tying me to the bed because if I don't hold onto something it feels like this orgasm is going to rip apart my body.

I howl a high-pitched scream and Abaddon growls and continues to loudly eat me out as the light of my orgasm tears through my chest outward to the tips of my toes. My legs shake, and shake, and shake with aftershocks.

"Another," Abaddon lifts from between my legs long enough to demand, before descending again.

I start to shake my head but then my head bangs backward against the mattress, immediately screeching again the second his tongue lands on my sensitive, swollen clitoris and he starts sucking.

Within fifteen seconds, he's brought me to the top of the mountain again.

And I've barely caught my breath, my heartbeat calmed down from racing like I'm competing at the Kentucky Derby, when he only rises long enough to declare, "Another."

And then the shadow of his head drops back down. "I don't think I can—"

Only to find my weak legs shaking with another orgasm moments later.

I think surely then, he's finished. I can't possibly come another time. My body can't take anymore. Surely, my over-sensitized clit will give up the ghost now!

I assume Abaddon has finally seen the light and decided the same when not only his head rises from between my legs, but I glimpse his shoulders, too.

Until I realize he's repositioning himself to get a better angle. I blink in confusion at all the different sensations of feeling him pry my ass cheeks apart and then his tongue is back, licking a long path from my clit, through my slit, all the way to my shy, dark little asshole.

"Abaddon!" I screech.

"That's right," his response comes from deep between my legs. "Get used to screaming my name."

And then his strong, probing tongue is back at my anus.

It's so wrong.

It's so dirty.

The tips of his wings curve around us and begin to flutter against my clitoris, fast as a bird's wings and angel-feather soft.

I squirt, I come so hard.

He chuckles, and the dark sound becomes the soundtrack to my next two orgasms. He eats my ass so good, and he pries me apart with his hands so he can get more of my darkest place. Promising when he comes up for breath, "I will fuck you here, soon. I will take all of you, and you will beg me for more."

Shaking from a run of orgasms beyond what I could have ever imagined, I can only nod. Because in this moment, I want everything he can do to me.

And I pray, as I try to inhale, and shudder instead with yet another aftershock, that I won't live to regret it.

The next morning, I wake up to Abaddon's warmth at my side. It is a little awkward sleeping on my back with my limbs stretched out and tied up.

But frankly, he exhausted me so much with the nonstop orgasms, I fell asleep within two seconds and slept like a log.

Now, though, I'm awake. And my body feels shockingly... amazing.

Except I'm starving. And I have to pee.

"You have to let me up at some point, you do realize, right?" I say when I feel him stir beside me. The entire bed creaks at his slightest motion.

"Fine," he growls but doesn't move.

"I'm serious. I have to pee."

Still he doesn't move, which pisses me off. "And I'm

hungry. You knocked me up, and pregnant women need to eat!"

This at least arouses some movement in him. Thank god. I sigh out a breath of relief as he shifts down the bed, and thank god, begins to untie my ankles.

My impatience to be free is briefly surprised into quiet when he gently massages the skin of my ankle after he frees it from the rough rope.

Surprise turns into squirming when he bends down to press his lips to my skin. Oh god, not this again.

He kisses every inch of skin where the rope chafed, lifting my leg in the air to reach the back near my Achilles tendon. We don't have time for this. I'm super hungry, and I really do have to p—

But annoyingly, as if his touch is tied to some magic sensual line connected to my belly, I have to fight not to make a noise at the sudden, searing arousal.

Now he's moving onto my second ankle. Thank god. I just need to get out of this bed. I've gotta get some distance from him. So I can clear my head. Obviously.

Because I want to be stubborn. I want to remind him that I'm hungry as he starts to kiss a similar path around my second ankle. But as he begins to climb up my body, his wicked tongue continuing to lick and suckle when he gets to my knees and then my thighs…Slowly, ever so slowly creeping around to my inner thighs…

Goddamn him.

I feel my sex begin to flush and moisten for him. And perversely, it's as if the fullness in my bladder only adds to the pressure and growing pleasure in my sex.

My ankles, now freed, seem to move of their own accord, driven by the need Abaddon is so good at sparking and then inflaming in me in ways I've never experienced before. My legs lift to wrap around the bulk of his lower back, beneath his wings.

"Fuck me," I whisper, my voice a tremble.

Abaddon's head lifts from where he's breathing over my sex.

His eyes search mine in question, and my need pulses higher. It's been so long since he's been inside me—he's just been incessantly driving me insane with his mouth and his wicked, wicked tongue.

And I realize in shock that for all his brutality, this is what he's been waiting for since our rift—for me to invite him back in. For me to beg, even. So I bite my lower lip then say it again, more urgently this time.

"Fuck me, Abaddon. I want you to fuck me."

His wings shoot out, flaring black night overhead to cover the morning light as he pounces up my body.

And I feel him there, ready and hard at my swollen, flushed sex.

His eyes gleam and glitter as a growl like a purr starts to come from the back of his throat. "I have been waiting for you."

I nod, my throat too full for words, as he leans down to nip at my neck.

"You will want none but me because I will fuck you so well." He breathes out in my ear.

I moan back in assent and finally manage some sort of words. "Yes, you fuck me so—"

He plunges in before I can finish.

My arms are still tied above my head so the only part of my body I'm able to cling to him with are my legs. I wrap them around his ass so tightly, my heels digging in as if I can pull him deeper into me.

"You are mine," he growls. "I will protect you."

He pulls out and then plunges in again, his huge cock splitting me open so that I feel him everywhere.

"I will worship you."

Pull.

"I will keep you safe and fuck you forever."

Thrust.

"Yes," I scream, so lost in him as the pleasure spawning at my core makes me feel insane with wanting him.

He pulls out again, and I feel like crying at the loss of pressure.

"I need you, and you need me," he growls, then thrusts in, grinding his groin against my swollen clit. My legs shake and spasm around him as I start to come.

"Yes!" I cry.

"Say it!" he demands as his thrusts increase in tempo. "Say you need me."

"I need you," I cry, tears of pleasure rolling down my cheeks as ecstasy crashes through me in waves. "I need you, and you need me."

He fucks me with even more intensity. Around us, his wings vibrate as his chest glows blindingly bright, shaking the hair and making my hair fly as my soul is torn to pieces as the blinding light of my orgasm shreds through me.

Oh my god. I feel him release, the hose of his cum pumping into me, which sends aftershocks as powerful as most regular orgasms quaking up and down my spine.

Oh shit. I think I'm in love with one of the Four Horsemen of the Apocalypse. My head falls back onto the pillow, and I laugh in a spent daze as Abaddon bows his head between my breasts, his wings falling like a shroud over the both of us.

ABBADON

CHAPTER FORTY-FOUR

There is something different in Hannah-consort's eyes when she looks at me ever since I untied her, and we fucked this morning.

I suppose I felt it first in how her legs clutched me to her and then as I took her—as if she did not want to let me go.

And now when she looks at me as we go down for breakfast… there is a smile in her eyes.

No one has ever looked at me this way before.

I would slay entire armies if only to keep that look in her eye.

My cold heart feels warmth it has never known before.

All in the castle notice as well.

I am glad to find it is Romulus present instead of his twin when we reach the main level in search of food.

Unlike his twin, Romulus simply looks first at Hannah-consort, notes her sated expression with surprise, and then at me, and then gives me a single, knowing smirk. But he leaves it at that.

Whereas Thing scampers directly to Hannah-consort. "Are you well? I heard you scream."

I am furious at him and want to tear off a pair of his arms as I rip him away from her.

But the way she blushes so prettily and voluntarily walks around him back to my side, sliding against my chest underneath the crook of my arm—well it shocks my system with such warmth that my anger instantly dissipates.

The surprise on Thing's face is also quite satisfactory to me.

"So," Hannah-consort says, clapping her hands. "Who's hungry?" She is bubbly and smiling, and if her cheeks are a tad bright, I know that it is our fucking that has put the color there.

I immediately want to take her back upstairs and fuck her again.

But her stomach grumbles with hunger noises. Ah. I must remember. She is carrying my kit, and he is demanding.

"I will blacken you some meat," I declare.

She squeezes my waist with her delicate arm. "How about I cook?" She blinks up at me in a sweet way with those smiling eyes I cannot deny. Especially with her body all pressed up against me, so warm.

I nod a little dazedly, and Romulus chuckles from somewhere behind me. But then I frown. I do not want her out of my sight, even if I will not worry her by telling her why.

"I will watch."

She laughs at this, then cocks one beautiful eyebrow. "You could learn a thing or two."

Which elicits another chuckle from Romulus. Whom I glare at. Since when has he had a sense of humor? Usually he is dour. Only his brother laughs, and what Remus finds funny is usually only the blood of his enemies.

"We all go," Thing says.

Hannah-consort immediately heads for the stairs, and we all follow, even Romulus.

He just shrugs when I look at him. "I could use some updated cooking lessons. I only know how to cook over an open campfire. And even then, pickings were usually slim when Layden was around."

"Layden?" Hannah-consort asks, inquiry in her eyes.

"Our other brother," Thing answers after loping down the stairs and opening the door to the kitchen.

Hannah-consort enters and flips on the lights.

I assume my brothers are smart enough to drop the topic of our lost brother, but Thing wouldn't know tact if it punched him in the face.

"Layden was Famine's name. We traveled with armies, and he spread famine in whatever country we passed through."

My jaw tightens. There's no need to rehash the past. Especially with my consort right when she has begun to look at me with eyes that don't see me as a monster.

But apparently her interest has been piqued because

she begins to ask one question after another as she pulls out pan after pan.

"So your father made you do those things? What made you finally stop?"

I try to caution Thing with my eyes, but either he does not notice or chooses to ignore me.

"We assumed it was our purpose," Thing continues recklessly. "Our Creator-Father said it was what we had been created for. And for too many centuries we did not question what he said."

Hannah-consort moves in a flurry between the refrigerator, the counter, and the stove.

She expertly cracks egg after egg into multiple pans on multiple burners. "So how did you know where to go and who to attack? Just whoever your dad pointed you at?"

Romulus nods, and suddenly he's in on story-time, too. "We did not see at the time, though, of course I ought to have. I was blinded by Remus's love of war itself." He looks down at the tiled floor. "And my own mind loved the chess game of winning each campaign, and on a more molecular level, each battle. Our father knew how to manipulate each of us to keep us too distracted to step back and question the larger picture. Or to question whether or not if he himself was a cause *worth* following all those years."

Thing picks right up. "He taught us gaining more power was everything. We were meant only to be his tools, but he made us believe we were sons."

Hannah-consort looks up from what she's doing at that. "I'm sorry."

"It was merely part of his clever manipulation tactics," Romulus spits. "Having us call him Father. To have us love him when he never felt it for us in return. To him, it made us more malleable."

Hannah-consort shudders. "He sounds like a cult-leader."

"Well, yes," Romulus says. "He had us call him God, though he was nothing of the sort."

"What was he, then?" Hannah-consort asks as she sprinkles something green into each pan of eggs.

Romulus shakes his head. "A powerful being of some kind. This earth is old. Powerful creatures from other planes have occasionally roamed here in ages past. But for the most part, they have quit this plane when it became poisoned by iron and when other metals began to be pulled from the depths and smelted together, to say nothing of the chemical compounds and combustibles humankind are now so fond of."

Then he narrows his eyes. "Some, like our father, however, were able to adapt and managed—or I should say *chose*—to stay."

Finally, I speak up, seeing that this history is determined to be told. "He gloried in being one of the last true powers, especially with us as his weapons. And so he amassed power—the only thing he ever truly cared about."

"Or at least he tried to," Romulus says. "Whatever he gained, he always eventually lost. He could only back one human despot at once or occasionally both sides. But eventually their armies were torn apart by us."

"We were unruly," Thing growls.

Romulus smiles. "Effective, but yes, unruly. Yet without us, Father was impotent."

"Something we failed to see until too late," I growl.

"Human rulers were ultimately fragile," Romulus continues, ignoring me. "Not to mention, our father was so full of hate, he delighted in their destruction as much as he did their victories. Any who dealt with him were making a deal with the devil."

Hannah-consort's eyes widen as she shifts various pans around the burners. "Did they know who they were dealing with? The human leaders?"

Romulus shrugs. "Some did. Some didn't. It just depended on what mood he was in. If he wanted to play with his food or not."

Hannah-consort frowns. "So did it feed him in some way?" she asks as she flips the eggs in the pans over to make a pocket upon itself. "Why did he do it all? How did it give him power?"

My brothers and I pause and look at one another. Ah, the ultimate question: Why?

Why, dear God, *why*?

Why all the senseless destruction?

Why did we tear apart the world, again and again?

"Because he could." My head snaps up, and it's Remus's wild eyes I'm staring into.

"He was a bully." Remus grins, teeth sharp. "He could have retired from this plane like all the others. But retire to what? To a land of peaceful meditation amongst equals for eternity? What attraction would that have held for one such as him?"

Remus shakes his head. "No. He saw that if he stayed, he would be the most powerful. He saw that if he stayed, and stole the angel-fire to create us—an act which would keep him barred from the Great Hall forever—he could *play*."

"Play by preying on those weaker than himself," Thing adds, nodding.

Hannah-consort is silent as she slides the egg pockets—she's made one for each of us—onto four plates.

"So what finally stopped him?"

"Layden." Thing's voice is quiet. "Our brother suffered more than any of us. The hunger... it was inside him, too."

"And sweet Layden especially didn't like it when Father murdered his own consort." Remus grins, eyes flicking toward me.

I feel my fur stiffen. What is he inferring? I would never—

"The food is ready," I growl. "We should eat."

But, naturally, Remus isn't done. "Our Father killed his consort," he repeats, and I want to smash his face in when I see my Hannah-consort's eyes go wide.

My impulse is to say: *It was an accident.* But then I am disgusted with myself, for Father did not accidently throw her down the stairs even if it was not his intent to kill her. He was not careful or gentle. He was violent, and she died. Those are the facts.

"Layden lost it," I say quietly. "He attacked our father. It shocked all of us. For all the wrong he'd done us, none of us had ever..."

"He'd made us such faithful dogs, you see," Remus

says. "And we obeyed. It was only after our father struck Layden down after torturing him slowly as an example to us—" Remus flashes his teeth. "But it had the opposite effect. Or perhaps it might have worked. Had at the last moment, he pulled back. We thought him slicing off Layden's wings and pouring burning hell-metal over his back so they'd never grow back would be as far as he would take it. Wasn't it punishment enough, after all?"

Then Remus answers his own question. "But of course that was not enough for our father. Still, I do not think any of us believed Father would go further until he took the hell-metal sword and drove it through our brother's heart right in front of us."

Hannah-consort gasps, and her hand goes to her own heart. Her food lies untouched in front of her. We should not have told her this gory story. She and my kit need sustenance. Not depressing stories of a long-gone past.

"What happened then?" she whispers.

"Then Abaddon moved faster than I've ever seen," Remus says. "There was no chance for our father to react. Abaddon yanked the sword out of his hand and drove it through our father's heart just as he had done to our brother." Remus cackles. "He looked so shocked that his most loyal dog would ever turn on him and bite so viciously. So fatally."

"He was the one who needed to be put down," I say.

It had been a simple decision in the moment, and one I've never regretted. If I have regrets, it is only that I did not act sooner. For then, I might be one brother richer.

And much suffering throughout the world might have been avoided.

"Wow," is all Hannah-consort says.

"Storytime is over," I say concisely. "You must eat."

"I don't know if I still have an appetite after that."

I growl disapprovingly. "We both know you do. Think of our kit. I will not tell you stories in the future if you will not eat." I do not intend to tell her any more stories of the past, no matter what, but she does not need to know that.

At my words, she quickly grabs her plate and some utensils, obviously realizing I'm right about her appetite because she doesn't even take her food upstairs to eat. Instead she tucks in right there, standing at the countertop.

Considering there is no longer a dining table upstairs after Romulus's scrying incident, I suppose this will do. For now. I make a note to send my brothers out later to get fresh wood so that we might build another.

For my part, I will not be leaving my consort's side.

ABBADON

CHAPTER FORTY-FIVE

The next week, we spend much time in that kitchen.
And in the bed.
And against the wall.
And in the bathtub.
Then back to the kitchen.

Then on the dining room floor against the cool cobblestones because I cannot not bear to wait for the whole climb back the six stories to our room. So, I throw my brothers out the door and tell them to go gather some trees for a new dining room table.

And then I toss my consort to the floor, flaring out my wings so she lands on feathers, then hike up her clothing, snuffle and tongue her to make sure she is slick enough for me, and at last thrust insight her tight little cunt.

Absolutely losing my goddamned mind as I whisper

over and over in her ear, "You're so fucking perfect. You're so fucking *mine*. You're so fucking *perfect*—"

All the while, she clenches and shudders around my cock, scrabbling for my horns to hold onto as I bring her to climax after climax with her tiny little hands—

So yes. There is lots of fucking. So much delicious fucking. Followed by meals that have *taste* to them. Followed by more of me clenching her knees to spread her sweet thighs apart and—

"Get your hand out of my goddamned face."

"Which one?"

"All of them!" Remus shouts at Thing from in front of where Hannah-consort and I stand at the sidelines watching on as they try to assemble the new table. "Whore son of a bastard's taint, if you don't get your motherfucking cunt hand out of my face, I'll slice it off!"

I look up reluctantly from Hannah-consort's thigh, and my reminiscing of all our recent fucking.

I want to tug on her hand and give her the look that's developed between us that communicates: *let's drop whatever we're doing and go fuck right now.*

But she just smiles and rolls her eyes at me before looking back to my brothers, where they're struggling to construct the new dining table, and have been for several days now.

The entire first day was just spent arguing alternately with Romulus and Remus—the first because Monsieur Tactician was certain he knew the best way to construct the table and the second because he sensed conflict in the air and delighted in fucking with us all.

Thing stood by, usually with all six of his hands full with either boards or tools. At least once Romulus and I finally agreed on the best way to plane the raw trees down into boards. Like usually, Thing allows larger personalities to dominate, which gladdens me because on the rare occasions he does decide to voice an opinion, he can make a mountainous ass of himself.

Such as pretending he was a ravenous beast for the past two hundred years. Even if he had genuinely lost his mind at the beginning, when he went on a murderous rampage after our losing our brother, why did he not tell me when he came back to his senses? I am still furious at him over this. Sure, I locked him in a dungeon for multiple centuries, but that doesn't mean I'm *unreasonable*.

After day one of fighting over the table's construction, I was happy to leave them to it and get back to fucking my consort since she is back to being happy to fuck.

But we're finally out of the bedroom, and Hannah-consort nudges me forward.

"Help them before Remus makes good on that promise, and Thing only has five arms left."

I give her a look. First, a *do-you-think-adding-a-match-to-a-lit-flame-is-a-good-idea?* look, followed one more time by the *wanna-drop-everything-and-go-upstairs-and-fuck* look.

But again she just rolls her eyes, and I allow her to shove me forward, if only because it's an excuse to have her hands on my lower back. I flare out my wings so she'll have better access.

But she notices me lingering and finally pulls back with

the most adorable little laugh that hits me somewhere between my chest and my nether regions.

I sigh and head into the fray with Thing and Remus.

For once, though, my brothers and I manage to do the impossible. We work together... *well*.

Last night, Romulus drew out the design plans in his head. With numbers and arrows and everything. Thing's able to both hold the boards, the nails, and hammer them in, as long as I take the other end of the long boards them for counterbalance.

We manage to get on well enough that somewhere along the way, Hannah-consort disappears, and I don't even notice. As soon as I do realize she is no longer watching on, my stomach drops out in alarm.

But Romulus grabs my arm before I can lose my shit and just says, "Smell."

Even as I prepare to yank away from him and launch off in search of my consort, I do unwittingly sniff the air, which is when I scent a complex delight of meaty smells wafting up from the kitchen below. Which immediately makes my alarm transform to warmth.

She has been cooking for us all week. Each time, she tells us not to get used to it. Yet every time I offer to char a slab of meat for her, she turns me down and stomps down to the kitchen herself.

Thing finishes pounding in a nail then Romulus declares, "It is finished!" with far more delight than is warranted by mere slabs of wood being stuck together and not falling apart when we all back away and hold up our hands.

But he is right. The table looks finished and seems as solid as the original. The fresh wood smells clean, as if the forest is right here in our dining room.

"Tomorrow, I'll stain it," Romulus says, "but we can still eat on it tonight. It smells like your consort is almost done with—"

"Dinner's ready," Hannah sing-songs as she enters the room carrying a stewpot that is far too large for her.

I rush over to her side, flying the last few feet across the expansive room. Quickly but carefully, I snatch the hot pot from her hands.

"Careful!" she says, "Don't burn your hands. It's hot!"

She needs to stop saying such things to me, or she will not get to eat, for I will have to take her upstairs and fuck her immediately.

No one has ever cared for me as she does. She feeds me and cares if my fingertips become a tad too warm?

Only knowing she needs the food for our shared kit growing in her belly overcomes my need to have my cock buried to the root inside her tight little cunt. I am glad I am carrying the large pot to cover my erection as I walk at her side back to the newly constructed table where my brothers sit. I have taken to wearing the cloth over my loins, as have my brothers, since we are all now together, but it is still often tented in her presence. She is also constantly covered now, either with aprons or furs, and I grudgingly acquiesce to it, because otherwise I would have to pluck out my brothers' eyes. Which would not likely add to our new-found tolerance for one another.

Along with the table, we have constructed two long

benches to replace the ones Romulus smashed to bits, along with the original table. After setting down the pot, I double check the seat is sanded smooth before allowing my consort to sit.

Thing has loped off to the kitchen to return with tableware and utensils.

How domesticated we have all become by her presence.

But I do not mind it.

For her presence in my life, there is much I would learn to put up with. In exchange for a good thing, change is not so bad, I suppose.

And perhaps it has been time for a little bit of civilizing.

It's certainly amusing watching Death scramble around like a trained puppy putting down table settings, and arranging forks, knives, spoons, and neatly folded cloth napkins carefully at each one even though thus far, it's only Hannah-consort and occasionally Romulus who even uses them.

More surprising, though, as Hannah-consort comes to sit beside me with a sweet, contented look on her face and the smile in her eyes that is for me alone—I find that I am...

Happy.

For the first time in my entire miserable fucking existence, I am happy.

I look at my brothers and their easy smiles, and I think they are, too. Like a sun that shines in winter after a bitter, endless night, Hannah-consort has brought us a new dawn.

For a moment, I am so choked, I can barely swallow the last of my deliciously spiced stew as I tip my bowl up and swallow the dregs. I snake my tongue out to lick the bowl, and I am eager for the taste to linger.

Which immediately strikes a foolish fear into my heart.

Because what if like the stew that is gone too soon, my Hannah-consort disappears as soon as the light of the happiness she has brought only begins to warm us?

Immediately, I glare toward Remus, who has spun to indolently enjoy the stew in Romulus's place. Dammit.

I need the more sober twin.

Because we have been foolishly toiling with tables when we ought to have been spending every moment working on his scrying shielding.

I must know what threats might be approaching.

Protecting this new happiness I have found is all I care about. And I will make it so it is all my brothers care about, too, until we succeed in seeing what might be hiding out there in the darkness, waiting to pounce and steal what is most precious to us.

HANNAH

CHAPTER FORTY-SIX

I am shocked that Abaddon's giving me a breather today. I woke up and blinked with a jolt of surprise to see Abaddon's side of the bed—aka most of the bed—empty. I blink some more, for a moment startled to be alone with my thoughts for the first time in a week, apart from briefly when I was cooking yesterday.

It's nice... I think. I frown. I sort of miss Abaddon's bossiness that I follow him as he drags me around the castle, never taking his eyes off me.

Not to mention how good the sex is—okay well it's *great*, beyond excellent, mind-and-body-shattering. Also to my great shock, I haven't been sore at all. To my further surprise, sometimes it's me tugging on *his* hand and giving *him* the look.

After my initial lackluster experiences with Drew, I never thought I'd be the one pushing for time in the bedroom. But I laugh out loud at even comparing Drew and Abaddon when it comes to sex. I mean Abaddon is— My mouth goes dry even thinking about him and the ways that man can manipulate my body. Even thinking about him and his hands and his *tongue* and his *wings*, dear God—

I place a hand on my heart to still it from its sudden quick clip just *thinking* about it all. I mean, sure, people talk about sex like this, but I never thought it would be anything little ol' *me* would experience. But dear god.

It's as if the universe has decided to make up for all the years my body was a cage by rewarding me with the most out-of-this-world sex it could think up for me. Don't get me wrong. I'm not complaining. I decided somewhere along the way, I guess, that I'm all in. Even if it hasn't exactly been a conscious decision.

It's sort of wild for once to let my body do the leading when it's for something *good*. I sigh. For something *wonderful*, actually. Who knew bodies could do something other than betray you?

My stomach grumbles audibly, and I laugh down at it. Then sober when I realize there's more than just a hungry belly in there. Well, apparently there are *two* hungry bellies—mine and...

I blink, still shocked every time I remember, holy shit, I'm pregnant. It hardly seems real. I'd think it was some elaborate prank the guys were playing on me... Except well, I'm starving every hour on the hour, it feels like. And while I haven't had any of the classic pregnancy symptoms I've always heard about my whole life—like day-long nausea or having to pee all the time (yet anyway), I do feel changes in my body.

Yes, it was hard to tell them apart from all the *other* big changes from, ya know, getting healed after a lifetime of being a certain way. Abaddon said he would only heal my body to a point. But it feels like my back has straightened even further since I got pregnant. When I flat-out asked Abaddon last night if he'd done it because I was carrying his kid, he just looked at me funny, then his eyes got all wide. "It is the kit doing it! From inside you. He is powerful already!"

Then his eyes got this weird happy glow like he was proud or something. I just rolled over in bed. He yanked me against him, purring contentedly into my hair. For my part, I was weirded out every time he referred to our child as a *kit*.

What the hell does that mean? Is a little chimera baby gonna be trying to claw its way out of me? Also, what is it with this *he* nonsense? We have no clue what gender the child will be, or how they will even identify. Patriarchal bullshit is what that is. It is time he joined the twenty-first century. I don't care how long he and his brothers have locked themselves away in this castle. If I am going to have a kid, then I am going to be loving and affirming and—

Oh shit. I'm gonna have a kid.

I rise and shake out my hands. I need to be in motion. I can't just keep sitting here all alone or I'll keep freaking out about this.

What do I know about kids? I've changed like two

diapers in my entire life! And the last time I tried, the kid peed in my face and all over the diaper I was trying to put on him. I had to call his mom—my friend from college—back from where she'd gone to answer the door so she could finish.

All this thinking is overwhelming. Time for food. I make a beeline for the kitchen. It's always my first stop, sometimes even before the bathroom, embarrassingly enough. Because whatever's inside my belly—be it an actual little monster-baby hybrid or a tapeworm—wants to inhale food on the regular. I baked bread yesterday, so I toast four pieces, slather them in butter and jam, then head upstairs. I don't have sharing in mind. These are all for me.

I'm surprised when I still don't run into Abaddon, who always seems to be underfoot wherever I am. I follow the noise of banging, like a hammer, down the hall from on the second floor, munching on my toast as I go. A sharp, whistled tune cuts through the quiet. It's a beautiful song, but very sad, in a minor key. Haunting.

I smile softly when I finally track down the source of the noise, and find Thing, by the light of a single, flickering candle, in a similar position to the last time I saw him. He has two hammers in hand, and his other four arms are variously holding nails and large boards he's hammering into place. Building a piece of furniture that's perhaps... a bedframe?

"Hello," I say. Apparently, this startles him so much he misses one of his frantic double swings and slams one of his thumbs.

"Oh no!" I hurry into the room and set my plate on the ground so that I can grab for his hand and observe the damage.

His entire body jerks the moment I touch him, and I realize too late that perhaps I'm taking liberties with his personal space.

"Crap, I'm sorry." I drop his hand and look up into his face. "Are you okay?"

He withdraws his hand and scampers back several steps, using one pair of his forearms to move on all fours like an ape. Then he lifts the thumb he smashed to his face, sniffs it, drops it, and stares at me.

Which makes me feel awkward and like I've intruded.

I take a step back. "Sorry to just come and invade your space."

I start to turn to go but his voice cuts through the space. "Wait. Do not go."

I pause and find Thing staring at me a little slack jawed. Then two of his hands go to his face, and I'm startled to discover that as he wipes them down his face, I swear it's as if his shape... *blurs* a little. I blink and step forward, not sure what I just saw. Was it just the darkness in the flickering candlelight? Or did I see what I thought I saw— and he *disappeared into* the darkness for a moment?

But then he moves slowly, looking fully solid again, approaching me as I approach him.

"Why do you stay?" he asks. "You should go. We are monsters."

I blink again, then force my eyes to stay open so I don't miss it again if he does that blur-into-the-darkness thing.

I shrug. "Monster is a subjective term. Kids used to call me things like that when I was younger because my back was bent, and I wasn't like them."

Thing tilts his head at me. "It is not our backs. It is our souls. Our insides are bent. Some monsters are real."

I look at the piece of furniture he's building. It's not quite up to the exacting engineering standards of Romulus, I imagine, but he's planed the wood down to a beautiful smoothness. And it looks sturdy, with a full headboard. Rustic, but quite well-made. Back in the city, they'd freak out over a piece like this.

"Maybe, but it sounds like if anyone was a monster, it sounds like it was your dad."

Thing's eyes dart toward me at my statement.

"Was that you I heard whistling when I was walking this way?"

He blinks in confusion, so I clumsily whistle a few bars of the song I heard.

He nods. "Oh. I did not realize it was out loud."

"I've never heard that song before. Where did you hear it?"

He shakes his head. "Just in here." With the hand of his middle left arm, he points to his temple.

"You just made it up?" I smile at him. "You're very talented. It was a beautiful song." Beautiful but sad. "You never studied music?"

He laughs at that. "We studied nothing but war." His eyes shift away from me toward the wall and then they go distant. "And death."

I don't like the haunted look in his eyes. "Well now it's

the time for music," I say gently. "And making beautiful furniture, it looks like. It's your renaissance."

He looks startled, then frowns down at the bedframe he's working on. "Just wanted a real bed. I never had one."

Well, shit, now I'm gonna cry. Maybe it's the pregnancy, or just everything else, but I swear I tear up at the drop of a hat now. And for this big, scary teddy bear of a guy to have never been given a bed his whole life just really tears my heart out.

But considering how Abaddon responds every time I try to express empathy, I swallow back my tears and instead ask, "You wanna dance?"

By the way Thing looks at me, I may as well have just told him I come from outer space. And it's official, I love managing to surprise one of them with kindness, when it's so obvious they've all been met with only brutality their entire lives.

So I nod and step closer. "You hum what you were humming, and we'll dance. I always wanted to dance, and I used to as much as I could before my limbs got too twisted. Even when they did, I was still the queen of the head bop and foot tap."

Now he's staring at me as every word coming out of my mouth is gobbledygook. Which is fair. So instead, I just grin my face off, walk up to him and take two of his hands. He freezes for a second when I touch him, but a moment later relaxes... ever so slightly.

"Now whistle," I instruct, but he shakes his head bashfully.

"Fine, then I'll sing, but I'm bad at it, I'm warning you."

I open my mouth and start to sing a Taylor Swift song I always loved, about Romeo and Juliet. Almost immediately, I begin to tear up again. Not because of the song lyrics, but because my illness made singing difficult to impossible for so many years. I haven't had the breath support, and it affected my speech patterns.

So, for a moment, I'm overwhelmed by that—being able to sing clearly—and being awash with gratefulness. And then I smile at Thing through my tears. He's just watching my mouth as if mesmerized by the sound coming out of it.

"Now we dance," I say quickly before picking up the melody again. I try to get him to move with me in a simple box pattern. He's clumsy at first, not understanding how I'm trying to get him to move.

And then suddenly, it clicks.

I'm astonished—for such a large man, he really can move with a beautiful fluidity. But then again, that's my fault for underestimating him.

After all, I'm dancing with Death.

I can't help but laugh delightedly at the idea, and my laugh pings and bounces off the walls. It seems to elicit something in Thing as well, for if my eyes don't deceive me, I begin to see the smallest of smiles appear on his face.

ABBADON

CHAPTER FORTY-SEVEN

I left my consort sleeping peacefully upstairs. And with all I did to her last night before she collapsed in sleep, she should be out for a little while longer yet.

Plenty of time to bring Romulus down to the basement dungeon where no one can look on while we continue his scrying lessons.

There are no distractions here. No wind or noise, and he needs to focus completely.

It still stinks to high heaven, but considering he spent most of the past few centuries here, I assume it will not bother him much.

And as he sits in the center of the room, in the lotus position as he lifts his arm to begin calling the runes, he does not seem much disturbed by the stench or anything else.

Good. He is focusing.

"Remember to shield yourself."

His face remains calm, eyes closed as he says, "Perhaps you should leave. I know what I have to do."

A growl from low in my throat is my only response. "Just see what comes for us. And try not to get blasted into the wall this time." At least there's no furniture to destroy down here. "We must know who you saw when you last scried."

"They were strong," Romulus murmurs, and it is only because I know him so well that I hear the hint of uncertainty in his tone.

"You will be stronger," I command. "Now focus."

He says no more, only keeps his eyes tightly shut as strained concentration overtakes his face. The vein in his forehead begins to pulse as the white-blue runes appear and vibrate in the stillness, flying in the air between his open hands like a vortex.

The stale air begins to stir in the room.

Well, he has lasted longer than the single moment he did before in the dining hall. Surely, that is a good sign. The runes whir faster and faster, and the concentration on Romulus's face becomes more and more strained.

I have seen such a look before—but only when Father was first training him, testing him by pushing back against him in the other plane where scrying is done.

The other presence is there with Romulus. It is only because Romulus is prepared and is shielding himself that he is able to maintain the runes, I know without being told. Even so, his face grows redder and redder. He might be managing, but only barely, it seems.

"Hold it!" I shout amid the growing roar of the air being whipped up by the flying runes.

But he only manages it for another moment before the controlled concentric circles tear apart, stray runes flying outward, smash me right in the face, and send *me* crashing against the flagstone wall. Dammit! If there is one thing I have made sure of about this dungeon, it is that it is *strong*. The walls are reinforced flagstone, two feet thick. And I feel every spine-crunching inch of those two feet as I'm slammed into them, wings first.

The bones in my wings don't snap or fracture, but if I were any less the monster that I am, I'd be broken to pieces.

But lucky for me—and Romulus—considering the growl of fury I can't help from escaping my chest as I climb back to my feet, I'm all but made of steel inside. I don't take kindly to being knocked on my ass even if he didn't intend it, and considering the source, I'll never really know, will I?

"Well did you see anything?" I growl.

And I immediately don't like how pale he is as he scrapes a hand down his face.

Or how, the next moment, his heads spin on their axis, and I'm eye to eye with Remus instead of the twin who just scried for me.

"What did he see?" I bark.

Remus looks around at where we are in surprise and obviously isn't happy about being back in the place he was caged, if the way his eyes narrow and his nostrils flare are any indication.

"First get me the fuck out of here and then maybe I'll be more in the sharing mood."

I grab him by his shoulders. "Tell me what the fuck Romulus saw." If this bastard knows my consort is in danger and fucking around with me—

But Remus just gets in my face while I still hold his shoulders. "I guess you don't actually want to know because you aren't moving the fuck out of the way." He smiles.

I roar in his face but pull back and storm out the door into the small hall and up a few stairs. Remus sweeps past me and halfway up the stairs back to the upper levels. But I snatch the base of his wing to stop him, spinning him back to me.

There's fire in his eyes at my daring the move, but I'm not fucking around here. "Is she in danger?" I demand.

His shoulders lift, and at first, I think he's going to continue being his asshole self. But then he pauses and says, "I don't know. I haven't looked yet."

"Well fucking *look*," I bark.

At first, I think he's going to keep being a little fuck, but in the dim unlit stairwell, I see the silhouette of his head tilt at an angle.

And then he exhales in a rush. "Fuck."

"What?" I rush up the stairs so that I'm at his level. "What is it?"

"You were right. All Romulus's training came back, so since he'd shielded himself, when he encountered... the other..." Remus shakes his head, eyes going distant.

"*What?*"

"He saw through its eyes."

"So? What did he see?"

Remus's eyes come to me, and for one of the few times in his life, he looks serious. "Looking through the other one's eyes, he saw this castle. The angel was right outside, looking in."

ABBADON

CHAPTER FORTY-EIGHT

I'm up the stairs in a shot, bounding and then flying the rest of the way when that feels too slow—all the way to our bedchamber.

But my consort is not asleep in our bed. The covers are pulled smooth in the funny habit she has of straightening bedclothes, I try to tell my hammering heart. She has not been kidnapped straight from my bed by an avenging angel whose name I do not even know.

I turn and race back down the stairs, yelling, "Hannah!" as I go. Then, when I do not get an immediate response, I roar again, "Hannah!"

And that is when I hear it. A screech.

My Hannah.

That which I have feared has come upon me, as some part of me always knew it would. I have not been strong enough to protect her.

But everything in me rejects the thought at the same time I burst into the room and find her grappling with—

Thing?

But I cannot care about the confusion at the specifics of the scene my eyes take in. There is danger near abouts. Perhaps Thing is working with the angel watching from the woods. He was angry at our imprisoning him for three hundred years and this is meant to be his revenge. Or he wants my consort for himself.

I do not care. The rage and fear in my heart have found a target.

Before my brother can react, I've flown across the chamber, ripped him away from my Hannah, and tossed him across the room.

"Abaddon!" Hannah-consort screams.

"Stay back!" I roar.

"No, stop!" she screams, but I've already leapt for my brother, wings flared wide and claws bared.

Thing has two of his six hands raised in surrender, but this motherfucker should have thought about that before he dared lay a hand on *my* consort.

I land by raking my clawed hand down his face, tearing the flesh of his cheeks into pieces. It is the one part of him that doesn't look as monstrous as the rest of him.

Until now.

I tear into him again.

And again. And again.

I hear screams behind me, but I've gone black. I will destroy him for daring to touch—

She's mine, and I will protect her.

Destroy. I have to destroy him.

Be who you are, dog. My father spits on my face after he has beaten me with the pipe made of hell-metal. It's the only thing that can make a dent in us, along with the cat-o-nine tailed whip that has hell-metal pieces tied into the leather strips. And my Creator-Father does so like to make dents.

I have tried for so many years, and I always fall short. And so he must punish me. Perhaps one day, I will learn.

But not today.

Maybe tomorrow you won't be such a miserable, disgusting fucking failure.

Then suddenly I flash back into the moment, and my brother who's lying in a bloody, disgusting mess of torn flesh and smashed-out teeth.

"Why aren't you fighting back?" I scream in his face.

Thing gurgles his in own blood but still manages to eventually say, "I am... no... dog."

I stumble backward from him as he coughs and turns over, spitting out several teeth. Then he continues, though he looks barely conscious. "And so... she sees who you are," he finishes in a rush.

Cold horror seeps up my spine, a creeping premonition even before I turn around to look.

Hannah-consort isn't there.

I run several steps forward and then stop and spin back toward Thing where he's still squirming and groaning on the floor in pain.

"Where is she?" I demand.

He lifts up on his elbows, and then drops back down.

But I still hear his voice, as if it echoes through the room in mockery when he says, "Gone."

CHAPTER FORTY-NINE

Remus sets me down on the back stoop in the dark outskirts of St. Paul. I ran into Remus as I fled from Abaddon and begged him to fly me home. I think he agreed more to cause havoc with his brother than to help me, but I'm happy to take what I can get.

I immediately drop my hand to my belly.

I will *not* raise children around such a violent father. I don't care what they come out looking like. They're *mine*, too, and I will protect them. Even if it means protecting them from *him*.

"What is this place?" Remus eyes the small, squat little property in the St. Paul suburbs.

I wrap my arms around myself, still wearing only one of the ancient aprons. "My mom's house."

"I will wait among the trees until you come to your senses." He steps off the porch, into the backyard.

"Don't waste your time. I'm not going back."

He shrugs. "Do not go back, then. Come with me. Be my consort. Together, we will raise the kit."

I all but choke on my tongue at his suggestion. "Yeah, right." I try to laugh it off.

But in an instant, he uses his wings to fly forward and is once again right in front of my face, manic grin wide. "Excellent. I will make you an excellent home to nest in while we await the arrival of the kit."

I shove him backward by his chest. "I was joking because I thought *you* were. Jesus!"

His eyebrows come together, and I raise a finger in his face. "Don't fuck with me, Remus. I'm a pissed-off pregnant lady, and if you try to kidnap me or some shit, I will be so angry, I will find a way to slit your throats in your sleep."

He just grins manically at me. "You are only making me want you more."

I roll my eyes and spin toward my mother's back door. Dear God, at least he brought me here and didn't just snatch me away immediately. I suppose that's something. I'm also happy to scoot inside with one last, "Thanks for bringing me," tossed over my shoulder right before I slam the door solidly *shut*.

"Who's there?" my mom calls, naturally startled.

"It's me, Mom." I head into the living room where I can usually find her stationed on the couch in front of the TV.

And she's there, all right.

But so is Drew.

I freeze as soon as I enter the room.

"Hannah!" My mother jumps up and hurries over to me. She pauses, her face awash with confusion as she looks me up and down. "What are you *wearing*?"

But then, as she looks again, her eyes widen. "Hannah." She breathes out, her eyes finally coming to mine.

My mother stares at me and she begins to cry. "Oh my God, I can't believe it worked. You're— You're actually *beautiful*."

She closes the last distance between us and embraces me. I swallow hard at the feeling of finally having the love and approval I've sought my entire life from my mother.

When she pulls back from me, her eyes are glistening with joy. "You and Drew are going to have such a beautiful life together. I just *know* it." She raises her eyes toward the ceiling. "Oh thank *God*."

And my heart shrivels and dies a little inside at the mother who could never see the beautiful dragon daughter who was always inside me. Instead, she only ever saw the paltry outer shell and judged my worth by that alone.

Then her eyes cloud over. "But I don't understand— How?"

And then Drew is there. "None of that matters. She's home."

Before I have a moment to squeak out a protest, Drew has wrapped his arms around me and is squeezing me in a possessive hug. "My baby's finally home where she belongs."

And into my hair, he whispers, "I forgive you for leaving."

Everything that happens in the next half hour is officially too much, too fast. My mother makes me go upstairs to shower and change, and when I come back down, things are far worse than I could have imagined.

Apparently, Drew and my mother have been meeting regularly since I took off to discuss "the problem"—that is, me.

"Isn't this wonderful," my mother declares, coming back in the room where Drew and I have been sitting semi-awkwardly since I got back downstairs after showering. "Now everything can go back to the way it was."

I swing my head toward her but she misses my what-the-hell-are-you-talking-about? look. Drew, on the other hand, just nods and beams at her as he takes his teacup from the tray she's brought. "Why, thank you so much, Mrs. Levine."

Finally, he looks my way. "I sure am looking forward to getting back to our life. Everyone's been asking about you. Don't worry, I made excuses. That your illness just had you feeling worse than usual, and you needed to rest at home. Everyone expressed such sympathy."

I blink at him. "But that's not what happened at all. You didn't tell them I broke off the engagement?"

He waves a hand. "I knew that was just you acting out.

I've read about how the grief of dealing with the realities of one's disability can make people do that."

My mouth drops open. So he just... *what?* Didn't take me breaking up with him *seriously*? As if I can't even be trusted to make my own choices with my life? My illness only affected my body, not my mind. And even if he misunderstood it to be an intellectual disability because of how it slowed my speech sometimes, then what the hell had he been doing with me in the first place?

Which was when I key back into what my mom's saying.

"So now that you're back, you can move back in with Drew, and the plans for the wedding won't even be interrupted because of how clever Drew's been with handling everything."

"What?" I choke out.

"Have some tea, honey, your throat's dry."

I take the cup of tea she hands me, but my hands are shaking. Which my mom notices and naturally misinterprets as having to do with my illness and not what it actually is—shaking rage.

I take a few long sips if only to try to calm myself.

When I finally speak, I talk with strong, clear syllables. "I'm so glad the two of you have been getting along so well. But Mom," I address her directly. "I was hoping to just spend some time here after my trip."

She just waves her hands. "Well I'm sorry but I just can't. I've already converted your room into my workout space and besides"—she beams at Drew—"it really is important to set a good example for people to see you two together again before the wedding. Drew's willing to let you come back to him right away."

My mouth drops open as I read between the lines. I'm no longer welcome here. I'm Drew's problem now.

He smiles at me, and maybe it's just me, but I swear there's some sort of satisfaction in the gaze that has nothing to do with love.

Has this always just been some weird power trip with him? Or like, being with me is the ultimate get as far as virtue signaling—look at *him*, everyone. What a good man he is—he even loves a *disabled girl*. That sense I got occasionally when we were together, that he cared more about how we looked together than who I was as a person... Yeah that's coming back in big vibes right now.

"Come on, honey," he says, standing. "It's time to go home. Now where are your arm crutches? Your walker?"

"Yes, yes," Mom says, also standing as if to usher me more quickly toward the door. "You two love birds should be off having time to reconnect without a third wheel around. Oh I'm so happy!" She claps in delight. "You two will have such beautiful babies, I can't wait."

I rise because I'll scream if I stay here another second.

What will my mother say when she finally sees the grandbaby that's already planted inside me? I choke on a half-hysterical laugh. Because this baby will likely have some assortment of wings, fangs, and claws.

But I do enjoy the surprise on Drew's face when I stand and come almost eye to eye with him. Hmm, he really is shorter than most men, isn't he? He was just always taller than me because of how slouched and bent my back was.

So I smile right at him when I say, "I don't need the crutches anymore. Or the walker."

He frowns but nods, gesturing toward the door. But before I can take the lead, he quickly walks ahead of me. He walks at a quick clip, too, seeming a little disconcerted when he glances over his shoulder only to find me easily keeping up.

The car ride home is quiet. "Everyone at work will be so excited to see you," he says.

I nod, offering nothing back. I can't help but feel like I have always been a burden to my mother that she has once again found a way to rid herself of. And that's... not a great feeling.

I clutch my stomach and promise the little being in there to do so much better. *I promise if nothing else, I'll love you extravagantly. I swear it. No matter if you're easy or difficult to deal with, I'll love you for everything you're worth.*

I turn my face toward the window and tears fall.

Drew turns on his favorite talk radio show and ignores me the rest of the drive to his apartment in the city.

HANNAH

CHAPTER FIFTY

"Do you need any help getting ready—"

Drew's question cuts off when he comes into the bedroom only to find me stepping out of the guest bedroom, already dressed.

He pauses, his gaze flicking up and down. "You look beautiful." But his voice is flat as he says it, and he turns around almost as quickly as he enters the room.

This is how it's been between us all week since my mother unceremoniously foisted me back upon him. I was able to get my job back, and I try to spend as little time in the apartment as possible. He was startled that first night when I informed him I'd be sleeping in the guest bedroom, but he didn't argue.

He doesn't say much of anything but seemed slightly enthusiastic yesterday when he came home and said some people from his division at work are having a dinner tonight he hoped I'll attend.

I feel nothing as I look at him, so handsome in a tailored black suit. Different, I think, from the tailored brown suit he wore to work. But I'm not sure.

My chest aches, looking at him, because all I've been able to think about all day has been Abaddon. How is he? Is Thing okay? Every time I close my eyes, the fight replays like this terrible, vicious loop behind my eyelids. Do they fight like that often?

And then, a thought slides in that I have absolutely no idea what to do with: does Abaddon miss me?

I rise, wearing low high heels for the first time in my adult life, and grab my purse from the floor. "Shall we go?" I can't quite manage to smile at Drew, and he doesn't look my way as he nods.

"We don't want to be late."

I let out a depressed sigh as I follow him.

The last thing I want to do is go be paraded out in front of his work friends around whom it always feels like we are playing a game of Who Deserves the Next Raise—with rules I've never been able to follow or understand. I just wanna curl up in bed, wrap my arms around my stomach, and cry for the lover and the strange future I've lost.

Even though now that I'm back in the real world, that castle and that life feels like a dream.

And I'm trying to be normal now. Except that's a fucking joke, because nothing's normal. Normally, my body isn't tall and straight up and down, or functional. Normally, Drew and I know how to say two words to each other. Normally, I am happy with my life, even with it being smaller than typical boundaries.

But now?

I barely know how to wrap my head around the now. Neither does Drew, apparently. He keeps trying to do things for me I can now do for myself. And I wonder: how much of our relationship was based on him being my caretaker? And what the hell about *that* was he even into? Because frankly, now that I know what it's like to be... well, vibrantly worshipped... I know the difference between love and indifference.

It's silent in the car all the way to the restaurant, except for the business podcast Drew puts on.

Maybe he's just still hurt because I left?

But if he is, then why doesn't he *say so* and not keep playing the silent martyr? And if he really loves me, wouldn't he be happy about the healing I found? Even if I found it on my own, separate from him?

I'm afraid there are no easy answers to these questions, so I stay silent, too.

And silently we drive, until we arrive, and Drew passes the keys off to the valet without so much as a word.

"Thank you so much!" I call after the valet as he hurries off with Drew's keys. Drew glances in my direction, as if annoyed at my outburst, then he's striding forward. He only pauses to wait for me at the door.

He brings his hand immediately to my elbow to support me as I head into the downtown restaurant's large turnstile doors. Except that I'm already heading confidently through, and he has to jerk his arm back so it doesn't get whacked by the quickly spinning door.

I freeze for a second, but then get moving so *I* don't get whacked by the big swiveling doors.

I wait on the other side for a slightly frustrated looking Drew. He tugs at his suitcoat, then glances up at me. Which is when I realize that, with the heels on, I'm taller than him. It's as if we both realize it at the same moment, too, I swear, because he gets this *look* on his face as he glares down at my heels. And then he stalks off ahead of me into the restaurant so that I have to hurry to keep up. Which I can, without problem. Something that also seems to constantly surprise him.

As soon as we pass the restaurant foyer, he takes my arm and puts it in the crook of his elbow. We've barely touched since I returned a week ago, so I'm a little confused by the gesture.

Until I realize that he's done it because we're now in view of his table of colleagues. And my stomach sinks. I have always hated these people. I never fit in with them. I don't know why I thought today would be any different. Putting on this pretty dress and these stupid high heels that I barely know how to walk in—

Drew drags me forward, a wide, plastic smile on his handsome face. I glance up at him as we walk. He really does look just like a Ken doll. Even his hair is pomaded into the same, smooth, stiff helmet as the Barbie companion.

Maybe I was just as shallow as he was—so dazzled to have someone so good-looking pay attention to me that I ignored how little actual chemistry there was between us. And well... also because no one else was offering and I believed no one *would*.

"Look who's up and around again," Drew says in an annoying announcer's voice as he proffers me forward like a prize animal at a fair. "We didn't want to tell anyone to get your hopes up, but Hannah's been to Europe for some experimental treatments and, well, voila!"

Exclamations erupt all around the table, and as usual, many stand up at my arrival. But instead of the awkward shuffling for the space everyone forgot to make for me, one of the partner's wives—Poppy— comes forward and hugs me. "Oh my god, I'm just *so* glad to see you finally doing better! I pray for you every *day*."

The woman who's always by her side at these things is next to greet me, eying me up and down. "Wow. Seriously, you look fabulous." She leans in with a smile. "Can you slip me the name of this miracle doctor? I need to get some work done."

I gape and just stare at her. Is she serious? I had a degenerative disease that would have resulted in my early death, and she's comparing it to her desire to get cosmetic surgery?

"Belinda!" Poppy grabs her by the elbow and yanks her back a step. Then Poppy turns toward me again. "We're *so* glad you're back. Drew's been an absolute wreck without you. Come"—she gestures—"come sit by me. Tell me all about where you're at with the wedding preparations."

I feel my eyes widen but try to cover it with a smile.

Wedding preparations? I glance at Drew. I seriously can't believe that he and my mother have been pretending that me leaving him was just...what? Some childish fit of temper?

As soon as we all get seated, I duck my hands under the table, ostensibly to arrange my cloth napkin over my lap. But I'm not wearing an engagement ring. Didn't Drew think someone would notice eventually?

But Drew's attention is already lost with his associates. They're talking shop on the other half of the circle table. So even though I'm seated beside him, I might as well be a world away. It's clear Poppy and Belinda mean to monopolize me for the moment, anyway, so I give in and try to scramble to remember everything a world away back when I was planning a wedding.

"Invitations-sminvitations," Belinda says, "let's get to what's important. Do you have the dress?"

I perk up. Because I do, indeed, have a dress. I had to get a replacement phone for the one lost on the mountain in Alaska when Abaddon whisked me away—which I'm totally *not* thinking about right now—but when I did, all my photos and everything downloaded from the cloud. All replaced as if I'd never been gone. So, I pull it out, except as I flip through the camera roll, all the photos of me throughout my travels around the world prove that I *did* go.

Even before Abaddon swept me off, I was already different from the person Drew seems to want me to go back to being—

"Here it is," I say, finally sweeping past the

chronological order of my life in reverse and coming to the beautiful wedding gown I picked out one Saturday afternoon with my mother.

I flip the phone around to show the women.

"It's lovely," Poppy says.

"But it's just on the rack," Belinda complains. "Do you have a picture of you in it?"

Poppy smacks her lightly on the shoulder. "It's bad luck to get pictures in the dress before the wedding. What if Drew saw?"

So, I guess I shouldn't tell them that Drew has already seen it? I mean, it is kinda hard for him not to see it, when he was the one who picked it up from the shop after the alterations were made. It's a big, poofy dress, and he said it would be easier if he just grabbed it on the way home from work. Besides, he said, he didn't believe in superstitions.

Right now, it's hanging in the back of the closet we used to share in his bedroom.

The whole thing makes a dark pit open up at the bottom of my stomach.

Because I can't imagine in a million years marrying Drew. And again I'm hit with wondering if Abaddon is missing me.

Which I finally recognize for what it really is.

I miss Abaddon.

Maybe I didn't give him enough time. He *was* changing. In a world where people never change, he *was*. Isn't that something?

I was asking for so much, so fast.

But then I remember him so brutally striking Thing, and my whole heart clenches. I can't stand to be around that kind of violence. And our child...

My hand below the table strays to my stomach.

"Hannah?"

I jerk my head toward Poppy. "Hmm?"

She nods toward the waiter standing behind me. "He's asking what you want?"

The waiter stands there, smiling genteelly.

And all of the sudden, I wonder what the hell I'm doing here.

What do I want?

What do I want?

I scoot my chair back, and the feet screech against the marble floor of the fancy restaurant in a way that grates.

Drew's head flies my direction. "Hannah, what are you *doing?*" His eyes are narrowed in a stop-acting-weird way.

"I'm leaving," I say, getting up.

He shoots out his hand to assist me, but I pull back before he can touch me. Briefly, I turn toward Poppy and Belinda. "It was so lovely to see you."

And then I all but flee the restaurant. I'm at the door before Drew catches up to me, where he snatches my elbow, but this time not to sweetly assist me. He yanks me around to face him. "What the hell are you doing? You made a fool of me back there!"

I blink at him. "Why did you ever want to be with me, Drew?"

He blinks, his mouth opening and then closing, but

at least he drops his hand from my elbow. "What are you talking about? I love you."

"But *why?*" I ask, genuinely wanting to know. "I'm not sure you even *like* me."

He waves a hand. "You're being ridiculous, and this is an important dinner. Now let's go sit back down and make a good impression. We can talk about this when we get home."

But for once in my life, I cross my arms and glare back at him. "I'm not going back to that table. I'll take an Uber home and pack up my things."

He looks shocked, and then furious. "You're going to leave me just because I won't respond to this hissy fit you're throwing all of the sudden? I took care of you for *years*. You owe me. Now go back to the table and sit down."

I *owe* him? Did he really just fucking say that I *owe* him?

"I can't believe I ever thought you actually loved me," I whisper, more angry than hurt in this moment. "But really, you just loved how I made you *look*."

I back away from him. "Enjoy your dinner, Drew."

And then I turn and leave by the revolving doors. Ready to begin the rest of my life. Wherever it may take me.

HANNAH

CHAPTER FIFTY-ONE

I pay the extra for the Uber that comes in two minutes rather than six, because now that I've made the decision to get the hell out of here, I want out *now*.

And unlike the last time I left Drew, I don't feel guilty or worry that I'm making the wrong decision. I *felt* something was off between us last time, I just couldn't put my finger on it. Now I can. And it's sad, and disheartening that someone I thought loved me really just—

Oh look, here's my Uber.

I hurry into the backseat, then put my earbuds in when the driver starts to make small talk. I'm *not* in the mood.

I listen to moody power ballads all the way home. And then laugh at the idea that Drew's apartment was ever my home.

Abaddon's castle felt more like home, even though I was only there a few weeks.

I lived a lifetime in those few weeks.

The ache in the pit of my stomach opens back up. God, I miss him.

I draw a deep breath as the city lights twinkle overhead and snow starts to tuft down from the sky. It doesn't matter that I miss him. I'm not making any more stupid romantic decisions. I'm obviously not trustworthy in that department.

I'm tired as I get out of the car, thank the driver, and then trudge through the fresh-fallen snow up to the apartment. The doorman greets me, and I nod back to him, then make my way to the elevator.

Even tiredness feels different now, in this new, strange body, though. I sink my head back against the wall as the elevator ascends. After living so long one way, even when I went in search of my miracle, I didn't really believe different was possible. And now...

Now everything's different... except also not. Because *I'm* still the same. Inside it's still me. A tear falls down my cheek, and angrily, I swipe it away. I'm tired of tears.

The elevator pings, and I pull out my keys. If I pack quickly, I can be gone before Drew gets back from dinner. I've said as many goodbyes to that man as I ever need to. What I fucking *owe* him. I'm still steamed over that comment. I probably will be for a while. As if my disability meant we were inherently uneven and him simply *being* with me was him doing me such a favor. He literally just said my worst fear out loud. And I might hate him for that.

Angrily, I push the door open, switch on the light, and stomp toward the guest bedroom where I moved all my stuff. Except on the way there, I frown, noticing a cold draft.

But before I can investigate, the door I just closed behind me swings open.

I turn around in alarm, but then I see it's Drew.

"What are you doing here?" I ask, surprised.

"What do you mean, what am I doing here? I couldn't just let you leave and not follow you. How would *that* look to my colleagues?" He tosses his hands in the air.

I roll my eyes. Of course. How would it *look*.

"Well you didn't need to bother. You could have just told them I'm leaving you. For good this time."

Drew sputters. "*You're* leaving *me*? Suddenly now that you look pretty, you're too good for me? I put in *time* with you."

I turn and head toward the guest bedroom to start packing, if only so I don't turn around and slap him. *I don't approve of violence, remember?*

But the bastard doesn't get the message and follows me.

Which is when a gigantic hulking shadow steps out from the corner of the bedroom, between me and Drew.

I shriek in surprise.

"My consort said she did not want you."

Oh shit.

Abaddon flares his wings and pounces toward Drew, who screams like he's a soprano in a choir.

CHAPTER FIFTY-TWO

"Don't hurt him!" Hannah-consort yells, and I growl in fury as I pin the puny mortal man to the ground with my wings, my claws extended, arm raised.

I want to rip his pretty face apart as I did Thing's.

But remembering what that moment cost me holds me in check. I lower my arm and look over my shoulder at my consort.

It feels like a lifetime since I have seen her.

I have never felt like more of an animal than this past week without her. It has been a long time since I lost my brother, and that was a different time. That is to say... I am unfamiliar with grief. Perhaps I did not understand many of the colors of emotions beyond red rage before meeting this soft creature who would show us a different way.

But this week, I have felt grief, and fear, and shame,

and embarrassment, and an aching, aching sadness at missing her sweet presence.

So, I lower my arm and turn back to my consort. The first creature in this life to ever show me kindness, and a better way. If only now I can make her understand.

"I am not my father," I say. "He did not love me, and so I believed in my center core I was not worthy of love."

I lower myself to my knees before her. "Even if I have battered any possibility of you ever loving me, I think I am finally beginning to stop hating myself. Because of you. No one in my existence showed me kindness until the day you came to my cave. And then every time you gifted your body to me—"

"What?" the small mortal man shrieks from behind me, but I ignore the gnat, my focus only on my Hannah.

"Over and over you proved to me that you cared more about who I was than what I looked like. And it made me believe that change was possible. Even for a monster like me. So now it is I will who will get on my knees before you, Hannah-consort. You who have always been my equal."

Then I shake my head. "No, not my equal, my *better*. I am here on my knees to beg you for the privilege of a life at your side to prove I can be the mate you deserve. Your strength gives me strength, and I bow before the person you are and always have been."

And then, already on my knees, I bow low to the floor before her.

I await her response with bated breath.

Only realizing my miscalculation too late. My eyes fly wide open at the cock of a trigger. Then gunfire explodes in the small apartment.

ABBADON

CHAPTER FIFTY-THREE

"Get behind me, Hannah!" cries the weak little human male as his bullets strike my wings that I flare out to protect her. Fury lights through me. He may have been firing at me, but she is also this direction.

I spin toward him at the same time Hannah sprints past me. My mouth drops in astonishment. Is she actually choosing *him*? Or perhaps just fleeing the gunfire, an instinct I wholly approve of.

But then I see my consort attack the small human male. "Hannah!" he shrieks. "What are you— Stop it!"

The beast inside me roars to life as he puts his hands on her to push her away. I leap to my feet and scamper toward the man, claws again bared. But unlike the fool, with Hannah in the way, I do not launch an attack.

The fool, however, abandons Hannah and scrambles

backward. I pounce. But again, right as my claws would tear through skin, Hannah screams, "Stop!"

My arm freezes. "Why?" I roar. "Do you love him?"

I look down at the beautiful man cowering below me, his whole human limbs as beautiful as most of the angels—

"No!" Hannah scoffs. "But what if I did? Have you changed, or haven't you? Will you commit violence every time something in life doesn't go your way?"

She moves so that she is in my line of sight, but I don't move off the human male this time, and also keep my eye on the gun where it fell several feet away. With my wing, I fling it even further.

Hannah sees my pause and draws a breath before continuing. "I want to come with you." Then she stands straighter. "But I refuse to be with someone whose temper scares me like yours does."

Shame sweeps me head to foot again, and I shake my head. "You will not need to be afraid or scared with me. It was Thing who scried for me that I might come find you."

Her eyebrows go up. "Thing can—"

"He is bad at it, but every so often, under certain circumstances, Death can call the runes. I begged him. We have had many long talks in your absence. I will change. I am changing. I *have*." I turn and lift a hand to her cheek, putting a foot on the male to hold him in place. "Hannah-consort never needs to be afraid when she is with me."

But I am proved to be a liar when I say I can protect her and yet *another* gunshot rings out, striking me in the back. It bounces off, but *still*.

I turn around with a roar, spin and grasp the second gun the human male has produced from somewhere, tearing it from his hand and in front of his face, crumpling the metal as if it is no more than a cotton ball.

His eyes widen at the distorted piece of metal I drop in his lap.

The beast inside me wants nothing more than to tear him to shreds for endangering my consort *again*, but I have just sworn to her than I am changing.

Only cowards use force.

So instead, I get right in his face, bear all of my fangs, and hiss, "Run."

The little male pisses his pants, scrambles to his feet, and flees out the door.

When I turn back to Hannah, she is beaming at me. She flings her arms around me, and then her sweet breath is on my ear. "Take me home, beloved."

ABBADON

CHAPTER FIFTY-FOUR

The orchestral music playing over the device Hannah-consort insisted on Romulus flying to the city to acquire fills the dining hall.

Though I suppose she will not be Hannah-consort for much longer. I smile, feeling pleasant heat inside my chest at the thought: soon she will be Hannah-*wife*.

As soon as I think it, my Hannah appears at the opposite end of the room in the large white dress that pools on the ground behind her. I was confused when she insisted on bringing it with us, along with many of her other clothing, but now I am filled with joy and pride.

My mouth goes dry at how beautiful she is.

I only brought her back here once Romulus assured me he had set an impenetrable net of protection runes over the entire castle. It took him a month to prepare himself, then to set all the runes and double and triple check them.

I have much to be grateful to my brothers for, in addition to him keeping watch over her from the shadows while she was away from me.

While Romulus did his work to protect the castle, I took Hannah-consort on vacation in Italy. There is an abandoned island there I know well. Hannah-consort could not believe such a place existed, so close to the mainland that we could see the bright lights of the city as we walked through the ghostlike structures of the old sanitorium.

There was no choice but to confess my long history with the island, but I had determined to no longer be afraid of my past, and to trust her with the truth. She had shared with me the words of a philosopher of her world, that a "wound is where the light enters." I think of the many wounds left all over my body made by my father and hope that one day, I may be full of light. Even though now, all I feel is full of wounds.

As we sat on the stone steps of what had once been a terrible hospital for the ill, I told her about how during Napoleon's time and before, this was a place where they brought those I'd given the plague to quarantine. And thus, to die.

"Following my father's orders, I brought sickness to many," I said, staring off into the sea beyond the shore. "Humans did not seem of much consequence and my father said their numbers must be cleansed on occasion. That was what he called my work. Cleansing."

And then I looked at her, feeling the weight of sadness in my soul I had so long ignored. "Perhaps it is wrong to bring you to a place full of such ghosts, but these are the only places in your world that welcome me any longer."

"You didn't know better."

I shrugged, stung by her words. "In my innermost heart I suppose I always felt it was wrong. But my father told me such thoughts were weakness, and he did his best to beat it out of me." Then I looked around and wondered if any spirits lingered here among the forgotten stone structures. "And the dead do not forgive."

But then my sweet consort stroked her fingers through the fur at the base of my neck. "They do not have to. All creatures are allowed to change. You get a second chance. So, take it, and do good now."

The sun was setting over the city in the distance, and I interlaced my hand with hers. "While you are by my side," I vowed, "I will be best."

She laid her head on my shoulder. And then, when the stars came out overhead, she climbed onto my lap and kissed me. Drawing out my passion until I finally flipped her and made love to her underneath the stars.

We spent the rest of the month among the ghosts, making love almost every moment we weren't sleeping, sun-bathing, or eating fish I caught and we cooked.

Only once Romulus said it was safe at the castle did I tell her it was time to go home.

She smiled up at me. "This has been like a wonderful honeymoon."

I frowned in curiosity. "What is this word?"

I became even more curious when her cheeks turned

red, and she averted her face from me. Which only made me demand more stridently, "Now you must tell me."

"Well," she said, "that's what people call the vacation that couples take after their wedding." Then her face fell a little. "But then, I guess we never exactly had a wedding..."

She absently rubbed her stomach.

"You are my consort," I stated.

Her eyes flashed my way. "Well that's not the most romantic title, is it? Is that what I'm supposed to tell my son or daughter? That I'm his father's *consort*?"

I frown at her. "What else would you be?"

She got to her feet and stalked away from me along the over-grown mossy ledge.

I leapt to my feet to follow her. "I have displeased you but I don't know why. Explain. This is a human custom you desire?"

She spun back to me. "Well I didn't bring that big, stupid wedding dress along for shits and giggles!"

Her outburst startled me, but her words rang old bells in my mind. Wedding... yes, I had heard this word before. "*Wedding*... is the human custom of binding?" I asked it tentatively since her eyes still spit fire.

But at my words, she softened slightly. "Yes."

I took a step closer. "And this binding ceremony. You would like this, with me?"

"Well we're about to be parents!" She threw her hands up in the air. "So it might be nice."

I swooped in on my consort and encased her in my arms, my wings wrapping around to cocoon her also.

"Beloved," I whispered, "I would be bound to you in every way possible. By both human and heavenly custom, and those of every other plane if I but knew them."

"Really?" she squeaked.

My sweet little fool. Did she doubt my love and obsession?

"You have but to tell me the details, and so it shall be done."

And now here we are, a week later at home. I stand waiting at the front of the dining hall with my brothers at my side as my bride approaches. Rose petals line her path to me.

A marriage is not a contract, or a deal, she explained. It is a ceremony where each partner makes promises— vows—of fealty to one another.

I was not sure I saw much difference until I began to prepare my promises. But then I did.

It seems to take forever for my most beautiful bride, moving slowly in time to the music, face hidden by a gauzy white veil, to finally reach me.

And when she finally does, the beast in me wants to rip aside her veil, and then tear away all the other many layers of white fluff hiding away the delectable prize of her body.

But I suppose anticipation is meant to be part of the ceremony. As is the later unwrapping of my bride.

Thing moves to stand in front of us. Perhaps some might find it morbid to have Death officiate their binding ceremony, but I certainly am not going to depend on Romulus, considering his wildcard twin. And I know more than most that we monsters hold within us both our gift and its opposite pendulum swing.

I am Pestilence, but I am also Healing. It is only because I had the father I did that I was forced to dwell only on the dark side of my gift and never able to find balance.

My brother, with whom I have reconciled, is not to be feared. And I want the energy of his blessing for a long, long *life* to this marriage.

It is still a shock to see the once ravenous beast of a brother so put together, standing upright and sane. In a suit no less, with tidy sleeves for each of his arms. Hannah sewed one for each of us, that we might match her in elegance if not beauty for this ceremony.

Remus grins on maniacally from the sidelines, but not even his smirking face can bother me today. And he and his twin *did* watch over my beloved during her time away from me, never allowing her out of their sight—not that she was aware of their constant vigil.

So, I find myself in the strange position of being grateful to each of my brothers and surprised by their kindness at this late stage in life. I suppose it is testament to the fact that we, who have known only violence, *can* truly change, though even six months ago I would have sworn such a thing impossible.

As I stand before my bride, preparing to take her as my wife, though, I know that should any come to threaten her or our coming kit, I will not hesitate to slay them. My family alone will see this kind face. All others will find me as merciless as ever. Perhaps more so, now that I know how much I have to lose.

I hold my beloved's hands tightly as she speaks her vows to me.

"I, Hannah Elizabeth Levine, take you, Abaddon, to be my husband before God and these witnesses." She smiles at me so sweetly as she says the words, and her eyes are full of emotion. "I promise to be a faithful and true wife."

Her hands shake as she holds forth a ring and I lift my hand. "This ring is a symbol of my love, devotion, and promise to be yours forever. With this ring, I thee wed."

My chest goes tight as her small fingers slip the thick gold ring past my claws and knuckles to land snuggly at the base of my fourth finger. She has bound herself to me truly.

"In sickness and health, in poverty and fortune, I am yours. Forever."

I swallow hard against an unexpected knot of emotion in my throat so that I am able to speak my own vows. "I promise to protect you and our kit, and to keep you safe and healthy." I press my palm with the glinting gold ring on it to her stomach, and her eyes glisten with unshed tears.

I hold her gaze as I continue. "I promise to bring you joy and not anguish, so far as I am able."

The tears fall down her cheeks, and I brush them away with my thumbs.

"With this ring, I thee wed." I take her tiny, delicate ring from my pocket and slide it onto her delicate finger, and then make my last vow. "I swear I will love you for eternity."

She grins at me so brightly it's like sunrise after the longest, darkest night.

Then Remus kicks Thing, who stands straighter and quickly swipes a tear from his eye with one of his hands before swallowing with a little cough. "I now declare you monster and wife. You may now kiss the bride."

I swing my wife into my arms and begin my claiming.

EPILOGUE

6 Months Later

HANNAH

"I feel like a whale." I toy with my food as we all sit around the dining room table.

"You are beautiful and round with kit," Abaddon reassures, moving to stand behind me and massage my sore shoulders.

I look down at my hugely distended stomach. I already look nine months pregnant. And just then, a horrible thought strikes, and I turn around to look up at Abaddon. "How long do angel-spawn babies or whatever last anyway? It's still just nine months, right?"

And still, looking down at myself, I can't imagine growing bigger for three more months. I won't be able to walk.

Which is when I look back just in time to catch Abaddon's eyes flick toward Thing. Who looks to Romulus. Who shrugs.

My eyes shoot open wide. "What does *that* mean?" I shriek. "Oh my god, we need to go get an ultrasound. We need to find out what's happening in there." My hands fly to my stomach.

"I thought you didn't want to—"

"Well now I do!" I yell. "I don't care if we terrify some clinicians somewhere, I have to see what's growing inside me!" I yell.

Grabbing the chair for support with one hand and the table with the other hand, I gingerly heft myself to my feet. "What are we going to do when the baby comes? We need an action plan. How have we not made an action plan?"

Abaddon takes my hand. "Breathe. Just breathe. It will all be all right. Romulus will go get a doctor."

I pause my pacing and look at him. "Really? But how?"

"I'll kidnap one." It's Remus's voice, and when I turn and look, it's to see the maniacal-faced twin grinning at me.

"Dear god, don't *kidnap* somebody—" But my sentence is cut off when a pain lancing through my stomach has me grabbing for Abaddon and screaming.

I'm almost knocked off my feet by the sudden, wrenching pain of it, but Abaddon catches me.

And then suddenly a pool of water releases and gushes at my feet.

I shake my head in terrified denial. "I can't have this baby now. It's too early!" I think it is, anyway. I look at Abaddon and scream in his face, "Get me to a hospital. Now!"

"What will they do at a hospital," Remus asks from behind me, "if you deliver a monster baby?"

My eyes go wide and my nails dig into Abaddon's arms as I imagine nurses screaming in fright and running as the head of my sweet little baby crowns... horns and all.

Plus, if we go to a hospital, I won't be able to have Abaddon at my side. I can't do this without him. I can't—

Pain tears across my stomach again and I screech, clawing for him. His strong arms are there for me, closing around me and holding me close. "*Fuuuuuuuuck!*" I holler.

"Get her to the bedroom!" Thing shouts.

Abaddon hefts me into his arms and starts to run. As soon as I have my breath again, I yell over his shoulder to Thing, "Boil some water!"

And then I screech again, this time not from a contraction, but because Abaddon leaps, with me still in his arms, out the *window*!

I scream directly into his ear as he flies the six stories up and back in through the window of our bedroom.

"Why didn't you take the stairs?" I yell at him as soon as he lands and deposits me on the bed.

"Faster," is all he says, helping to get me situated.

I would yell at him some more, except right then another contraction hits. *Too soon, too fast*, I think, but then I'm screaming and clutching my stomach to be thinking about anything else than combatting the pain.

I can't say I'm delighted when Thing and Remus appear in the bedroom minutes later. My dream birthing scenario certainly never included having my brothers-in-law present.

But I don't know anything about what's going on.

I don't know if this labor is premature.

Or if this is the kind of birth I'll be able to survive.

Or if—

I was supposed to have more time to figure things out. The past six months have passed so peacefully. Yes, Abaddon's been annoyingly overly protective, and he wouldn't even bring me back to the castle for a month after what happened at Drew's.

And ever since we've been home, he and his brothers have been behaving well with one another. Thing and Abaddon do genuinely seem to have buried the hatchet, though Thing's face still bears the scars of Abaddon's claws.

Even Remus has been behaving... for the most part.

Now, dear god, if only my child may be born safely—

I scream and bunch the covers in my fist as pain, worse than what came before, wrenches across my stomach.

Thing sets down a pot of steaming water. "I must check for the child," he says, and Abaddon roars at him as he moves between my legs.

"Let him!" I scream with the last of the contraction, before sagging into the mattress, tears streaming down my cheeks. This is all happening so fast. Too fast. And it hurts too much. Dear god, does that mean there's something wrong with the baby? I need to be in a hospital! I need the familiar click and beep of monitors telling me what the hell is going on!

But then Abaddon puts his knees on the bed beside me and lays one hand on my forehead, and another on my stomach. "Brother!" he barks, "keep my wife and child safe and away from the gates of Death!"

Thing nods, moving between my legs and nudging them open wider.

Oh dear god. I forget about their powers, they have become so dear to me. But I am bringing a life into the world with Pestilence and Death hovering over me. And yet… it is also one of their kind I am birthing, so maybe it is only right—

And then another contraction wipes out the possibility of any further thought.

"Push," Thing says. "It is time."

What? It can't be time already!

But god help me, I do. I push.

As I do, light erupts from Abaddon's hands, surrounding me like a penumbra. I push and I push even as the pain lightens, and then—

The pressure between my legs pops like a cork, and then Thing is pulling—

A baby's cry suddenly fills the room and I begin to weep with joy.

Moments later Thing hands the baby to Abaddon who immediately climbs into bed with me as he puts our child to my chest.

She's a beautiful, pink-faced little cherub, who looks totally human except for her curved ears and beautiful gossamer black wings folded neatly against her back.

I sob even harder as Abaddon helps position her against my breast so that she can begin to feed. She is eager, and as her little rosebud lips begin to pull, slowly at first and then more urgently, her eyes blink open and she looks at me with irises that are an almost translucent gray.

I try to slow my sobbing as I say hello to my baby girl, and clutch my family close to me, happier than I ever knew was possible.

CREATOR-FATHER

He has done it!

I am tempted to continue watching through the scry, but it is best not to press my luck. My foolish, stubborn son has finally managed to do *something* right in his entire miserable existence!

A child.

A perfect little angel. *Finally*.

My life's work is not lost after all. I knew it could not have all been for nothing.

I was merely short-sighted. Of course I should have tried breeding them to create a more perfect creature! I simply assumed they would be sterile like donkeys. Like... me.

And also, I assumed they took their pleasures among the women of the conquered lands like all other soldiers did. But then, my sons always were a peculiar lot. And they were certainly too monstrous to seduce any of the easily frightened human women into bed *willingly*.

But it is such an obvious oversight that I can only smack my forehead for not attempting it sooner. Of course, the intermingling of angel-kind and the humans of this plane is how beings such as I came to be in the first place. Granted, the angels were beautiful when they first came, and human women were happy to offer their bodies to such creatures, especially since they assumed my forebearers to be gods.

They called the offspring of these unions such as me Nephilim in their sacred texts. We were worshipped and lived lives of such glory back in those days. Before, one by one, we were either killed off or retired to the eternal plane during the ascension. But I knew the eternal beings took the rest of my brethren more from duty than desire, and in that other plane, there would be no true glory for me. Not like I could have if I remained, the last of my kind.

So I stayed behind. But I was not powerful enough on my own. I needed soldiers.

Does it leave a bitter flavor on my tongue to realize it is me alone who is the donkey who cannot procreate? For oh how I did try.

Instead, I was forced to be a thief, to steal the light from beyond the gates. And then I used up almost all the creative force left inside myself to fashion these children of mine.

These ungrateful, backstabbing sons who never appreciated the sacrifices I made to give them the greatest gift of all: life and existence on this sumptuous earthly plane.

Ah, but a father's work is never done, it turns out.

And now, a *Grandfather's*.

Long have I watched my sons from afar, regaining my strength. All these centuries after they betrayed me, I have waited, diminished. And oh, I have watched.

Times have changed, and I have allowed it. I knew one

day, something would change, and our true glory could finally be obtained.

And look, here it finally is.

Wastefully, they imprisoned themselves in that castle, allowing the world of men to thrive. Allowing glory to pass them by. Fools.

So I could hardly believe the day I saw my son bearing the small human woman in his arms as he flew her back to his castle tomb.

When she fled him days later, I laughed, and went to intercept her without fully knowing my own mind as to what I would do with her. Except I felt in the air that finally, *finally*, change was on the wind after our long stasis.

It was arriving right on time, too, for I had almost regained my full strength after my long convalescence. My son may not have killed me, but he had diminished the life force within me from a blazing fire to a mere ember in the ashes. And it has taken this long to rebuild the flame to full light.

I am now ready.

But all thoughts on how I might use the small human woman as a captive against my son evaporated as soon as I caught her scent and realized the fool had managed it!

She was with child.

There would be a new generation.

Oh, how I gloried. That which I was never able to do— recreate the perfect angelic specimen—he had done by foolish happenstance! Through fatherhood, no less. He, who should not be able to procreate at all!

So I protected her, remaining a kindly stranger only so that when she went back out, she might continue back to him, and bear him the child.

My plans are not so short-sighted as to take the child as a baby... though I was tempted. The suffering it would inflict on the son who wounded and meant to kill me... oh it was *so* tempting.

But if the past two hundred years have taught me anything, it is patience.

For why would I stop at only having *one* new soldier in my army when a vista of possibility has suddenly opened before me?

My sons need consorts. And considering how long it has taken one of them to find himself a mate, I will not trust them to the task.

After all, Creator-Father knows best.

Coming this summer, THING's story.

Being the angel of death's a lonely gig,
and Thing's been alone all his life,
even when he wasn't chained to a
dungeon wall half-mad for two centuries.

He's not like his brothers.
He's come to prefer his solitude.
Or so he thinks.

Because when a fierce woman covered
in blood comes crashing through the forest
into his many arms,
he begins to wonder if he might just want
a consort of his very own...

Also by
STASIA BLACK

BREAKING BELLES SERIES
Elegant Sins
Beautiful Lies
Opulent Obsession
Inherited Malice
Delicate Revenge
Lavish Corruption

DARK MAFIA SERIES
Innocence
Awakening
Queen of the Underworld
Innocence Boxset: Hades & Persephone

LOVE SO DARK DUOLOGY
Innocence
Awakening
Queen of the Underworld
Innocence Boxset: Hades &
Persephone

BEAUTY AND THE ROSE SERIES
Beauty's Beast
Beauty and the Thorns
Beauty and the Rose

Also by
STASIA BLACK

STUD RANCH SERIES
The Virgin and the Beast
Hunter
The Virgin Next Door
Reece
Jeremiah

TABOO SERIES
Daddy's Sweet Girl
Hurt So Good
Without Remorse
Taboo: a Dark Romance Boxset Collection

MARRIAGE RAFFLE SERIES
Theirs To Protect
Theirs To Pleasure
Theirs To Wed
Theirs To Defy
Theirs To Ransom

DRACI ALIEN SERIES
My Alien's Obsession
My Alien's Baby
My Alien's Beast

ABOUT THE AUTHOR

STASIA BLACK grew up in Texas, recently spent a freezing five-year stint in Minnesota, and now is happily planted in sunny California, which she will never, ever leave. She loves writing, reading, listening to podcasts, and going to concerts any time she can manage.

Stasia's drawn to romantic stories that don't take the easy way out. She wants to see beneath people's veneer and poke into their dark places, their twisted motives, and their deepest desires. Basically, she wants to create characters that make readers alternately laugh, cry ugly tears, want to toss their kindles across the room, and then declare they have a new FBB (forever book boyfriend).

Website: stasiablack.com
Facebook: facebook.com/StasiaBlackAuthor
Instagram: instagram.com/stasiablackauthor
Goodreads: goodreads.com/stasiablack
BookBub: bookbub.com/authors/stasia-black

Made in USA - Crawfordsville, IN
23295_9781639002085
05.20.2023 1817